CLOUDIA & REX

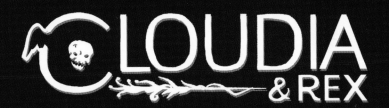

BY
ULISES FARINAS
ERICK FREITAS
DANIEL IRIZARRI

EDITING AND LAYOUT BY MIKE KENNEDY

CLOUDIA AND REX (COLLECTED EDITION)
PUBLISHED 2017, BY THE LION FORGE, LLC.
FIRST PRINTING

© 2017 ULISES FARINAS, ERICK FREITAS, DANIEL IRIZARRI.

PRINTED IN CHINA.

www.LIONFORGE.com

NAMES: FARINAS, ULISES. | FREITAS, ERICK. | IRIZARRI, DANIEL. | KENNEDY, MIKE (GRAPHIC NOVELIST), EDITOR.
TITLE: CLOUDIA & REX / BY ULISES FARINAS, ERICK FREITAS, DANIEL IRIZARRI ; EDITED BY MIKE KENNEDY.
OTHER TITLES: CLOUDIA AND REX
DESCRIPTION: COLLECTED EDITION. | [GREENVILLE, SOUTH CAROLINA] : BUÑO ; [ST. LOUIS, MISSOURI] : THE LION FORGE, LLC, 2017. | "PORTIONS OF THIS BOOK WERE
    PREVIOUSLY PUBLISHED IN CLOUDIA & REX, VOL. 1, ISSUES 1-3." | SUMMARY: "12-YEAR-OLD CLOUDIA AND HER KID SISTER REX ARE IMBUED WITH STRANGE POWERS BY TWO DEITIES
    FLEEING AN INTERDIMENSIONAL APOCALYPSE. AS IF GROWING UP ISN'T ENOUGH TO DEAL WITH!"--PROVIDED BY PUBLISHER.
IDENTIFIERS: ISBN 978-1-942367-30-7
SUBJECTS: LCSH: PRETEEN GIRLS--COMIC BOOKS, STRIPS, ETC. | SISTERS--COMIC BOOKS, STRIPS, ETC. | END OF THE WORLD--COMIC BOOKS, STRIPS, ETC. | CYAC: PRETEEN
    GIRLS--CARTOONS AND COMICS. | SISTERS--CARTOONS AND COMICS. | END OF THE WORLD--CARTOONS AND COMICS. | SUPERNATURAL--CARTOONS AND COMICS. | LCGFT:
    PARANORMAL FICTION. | GRAPHIC NOVELS.
CLASSIFICATION: LCC PZ7.7.F37 CL 2017 | DDC [FIC]--DC23

CHAPTER ONE

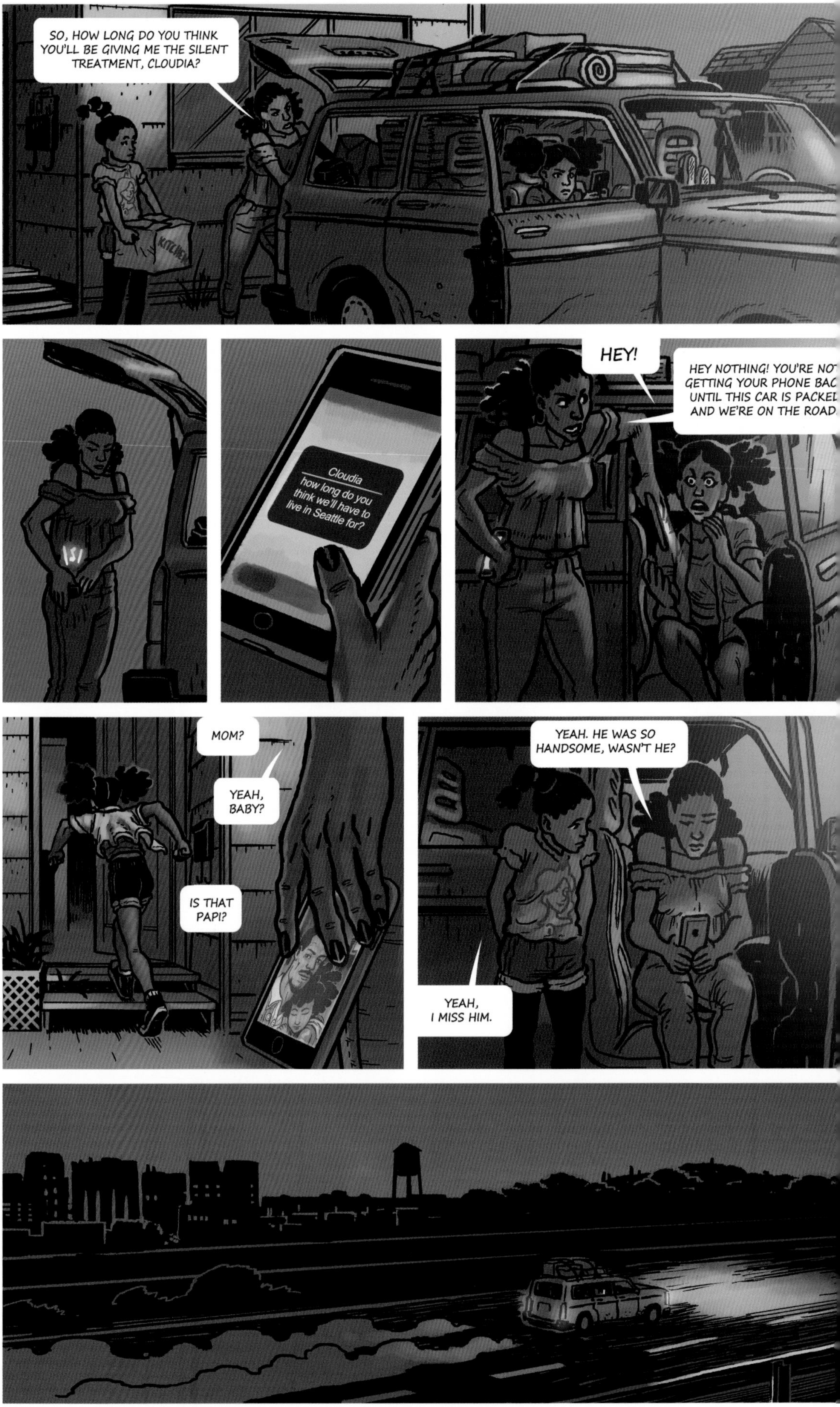
SO, HOW LONG DO YOU THINK YOU'LL BE GIVING ME THE SILENT TREATMENT, CLOUDIA?
KITCHEN
Cloudia
how long do you think we'll have to live in Seattle for?
HEY!
HEY NOTHING! YOU'RE NOT GETTING YOUR PHONE BAC UNTIL THIS CAR IS PACKED AND WE'RE ON THE ROAD.
MOM?
YEAH, BABY?
IS THAT PAPI?
YEAH. HE WAS SO HANDSOME, WASN'T HE?
YEAH, I MISS HIM.

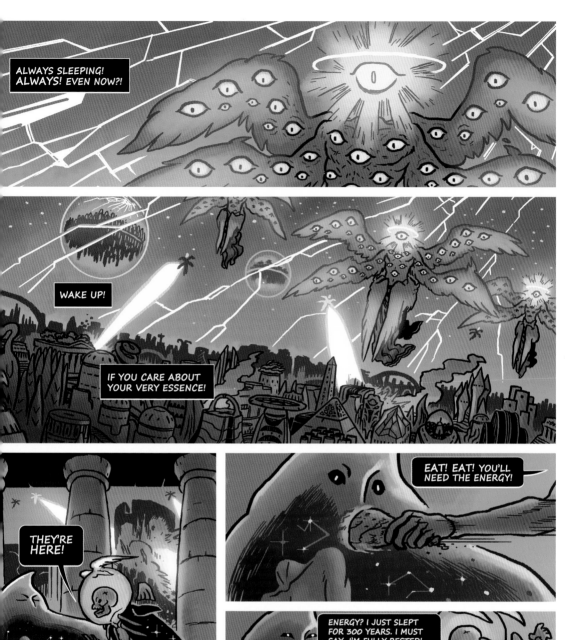

ALWAYS SLEEPING! ALWAYS! EVEN NOW?!

WAKE UP!

IF YOU CARE ABOUT YOUR VERY ESSENCE!

THEY'RE HERE!

EAT! EAT! YOU'LL NEED THE ENERGY!

ENERGY? I JUST SLEPT FOR 300 YEARS. I MUST SAY, I'M FULLY RESTED!

YOU FOOL! THE SERAPHIM ARE ANNIHILATING THE CITY! CONSUMING OUR BRETHREN!

QUICKLY! WE NEED TO LEAVE THIS PLACE! PERHAPS WE CAN FIND A LIGHT-BEAM TO CROSS THE QUINTESSENCE?

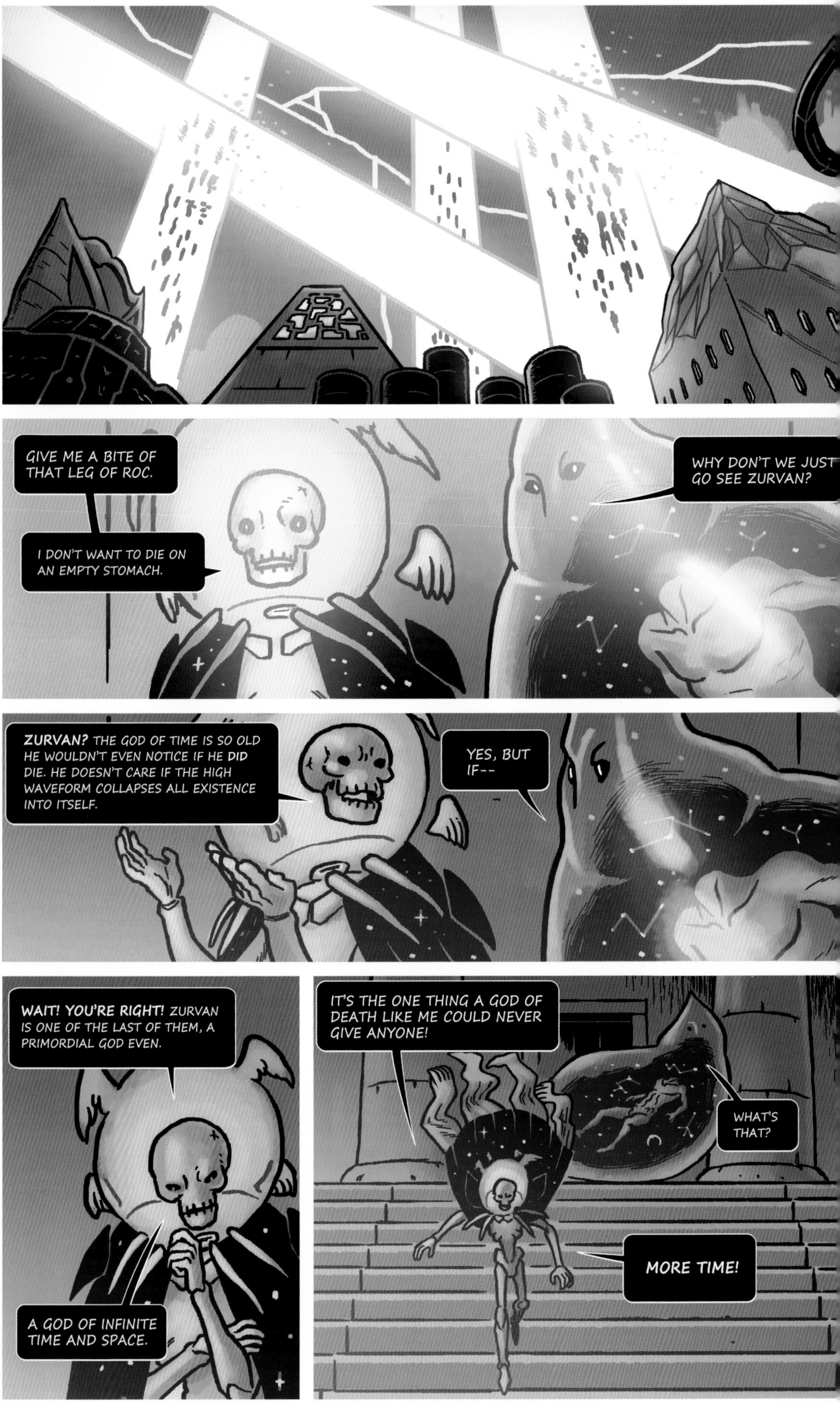
GIVE ME A BITE OF THAT LEG OF ROC.
I DON'T WANT TO DIE ON AN EMPTY STOMACH.
WHY DON'T WE JUST GO SEE ZURVAN?
ZURVAN? THE GOD OF TIME IS SO OLD HE WOULDN'T EVEN NOTICE IF HE **DID** DIE. HE DOESN'T CARE IF THE HIGH WAVEFORM COLLAPSES ALL EXISTENCE INTO ITSELF.
YES, BUT IF--
WAIT! YOU'RE RIGHT! ZURVAN IS ONE OF THE LAST OF THEM, A PRIMORDIAL GOD EVEN.
A GOD OF INFINITE TIME AND SPACE.
IT'S THE ONE THING A GOD OF DEATH LIKE ME COULD NEVER GIVE ANYONE!
WHAT'S THAT?
MORE TIME!

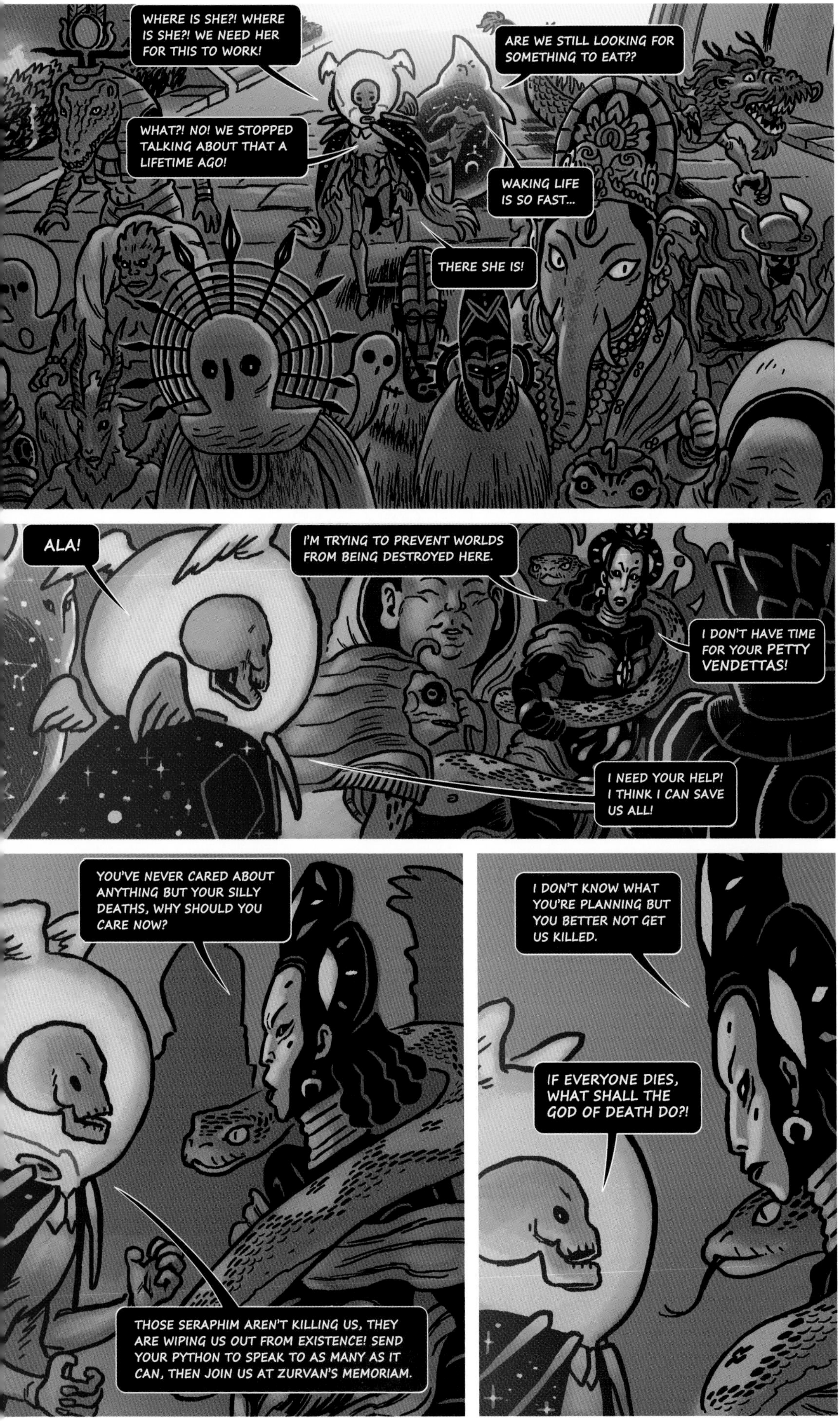
WHERE IS SHE?! WHERE IS SHE?! WE NEED HER FOR THIS TO WORK!
ARE WE STILL LOOKING FOR SOMETHING TO EAT??
WHAT?! NO! WE STOPPED TALKING ABOUT THAT A LIFETIME AGO!
WAKING LIFE IS SO FAST...
THERE SHE IS!
ALA!
I'M TRYING TO PREVENT WORLDS FROM BEING DESTROYED HERE.
I DON'T HAVE TIME FOR YOUR PETTY VENDETTAS!
I NEED YOUR HELP! I THINK I CAN SAVE US ALL!
YOU'VE NEVER CARED ABOUT ANYTHING BUT YOUR SILLY DEATHS, WHY SHOULD YOU CARE NOW?
THOSE SERAPHIM AREN'T KILLING US, THEY ARE WIPING US OUT FROM EXISTENCE! SEND YOUR PYTHON TO SPEAK TO AS MANY AS IT CAN, THEN JOIN US AT ZURVAN'S MEMORIAM.
I DON'T KNOW WHAT YOU'RE PLANNING BUT YOU BETTER NOT GET US KILLED.
IF EVERYONE DIES, WHAT SHALL THE GOD OF DEATH DO?!

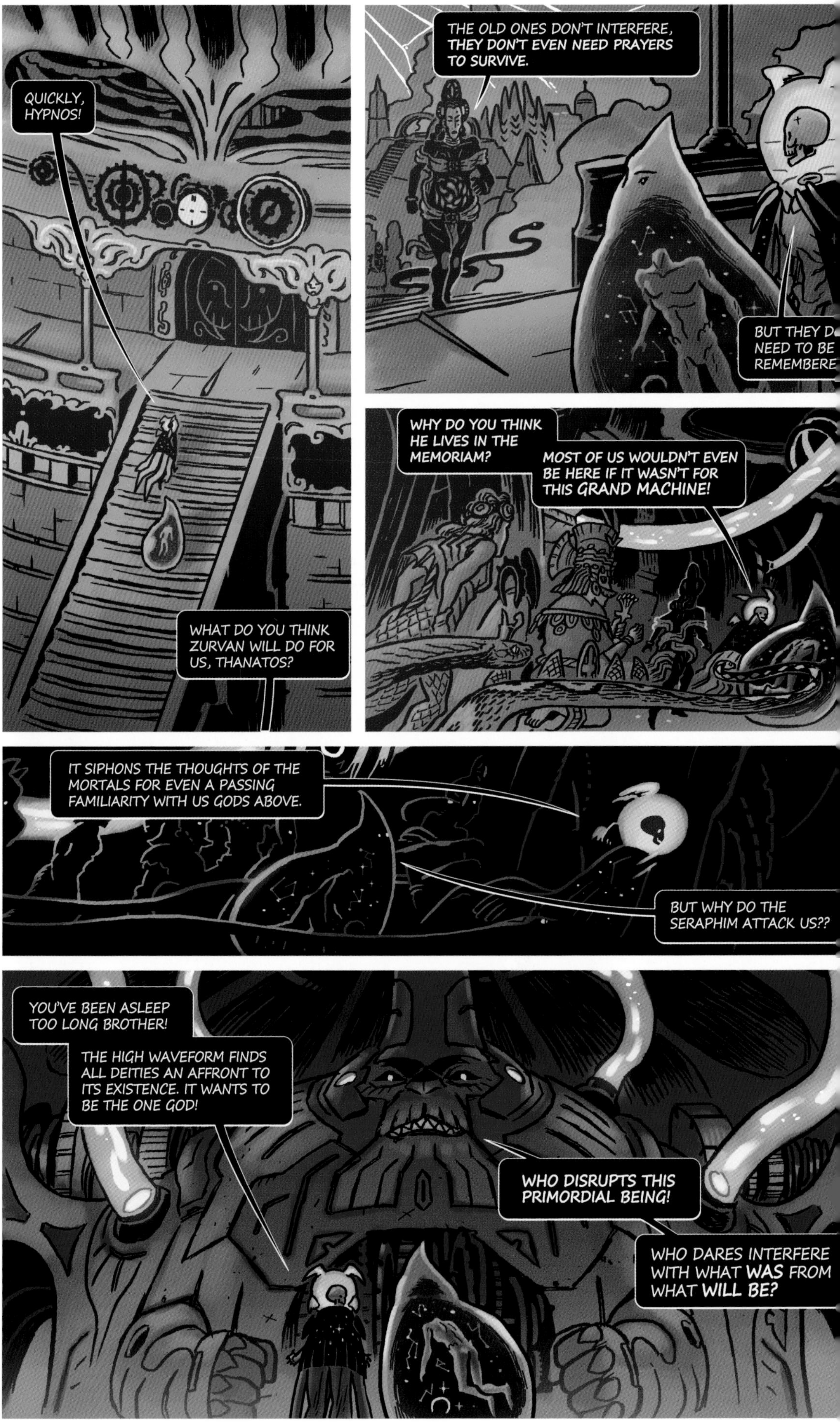
QUICKLY, HYPNOS!
WHAT DO YOU THINK ZURVAN WILL DO FOR US, THANATOS?
THE OLD ONES DON'T INTERFERE, THEY DON'T EVEN NEED PRAYERS TO SURVIVE.
WHY DO YOU THINK HE LIVES IN THE MEMORIAM?
MOST OF US WOULDN'T EVEN BE HERE IF IT WASN'T FOR THIS GRAND MACHINE!
IT SIPHONS THE THOUGHTS OF THE MORTALS FOR EVEN A PASSING FAMILIARITY WITH US GODS ABOVE.
BUT WHY DO THE SERAPHIM ATTACK US??
YOU'VE BEEN ASLEEP TOO LONG BROTHER!
THE HIGH WAVEFORM FINDS ALL DEITIES AN AFFRONT TO ITS EXISTENCE. IT WANTS TO BE THE ONE GOD!
WHO DISRUPTS THIS PRIMORDIAL BEING!
WHO DARES INTERFERE WITH WHAT WAS FROM WHAT WILL BE?

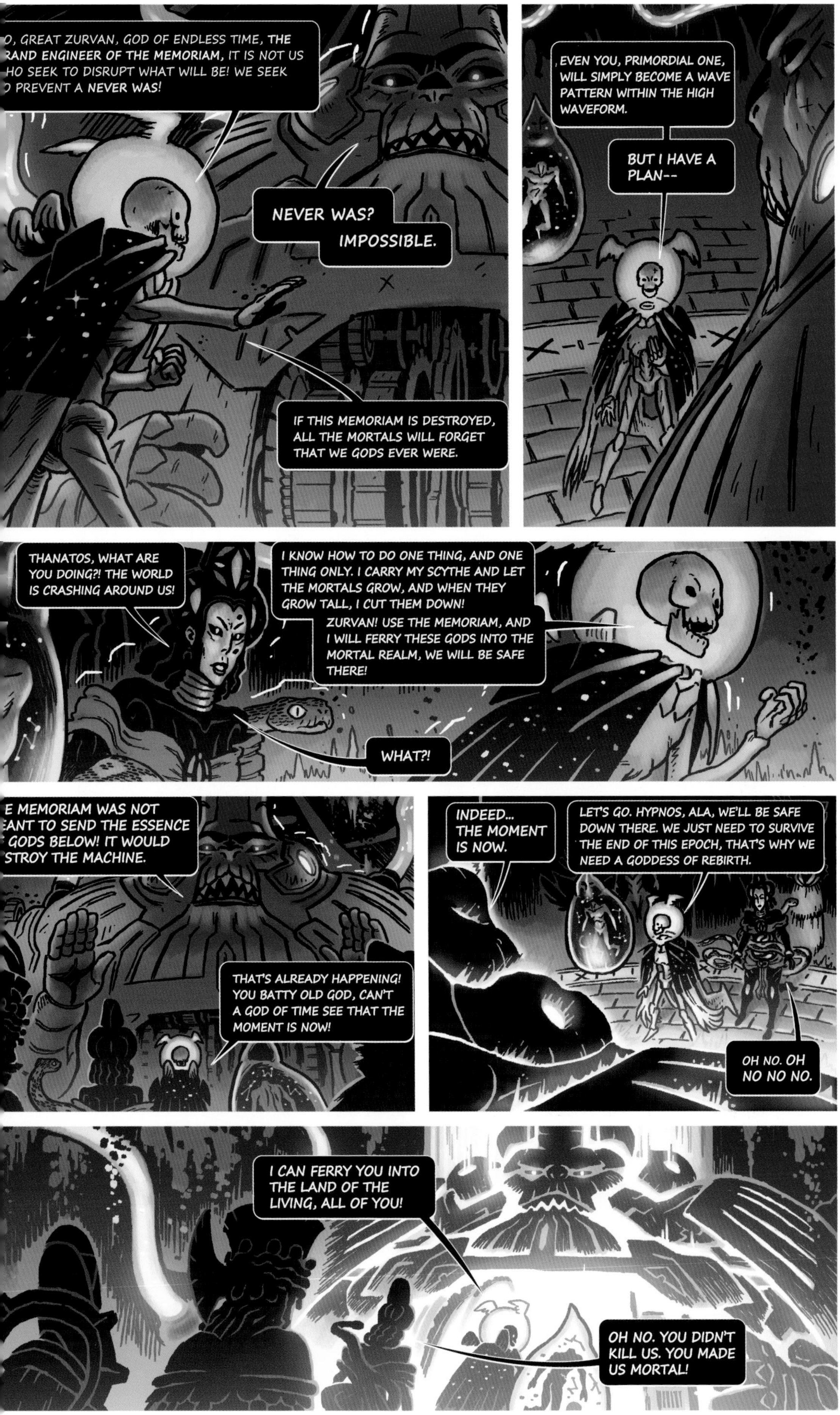

O, GREAT ZURVAN, GOD OF ENDLESS TIME, THE RAND ENGINEER OF THE MEMORIAM, IT IS NOT US HO SEEK TO DISRUPT WHAT WILL BE! WE SEEK PREVENT A NEVER WAS!
NEVER WAS?
IMPOSSIBLE.
IF THIS MEMORIAM IS DESTROYED, ALL THE MORTALS WILL FORGET THAT WE GODS EVER WERE.
EVEN YOU, PRIMORDIAL ONE, WILL SIMPLY BECOME A WAVE PATTERN WITHIN THE HIGH WAVEFORM.
BUT I HAVE A PLAN--
THANATOS, WHAT ARE YOU DOING?! THE WORLD IS CRASHING AROUND US!
I KNOW HOW TO DO ONE THING, AND ONE THING ONLY. I CARRY MY SCYTHE AND LET THE MORTALS GROW, AND WHEN THEY GROW TALL, I CUT THEM DOWN!
ZURVAN! USE THE MEMORIAM, AND I WILL FERRY THESE GODS INTO THE MORTAL REALM, WE WILL BE SAFE THERE!
WHAT?!
E MEMORIAM WAS NOT ANT TO SEND THE ESSENCE GODS BELOW! IT WOULD STROY THE MACHINE.
THAT'S ALREADY HAPPENING! YOU BATTY OLD GOD, CAN'T A GOD OF TIME SEE THAT THE MOMENT IS NOW!
INDEED... THE MOMENT IS NOW.
LET'S GO. HYPNOS, ALA, WE'LL BE SAFE DOWN THERE. WE JUST NEED TO SURVIVE THE END OF THIS EPOCH, THAT'S WHY WE NEED A GODDESS OF REBIRTH.
OH NO. OH NO NO NO.
I CAN FERRY YOU INTO THE LAND OF THE LIVING, ALL OF YOU!
OH NO. YOU DIDN'T KILL US. YOU MADE US MORTAL!

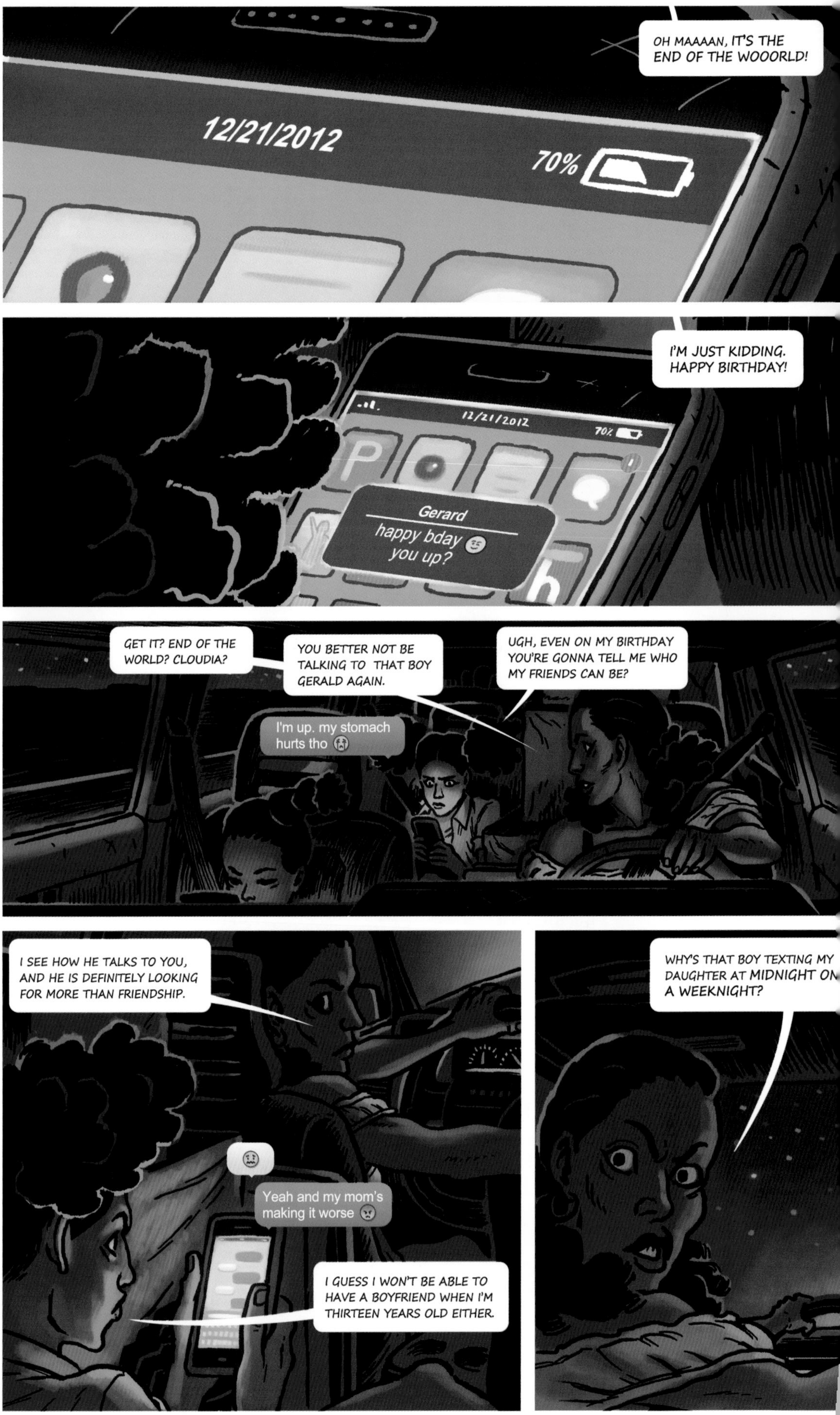

OH MAAAAN, IT'S THE END OF THE WOOORLD!
12/21/2012
70%
I'M JUST KIDDING. HAPPY BIRTHDAY!
12/21/2012
70%
Gerard
happy bday
you up?
GET IT? END OF THE WORLD? CLOUDIA?
YOU BETTER NOT BE TALKING TO THAT BOY GERALD AGAIN.
UGH, EVEN ON MY BIRTHDAY YOU'RE GONNA TELL ME WHO MY FRIENDS CAN BE?
I'm up. my stomach hurts tho
I SEE HOW HE TALKS TO YOU, AND HE IS DEFINITELY LOOKING FOR MORE THAN FRIENDSHIP.
Yeah and my mom's making it worse
I GUESS I WON'T BE ABLE TO HAVE A BOYFRIEND WHEN I'M THIRTEEN YEARS OLD EITHER.
WHY'S THAT BOY TEXTING MY DAUGHTER AT MIDNIGHT ON A WEEKNIGHT?

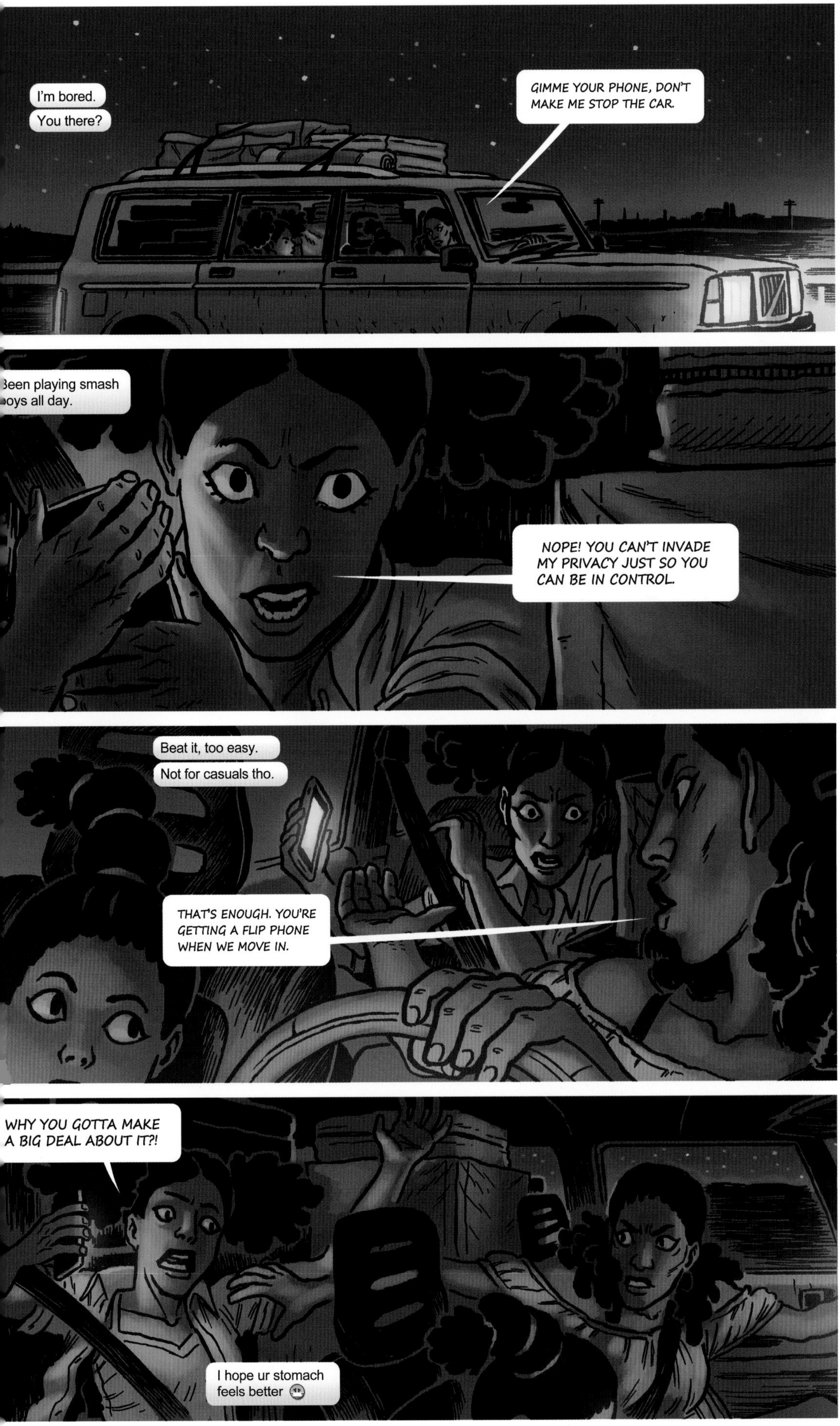
I'm bored.
You there?
GIMME YOUR PHONE, DON'T MAKE ME STOP THE CAR.
Been playing smash boys all day.
NOPE! YOU CAN'T INVADE MY PRIVACY JUST SO YOU CAN BE IN CONTROL.
Beat it, too easy.
Not for casuals tho.
THAT'S ENOUGH. YOU'RE GETTING A FLIP PHONE WHEN WE MOVE IN.
WHY YOU GOTTA MAKE A BIG DEAL ABOUT IT?!
I hope ur stomach feels better

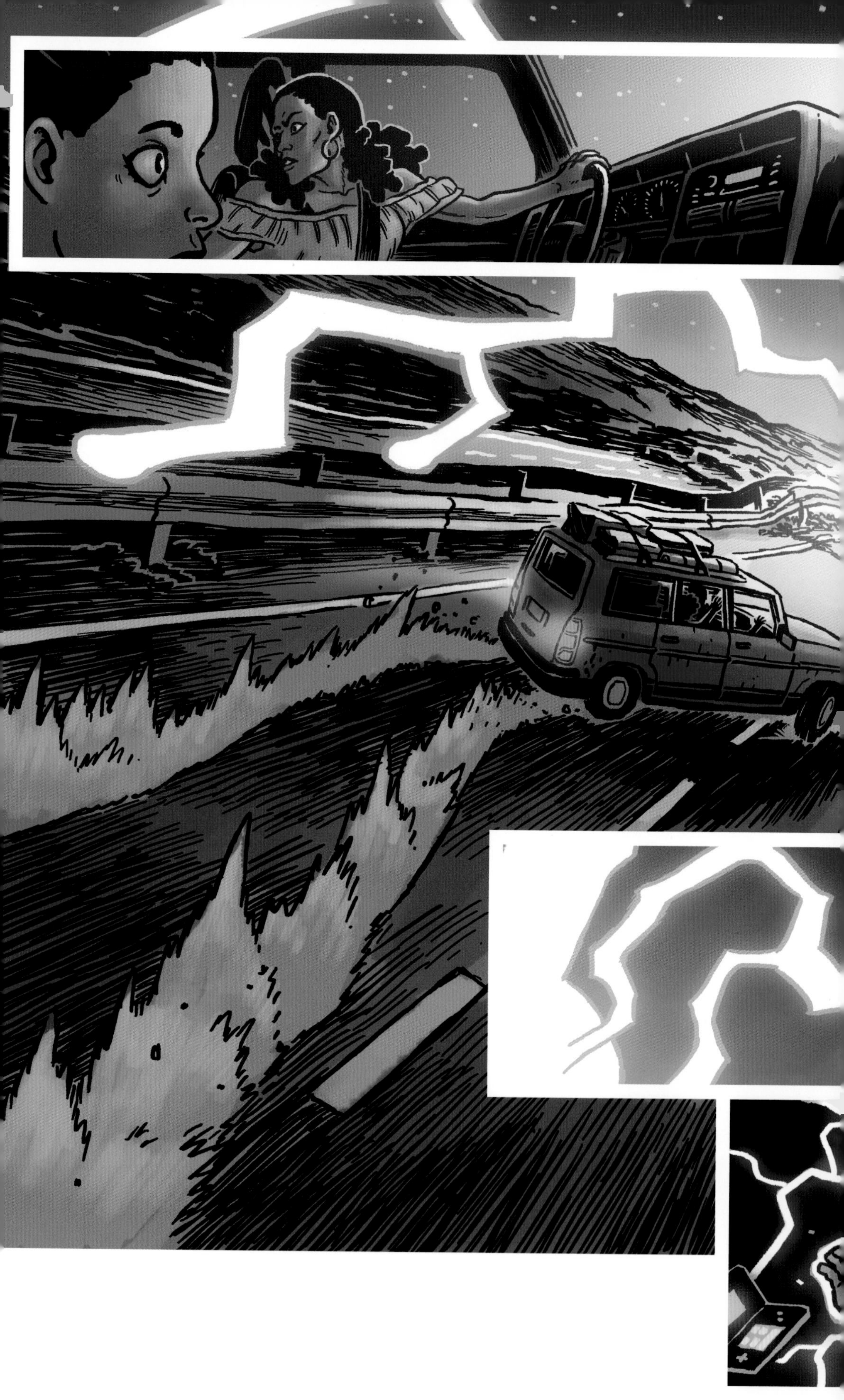

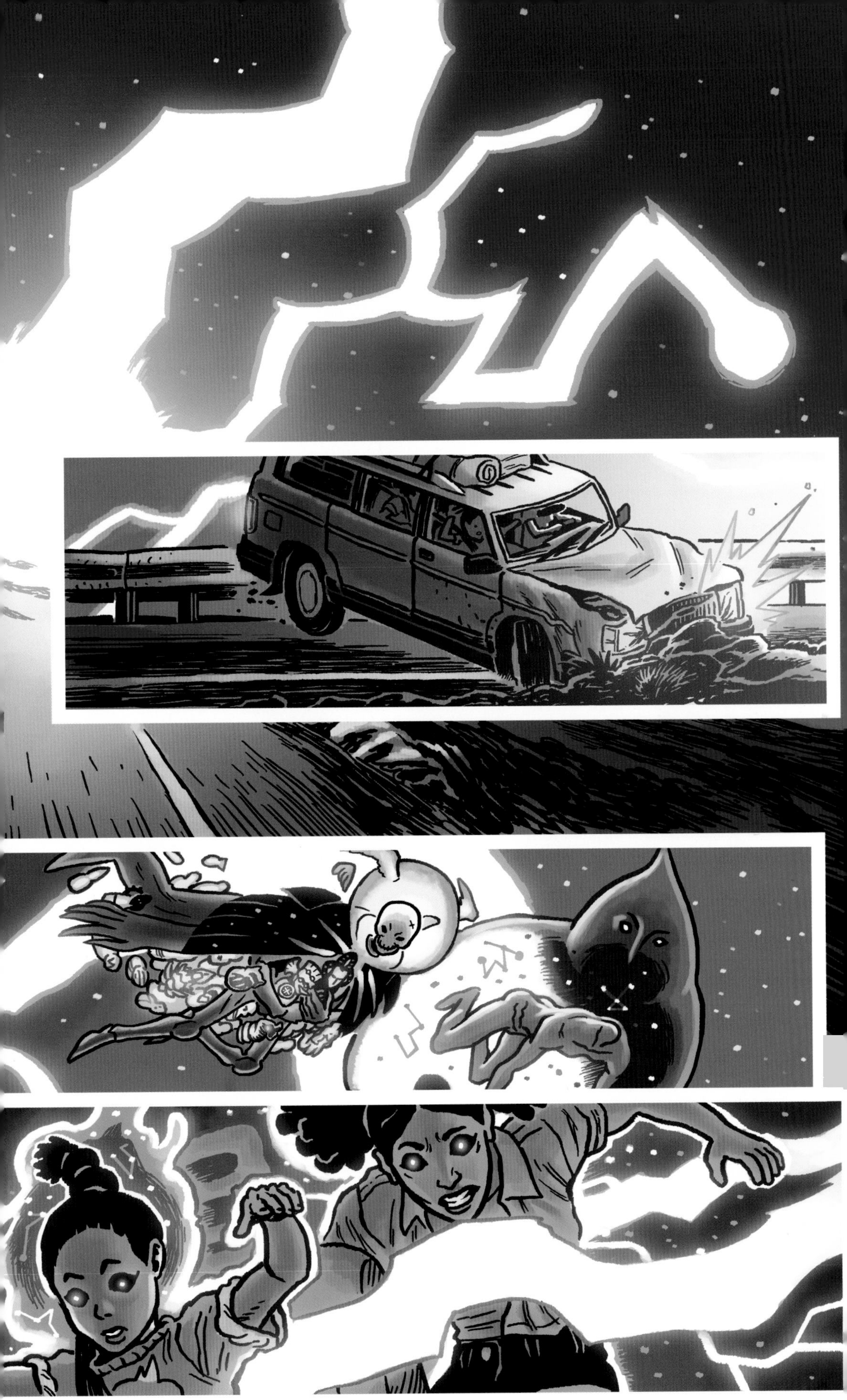

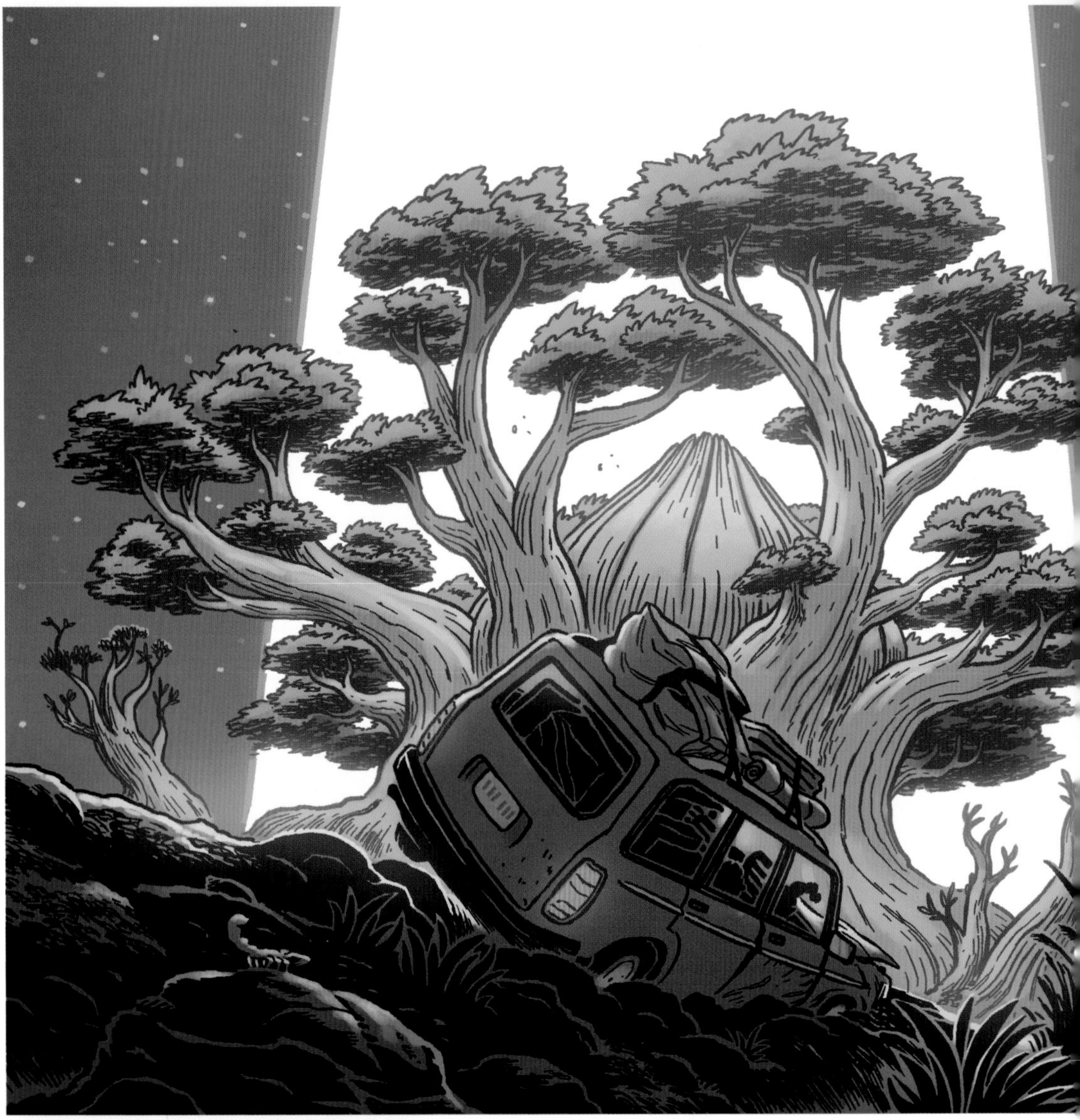
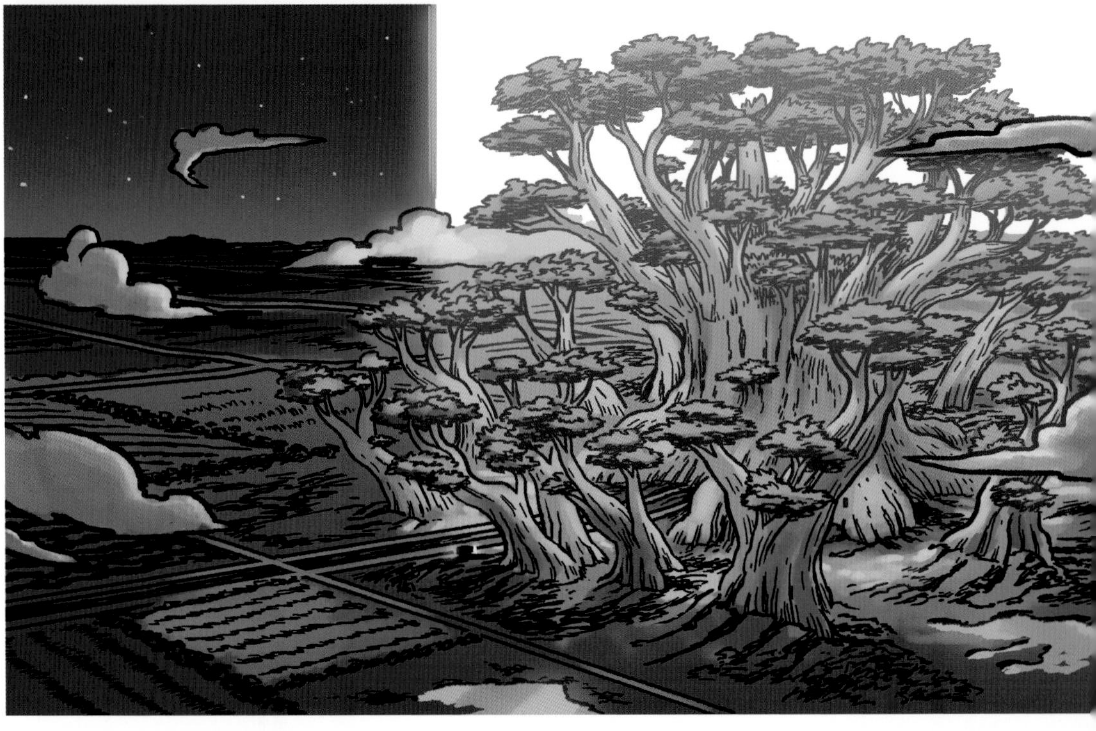

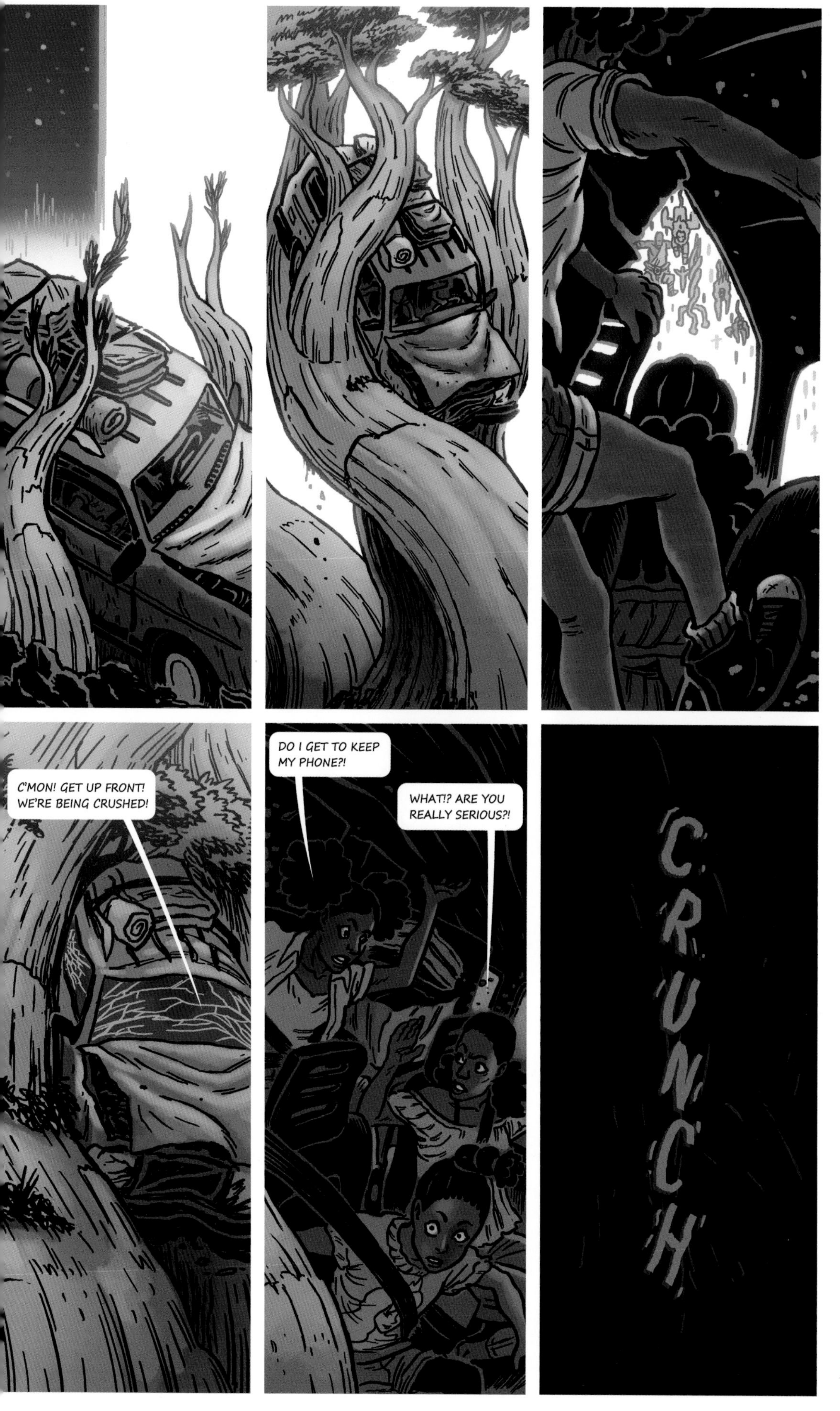
C'MON! GET UP FRONT! WE'RE BEING CRUSHED!
DO I GET TO KEEP MY PHONE?!
WHAT!? ARE YOU REALLY SERIOUS?!
CRUNCH

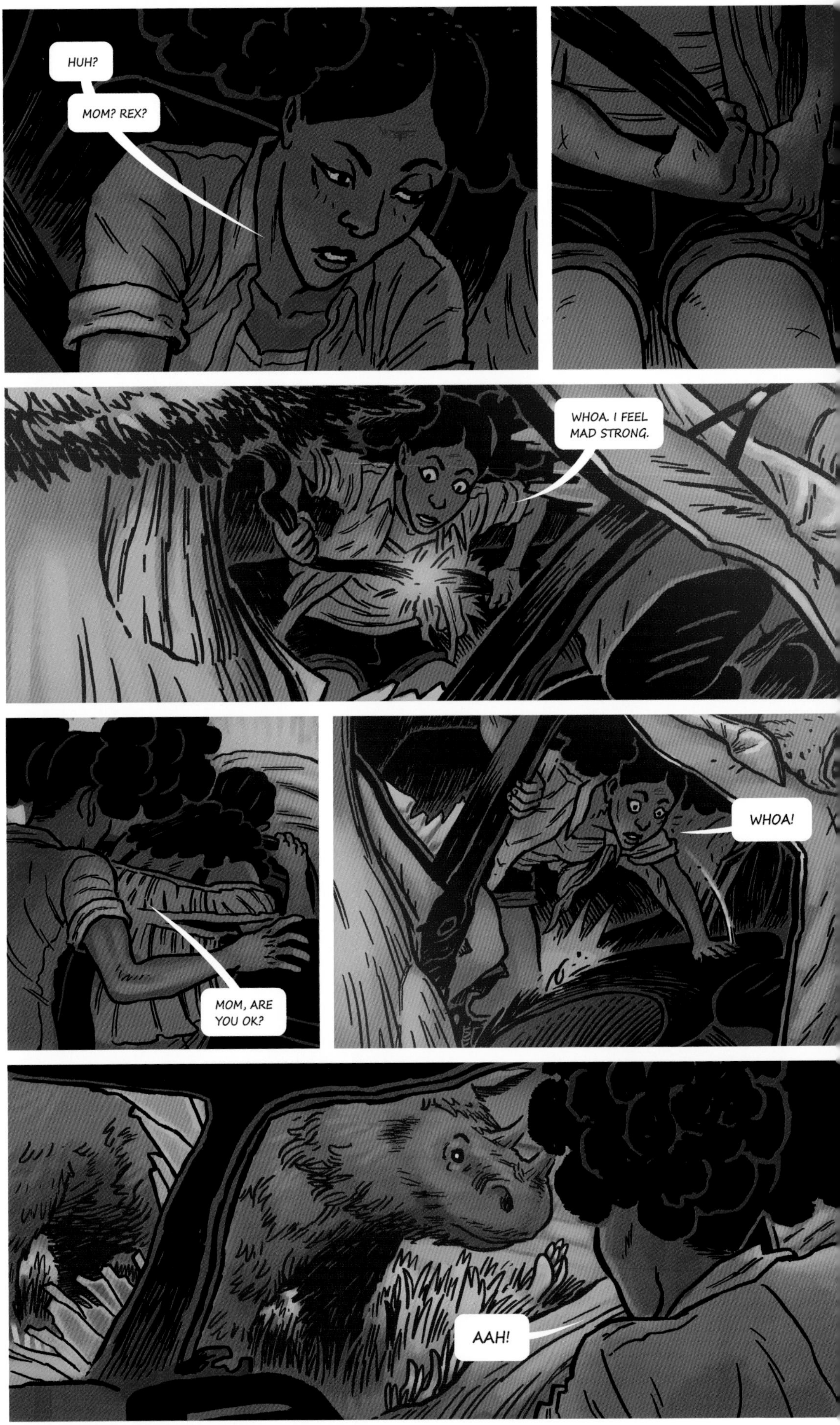
HUH?
MOM? REX?
WHOA. I FEEL MAD STRONG.
MOM, ARE YOU OK?
WHOA!
AAH!

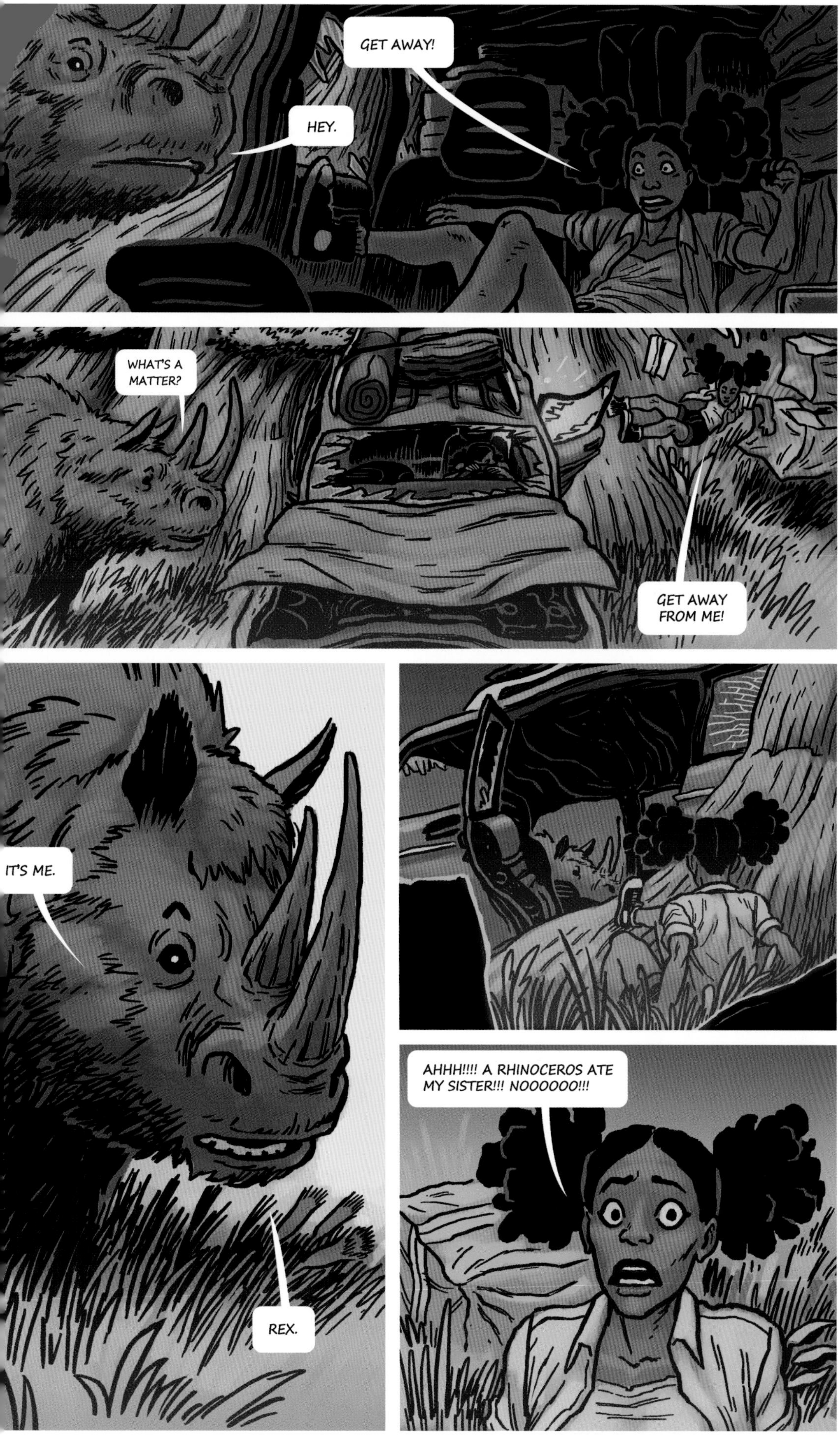
GET AWAY!
HEY.
WHAT'S A MATTER?
GET AWAY FROM ME!
IT'S ME.
REX.
AHHH!!!! A RHINOCEROS ATE MY SISTER!!! NOOOOOO!!!

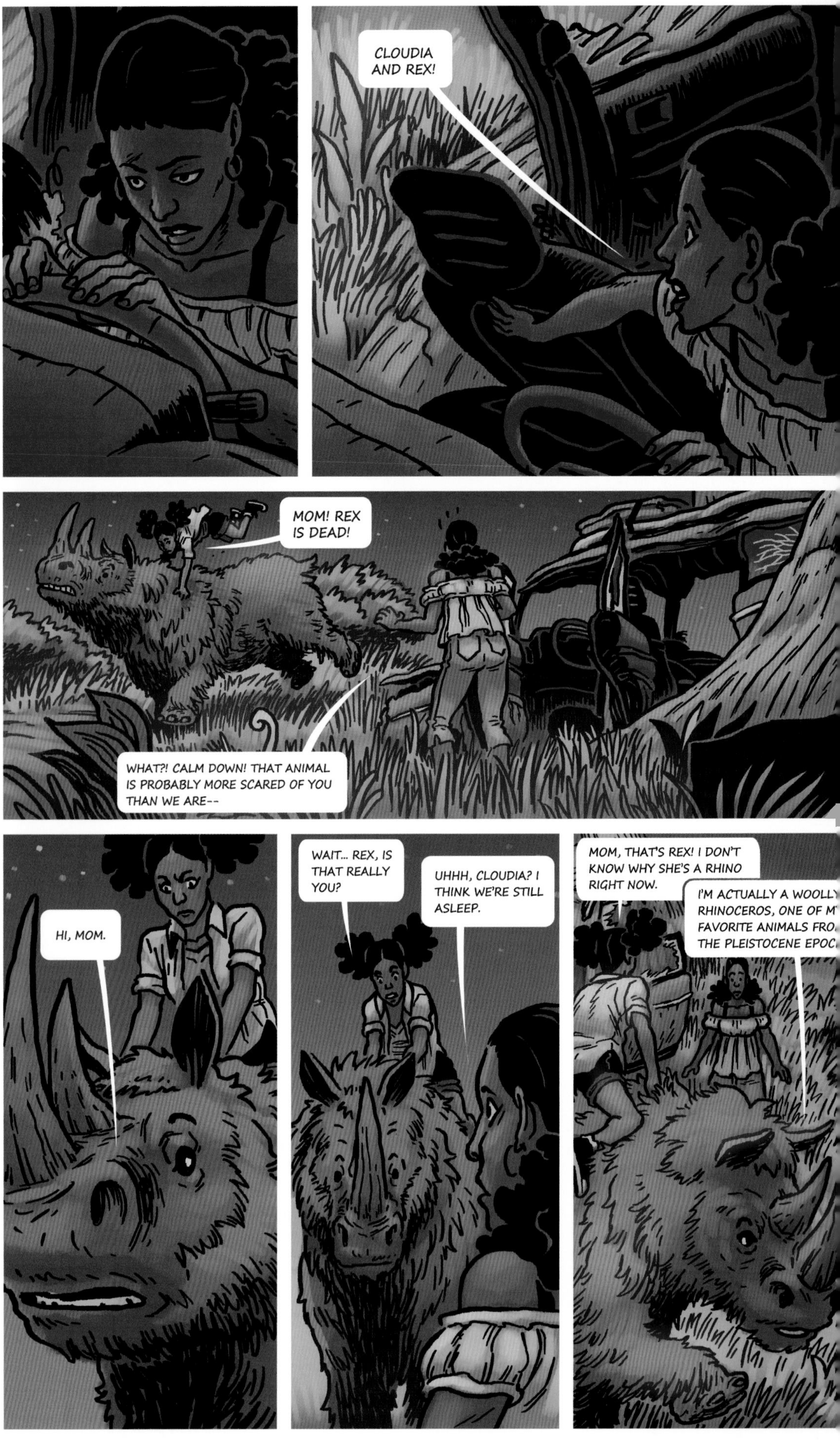
CLOUDIA AND REX!
MOM! REX IS DEAD!
WHAT?! CALM DOWN! THAT ANIMAL IS PROBABLY MORE SCARED OF YOU THAN WE ARE--
HI, MOM.
WAIT... REX, IS THAT REALLY YOU?
UHHH, CLOUDIA? I THINK WE'RE STILL ASLEEP.
MOM, THAT'S REX! I DON'T KNOW WHY SHE'S A RHINO RIGHT NOW.
I'M ACTUALLY A WOOLLY RHINOCEROS, ONE OF MY FAVORITE ANIMALS FROM THE PLEISTOCENE EPOCH

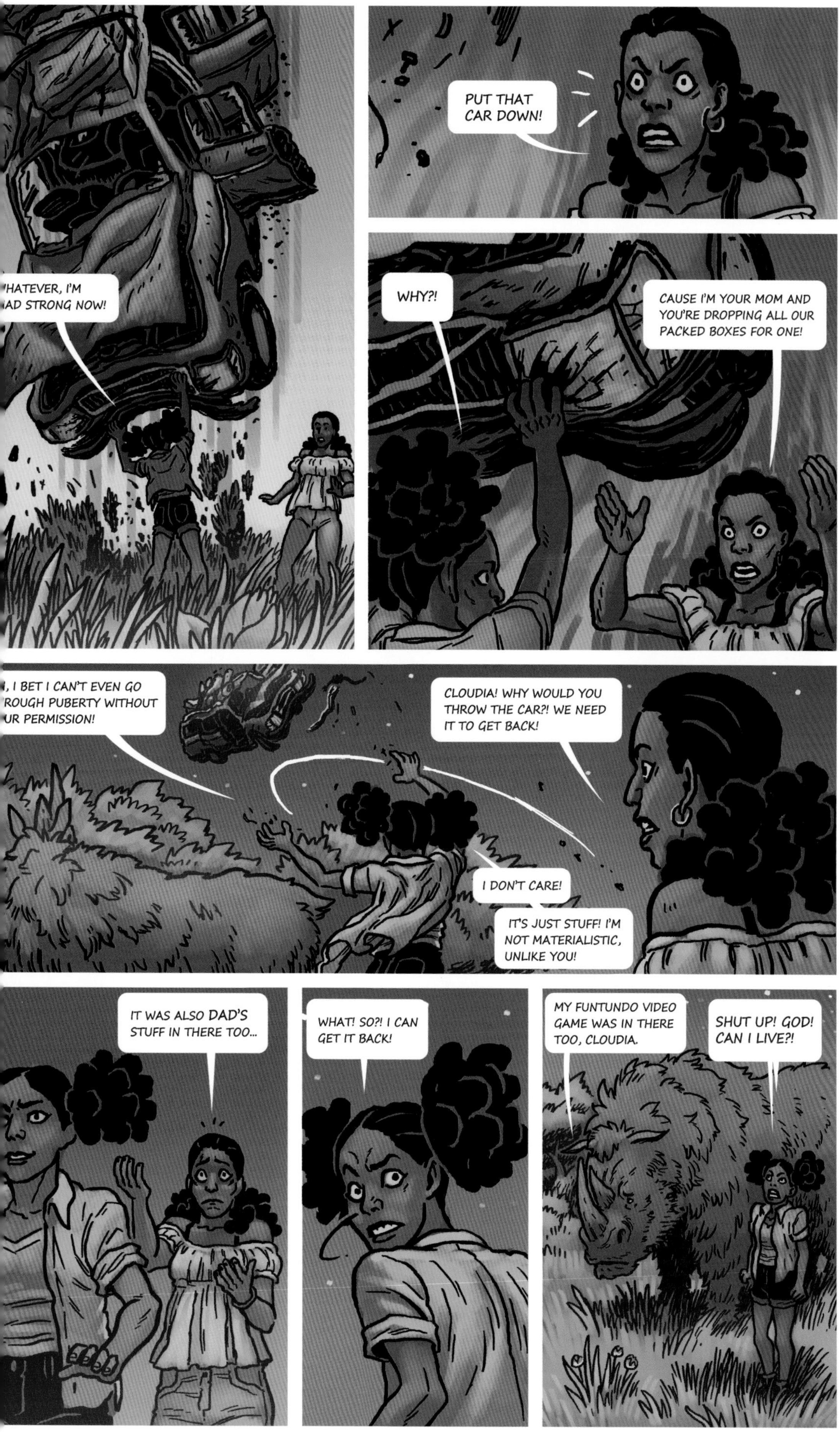

'HATEVER, I'M
AD STRONG NOW!
PUT THAT CAR DOWN!
WHY?!
CAUSE I'M YOUR MOM AND YOU'RE DROPPING ALL OUR PACKED BOXES FOR ONE!
, I BET I CAN'T EVEN GO ROUGH PUBERTY WITHOUT UR PERMISSION!
CLOUDIA! WHY WOULD YOU THROW THE CAR?! WE NEED IT TO GET BACK!
I DON'T CARE!
IT'S JUST STUFF! I'M NOT MATERIALISTIC, UNLIKE YOU!
IT WAS ALSO DAD'S STUFF IN THERE TOO...
WHAT! SO?! I CAN GET IT BACK!
MY FUNTUNDO VIDEO GAME WAS IN THERE TOO, CLOUDIA.
SHUT UP! GOD! CAN I LIVE?!

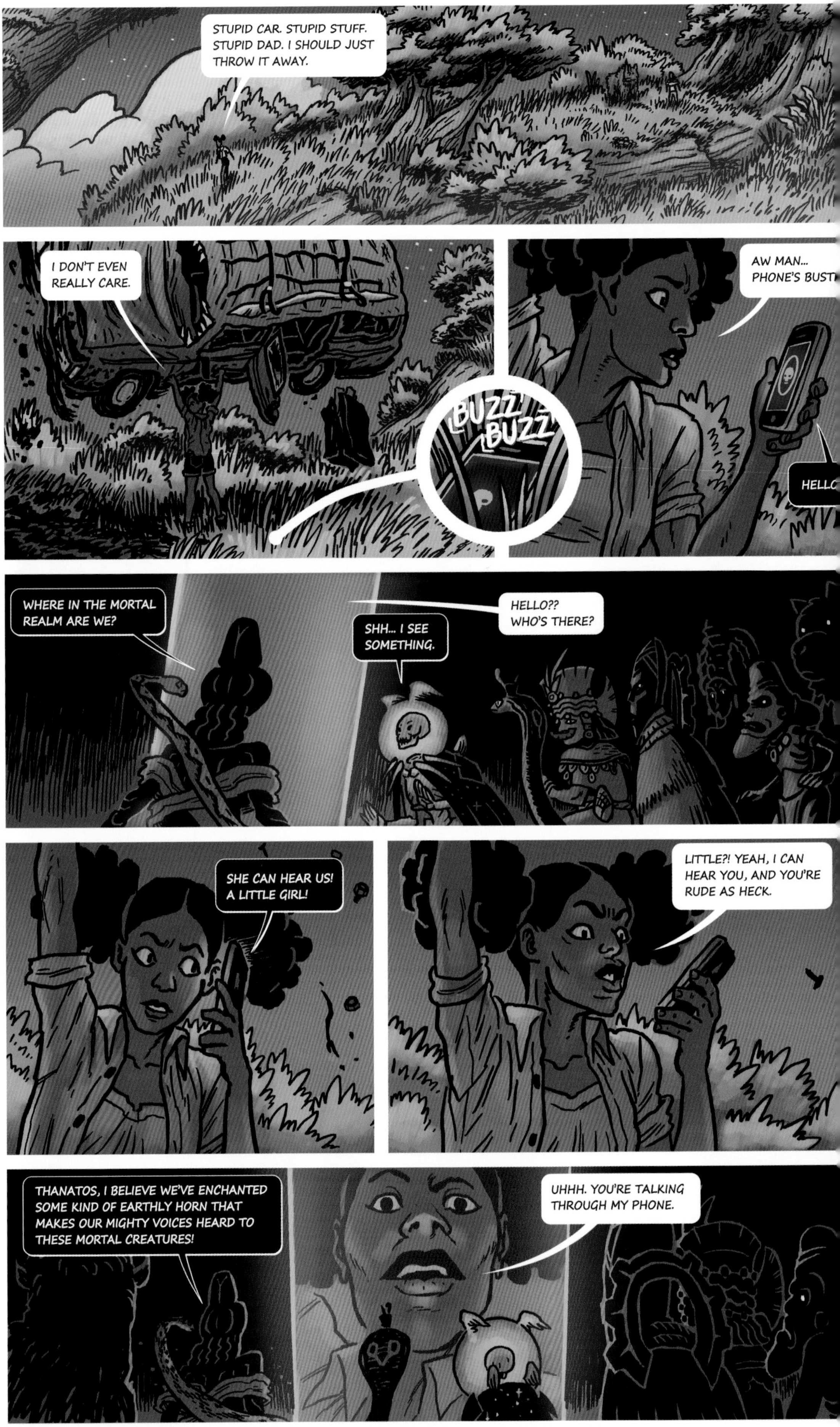
STUPID CAR. STUPID STUFF. STUPID DAD. I SHOULD JUST THROW IT AWAY.
I DON'T EVEN REALLY CARE.
BUZZ BUZZ
AW MAN... PHONE'S BUST
HELLO
WHERE IN THE MORTAL REALM ARE WE?
SHH... I SEE SOMETHING.
HELLO?? WHO'S THERE?
SHE CAN HEAR US! A LITTLE GIRL!
LITTLE?! YEAH, I CAN HEAR YOU, AND YOU'RE RUDE AS HECK.
THANATOS, I BELIEVE WE'VE ENCHANTED SOME KIND OF EARTHLY HORN THAT MAKES OUR MIGHTY VOICES HEARD TO THESE MORTAL CREATURES!
UHHH. YOU'RE TALKING THROUGH MY PHONE.

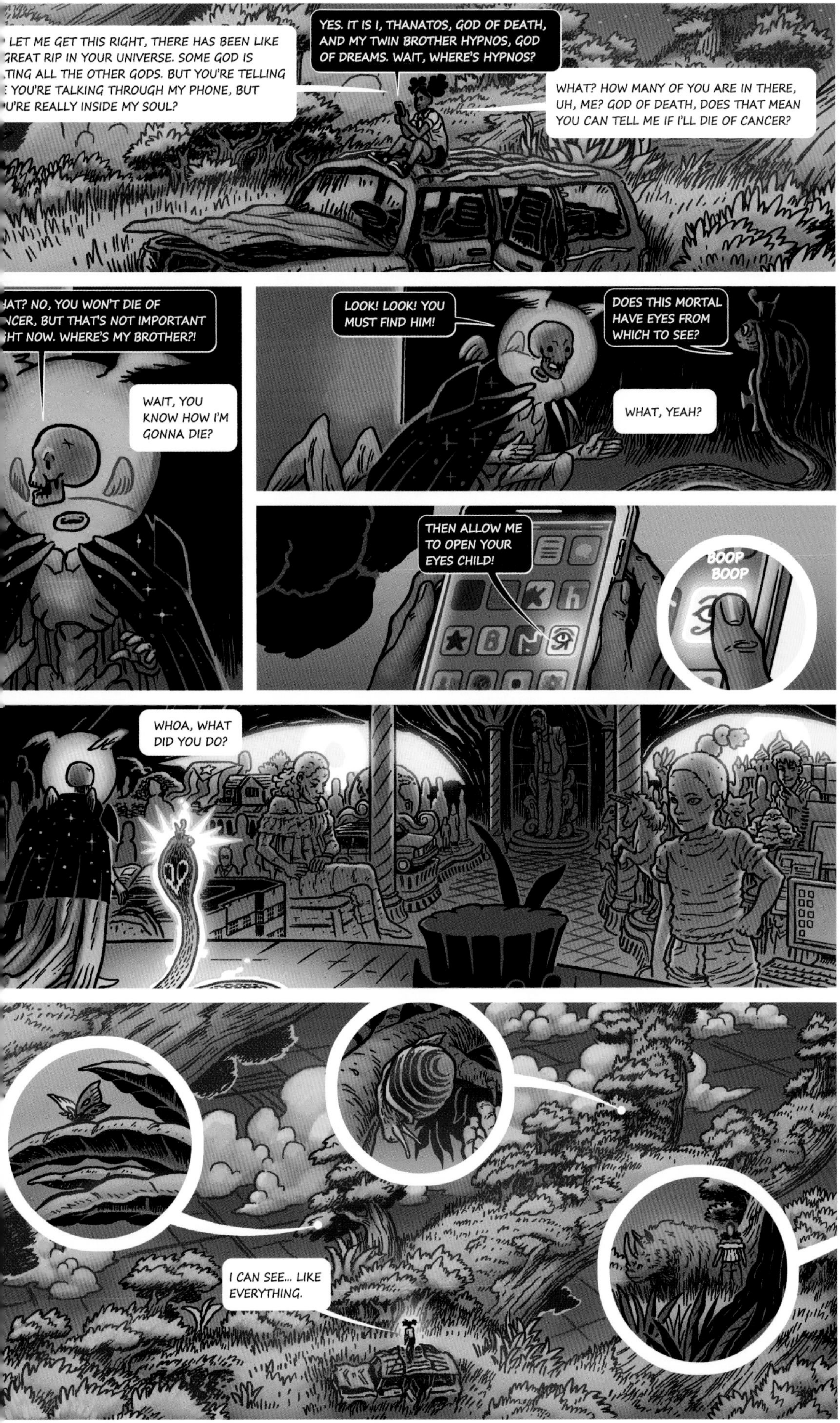
LET ME GET THIS RIGHT, THERE HAS BEEN LIKE
GREAT RIP IN YOUR UNIVERSE. SOME GOD IS
TING ALL THE OTHER GODS. BUT YOU'RE TELLING
YOU'RE TALKING THROUGH MY PHONE, BUT
U'RE REALLY INSIDE MY SOUL?
YES. IT IS I, THANATOS, GOD OF DEATH, AND MY TWIN BROTHER HYPNOS, GOD OF DREAMS. WAIT, WHERE'S HYPNOS?
WHAT? HOW MANY OF YOU ARE IN THERE, UH, ME? GOD OF DEATH, DOES THAT MEAN YOU CAN TELL ME IF I'LL DIE OF CANCER?
IAT? NO, YOU WON'T DIE OF
NCER, BUT THAT'S NOT IMPORTANT
HT NOW. WHERE'S MY BROTHER?!
WAIT, YOU KNOW HOW I'M GONNA DIE?
LOOK! LOOK! YOU MUST FIND HIM!
DOES THIS MORTAL HAVE EYES FROM WHICH TO SEE?
WHAT, YEAH?
THEN ALLOW ME TO OPEN YOUR EYES CHILD!
BOOP BOOP
WHOA, WHAT DID YOU DO?
I CAN SEE... LIKE EVERYTHING.

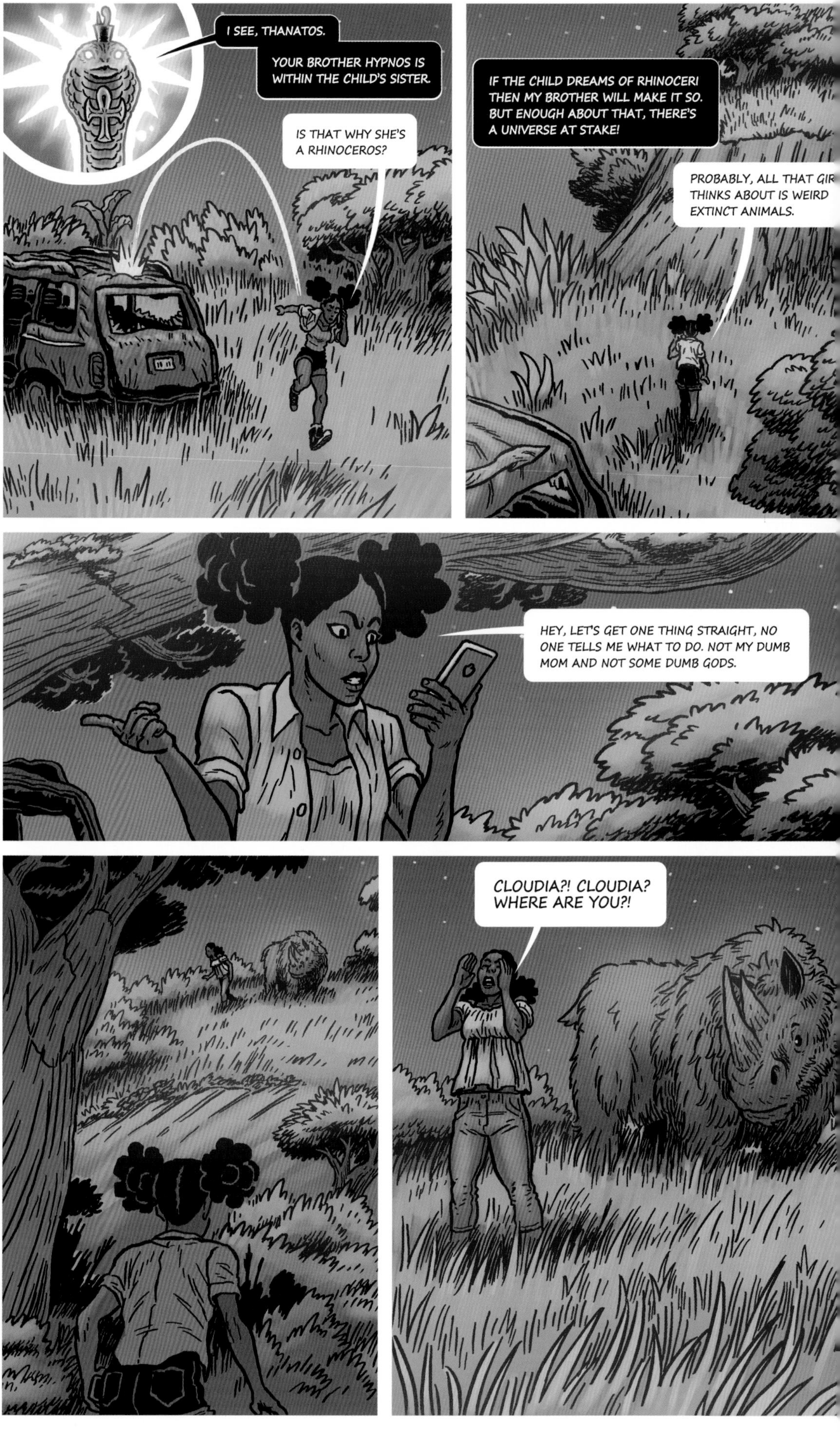
I SEE, THANATOS.
YOUR BROTHER HYPNOS IS WITHIN THE CHILD'S SISTER.
IS THAT WHY SHE'S A RHINOCEROS?
IF THE CHILD DREAMS OF RHINOCERI THEN MY BROTHER WILL MAKE IT SO. BUT ENOUGH ABOUT THAT, THERE'S A UNIVERSE AT STAKE!
PROBABLY, ALL THAT GIR THINKS ABOUT IS WEIRD EXTINCT ANIMALS.
HEY, LET'S GET ONE THING STRAIGHT, NO ONE TELLS ME WHAT TO DO. NOT MY DUMB MOM AND NOT SOME DUMB GODS.
CLOUDIA?! CLOUDIA? WHERE ARE YOU?!

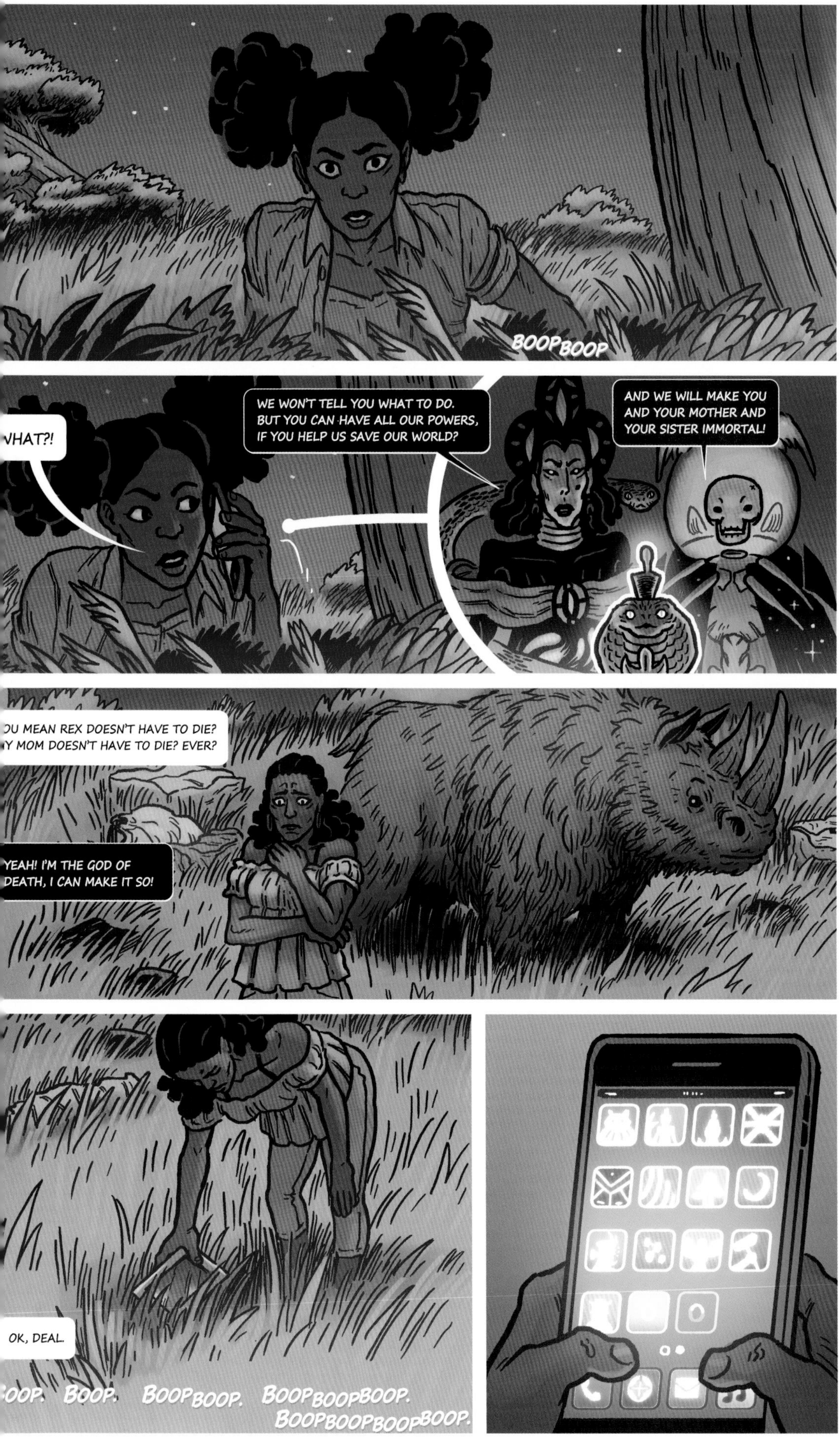
BOOPBOOP
WHAT?!
WE WON'T TELL YOU WHAT TO DO. BUT YOU CAN HAVE ALL OUR POWERS, IF YOU HELP US SAVE OUR WORLD?
AND WE WILL MAKE YOU AND YOUR MOTHER AND YOUR SISTER IMMORTAL!
OU MEAN REX DOESN'T HAVE TO DIE? Y MOM DOESN'T HAVE TO DIE? EVER?
YEAH! I'M THE GOD OF DEATH, I CAN MAKE IT SO!
OK, DEAL.
OOP. BOOP. BOOPBOOP. BOOPBOOPBOOP. BOOPBOOPBOOPBOOP.

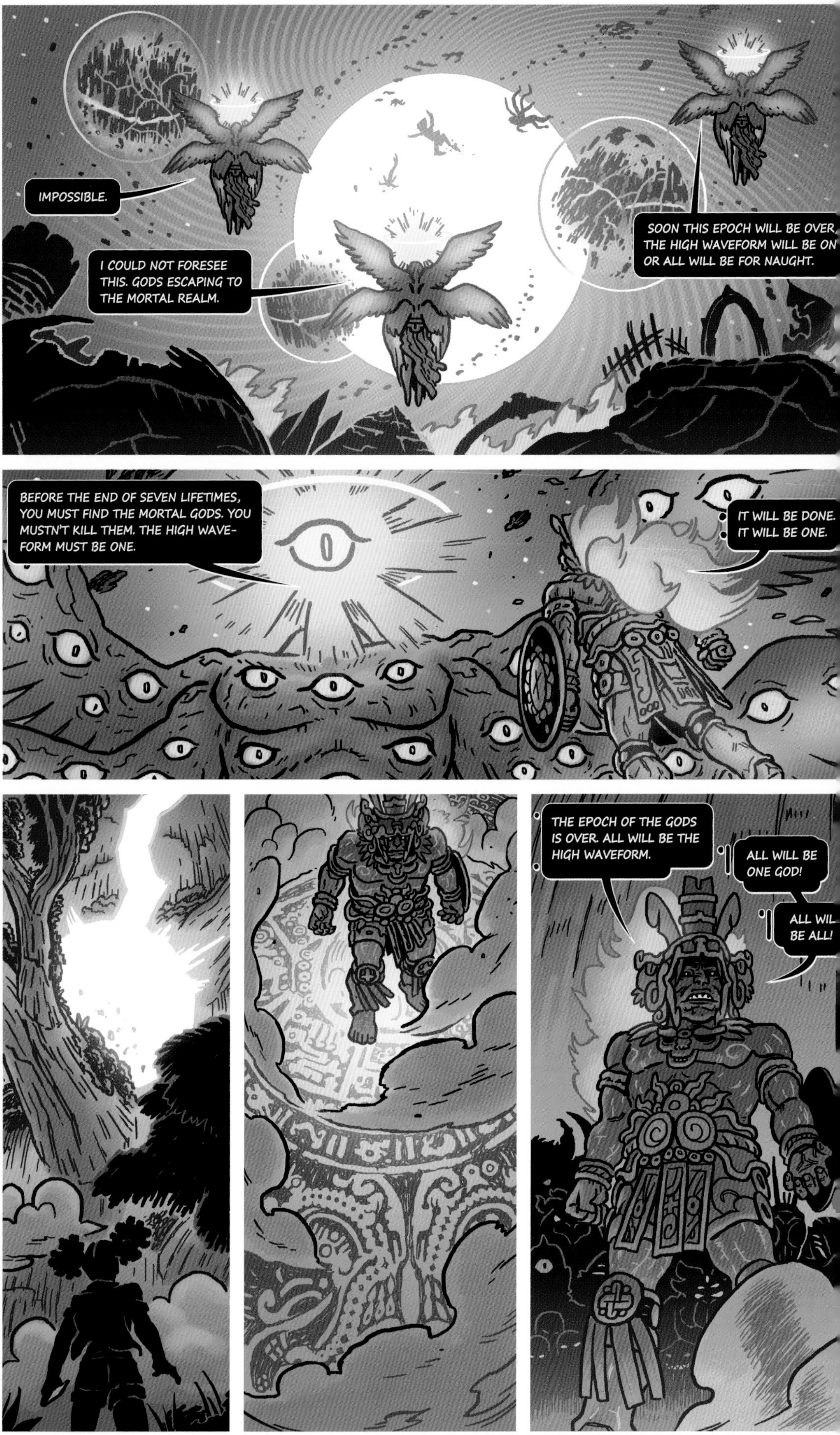
IMPOSSIBLE.
I COULD NOT FORESEE THIS. GODS ESCAPING TO THE MORTAL REALM.
SOON THIS EPOCH WILL BE OVER THE HIGH WAVEFORM WILL BE ON OR ALL WILL BE FOR NAUGHT.
BEFORE THE END OF SEVEN LIFETIMES, YOU MUST FIND THE MORTAL GODS. YOU MUSTN'T KILL THEM. THE HIGH WAVE-FORM MUST BE ONE.
IT WILL BE DONE. IT WILL BE ONE.
THE EPOCH OF THE GODS IS OVER. ALL WILL BE THE HIGH WAVEFORM.
ALL WILL BE ONE GOD!
ALL WIL BE ALL!

CHAPTER TWO

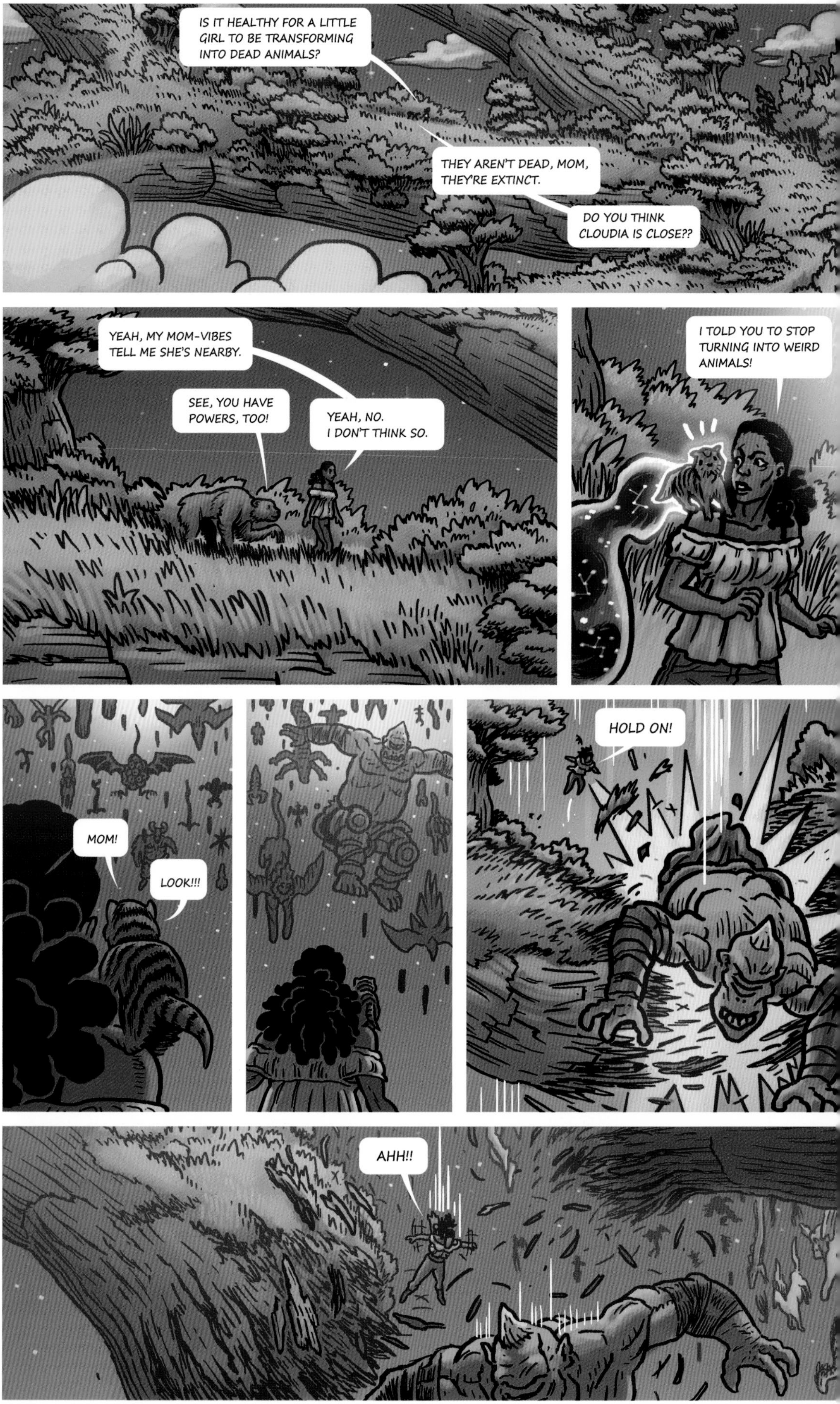
IS IT HEALTHY FOR A LITTLE GIRL TO BE TRANSFORMING INTO DEAD ANIMALS?
THEY AREN'T DEAD, MOM, THEY'RE EXTINCT.
DO YOU THINK CLOUDIA IS CLOSE??
YEAH, MY MOM-VIBES TELL ME SHE'S NEARBY.
SEE, YOU HAVE POWERS, TOO!
YEAH, NO. I DON'T THINK SO.
I TOLD YOU TO STOP TURNING INTO WEIRD ANIMALS!
MOM!
LOOK!!!
HOLD ON!
AHH!!

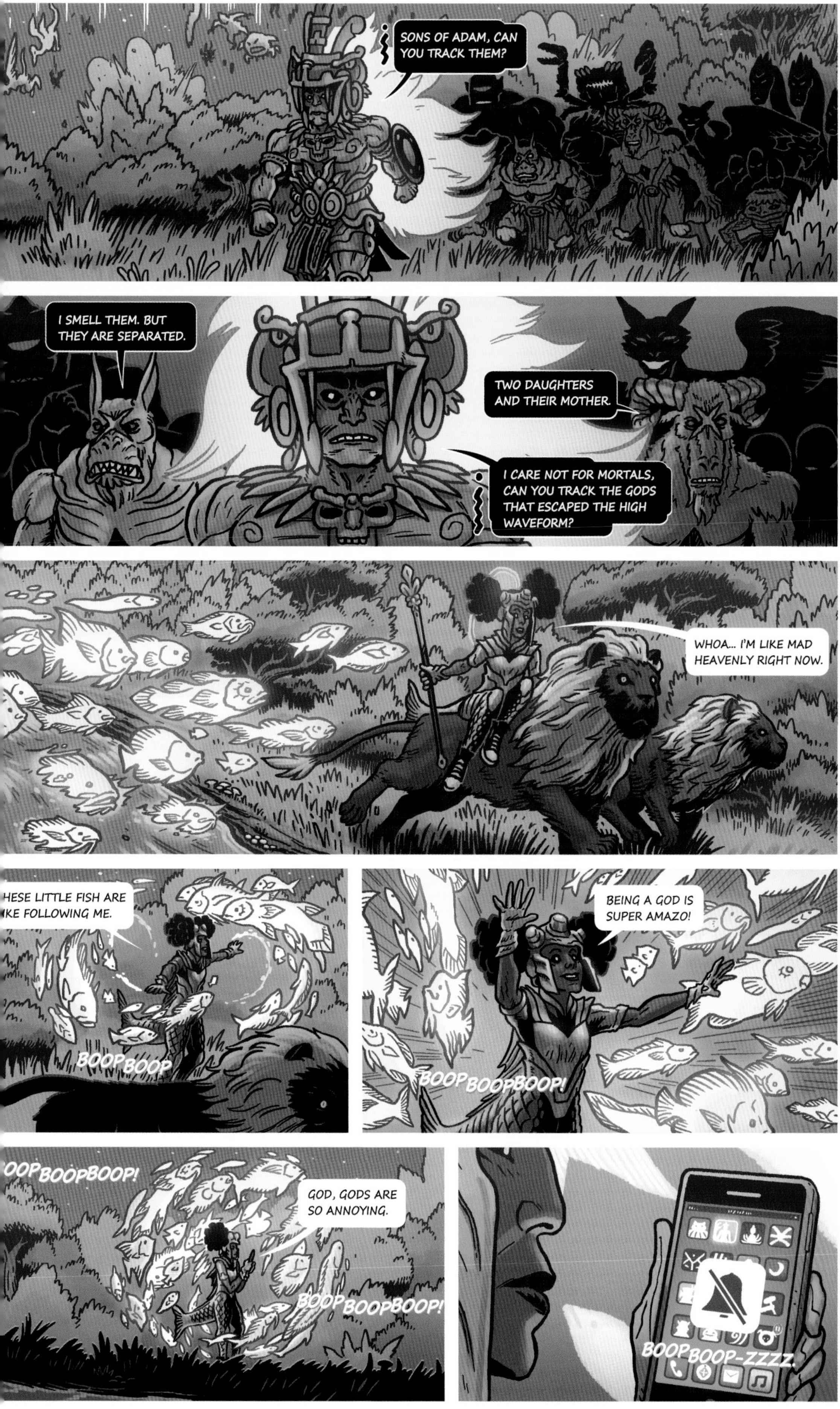
SONS OF ADAM, CAN YOU TRACK THEM?
I SMELL THEM. BUT THEY ARE SEPARATED.
TWO DAUGHTERS AND THEIR MOTHER.
I CARE NOT FOR MORTALS, CAN YOU TRACK THE GODS THAT ESCAPED THE HIGH WAVEFORM?
WHOA... I'M LIKE MAD HEAVENLY RIGHT NOW.
HESE LITTLE FISH ARE IKE FOLLOWING ME.
BOOPBOOP
BEING A GOD IS SUPER AMAZO!
BOOPBOOPBOOP!
OOPBOOPBOOP!
GOD, GODS ARE SO ANNOYING.
BOOPBOOPBOOP!
BOOPBOOP-ZZZZ.

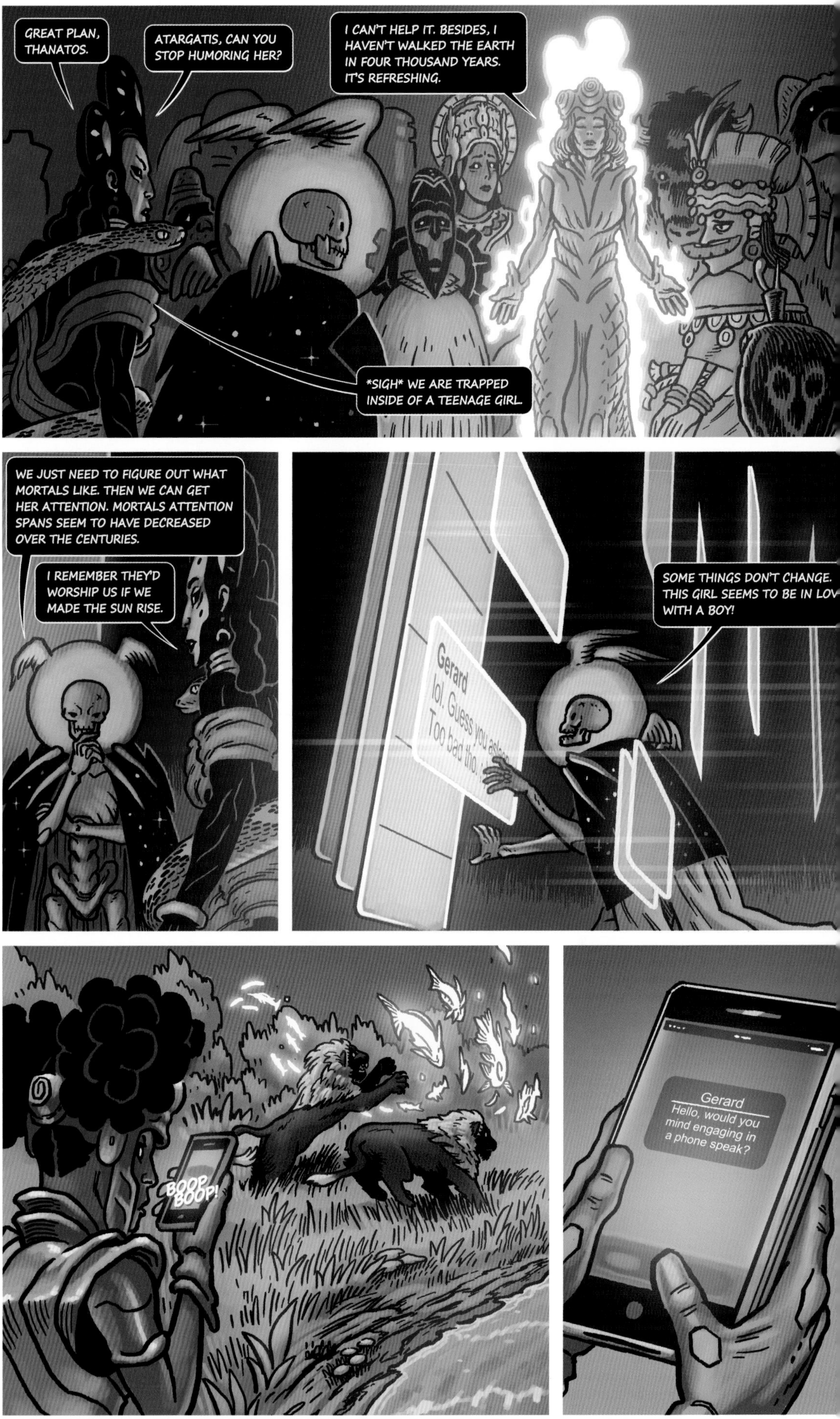
GREAT PLAN, THANATOS.
ATARGATIS, CAN YOU STOP HUMORING HER?
I CAN'T HELP IT. BESIDES, I HAVEN'T WALKED THE EARTH IN FOUR THOUSAND YEARS. IT'S REFRESHING.
SIGH WE ARE TRAPPED INSIDE OF A TEENAGE GIRL.
WE JUST NEED TO FIGURE OUT WHAT MORTALS LIKE. THEN WE CAN GET HER ATTENTION. MORTALS ATTENTION SPANS SEEM TO HAVE DECREASED OVER THE CENTURIES.
I REMEMBER THEY'D WORSHIP US IF WE MADE THE SUN RISE.
Gerard
lol. Guess you
SOME THINGS DON'T CHANGE. THIS GIRL SEEMS TO BE IN LOV
WITH A BOY!
BOOP BOOP!
Gerard
Hello, would you mind engaging in a phone speak?

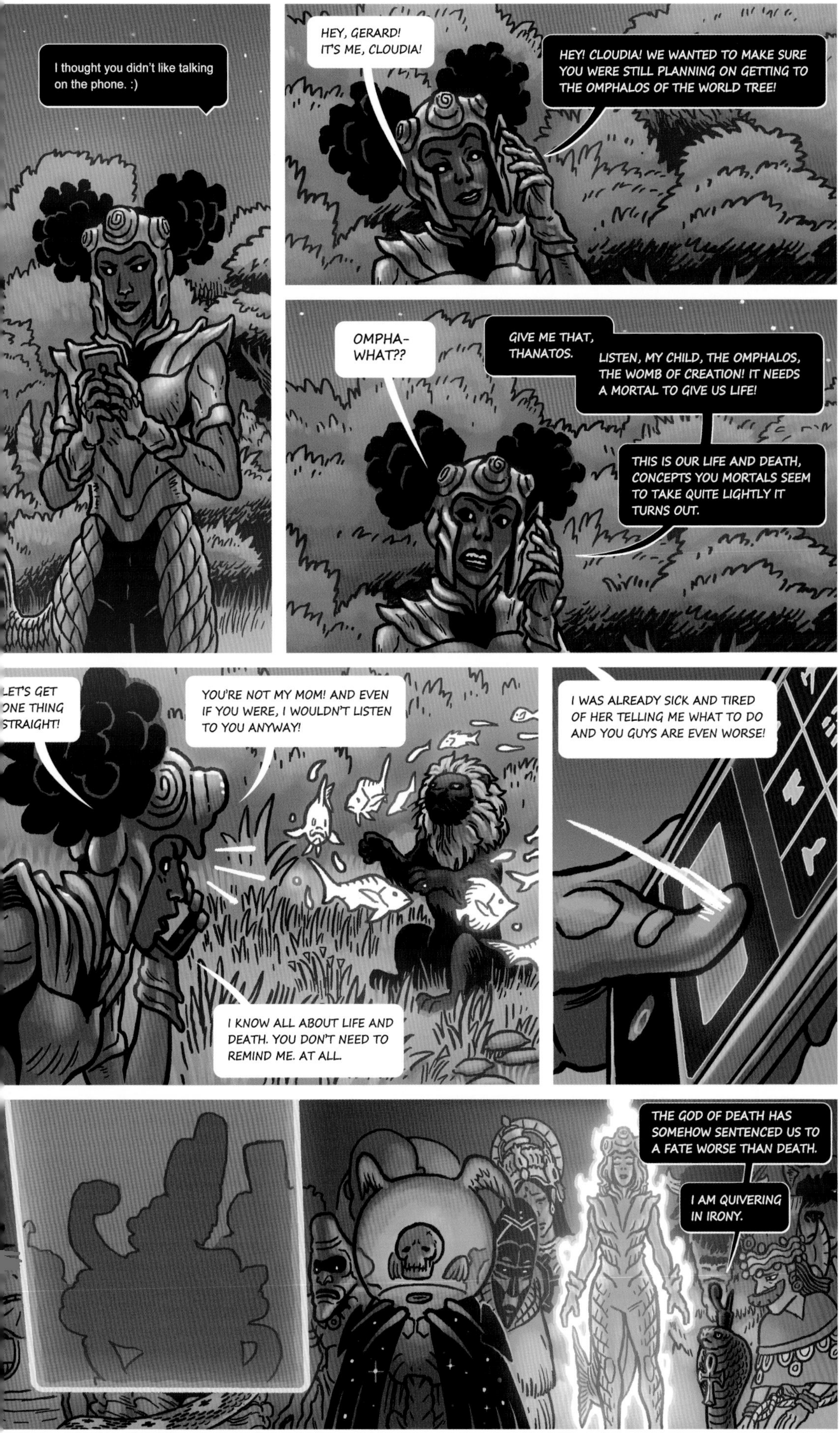
I thought you didn't like talking on the phone. :)
HEY, GERARD! IT'S ME, CLOUDIA!
HEY! CLOUDIA! WE WANTED TO MAKE SURE YOU WERE STILL PLANNING ON GETTING TO THE OMPHALOS OF THE WORLD TREE!
OMPHA-WHAT??
GIVE ME THAT, THANATOS.
LISTEN, MY CHILD, THE OMPHALOS, THE WOMB OF CREATION! IT NEEDS A MORTAL TO GIVE US LIFE!
THIS IS OUR LIFE AND DEATH, CONCEPTS YOU MORTALS SEEM TO TAKE QUITE LIGHTLY IT TURNS OUT.
LET'S GET ONE THING STRAIGHT!
YOU'RE NOT MY MOM! AND EVEN IF YOU WERE, I WOULDN'T LISTEN TO YOU ANYWAY!
I KNOW ALL ABOUT LIFE AND DEATH. YOU DON'T NEED TO REMIND ME. AT ALL.
I WAS ALREADY SICK AND TIRED OF HER TELLING ME WHAT TO DO AND YOU GUYS ARE EVEN WORSE!
THE GOD OF DEATH HAS SOMEHOW SENTENCED US TO A FATE WORSE THAN DEATH.
I AM QUIVERING IN IRONY.

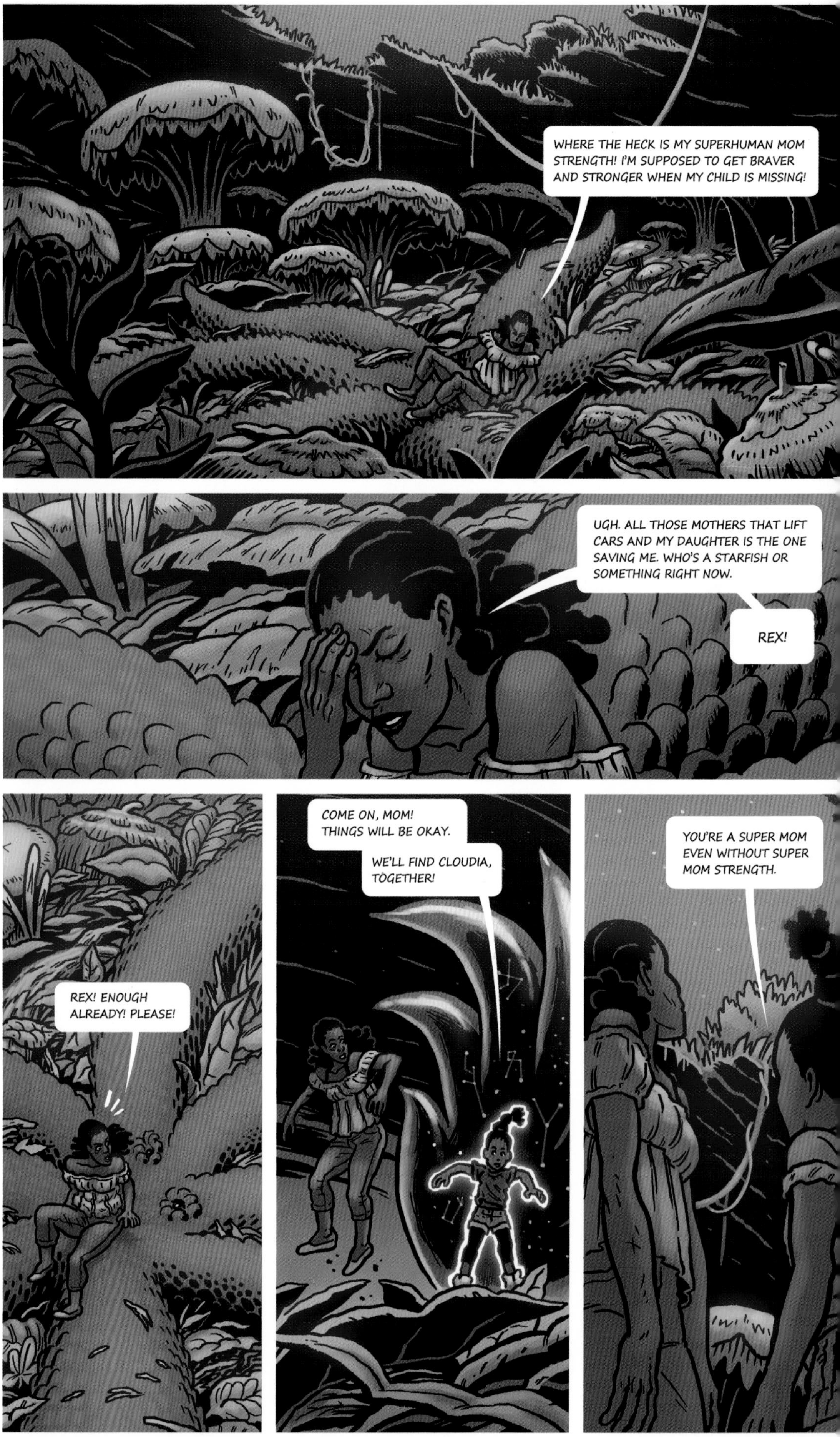
WHERE THE HECK IS MY SUPERHUMAN MOM STRENGTH! I'M SUPPOSED TO GET BRAVER AND STRONGER WHEN MY CHILD IS MISSING!
UGH. ALL THOSE MOTHERS THAT LIFT CARS AND MY DAUGHTER IS THE ONE SAVING ME. WHO'S A STARFISH OR SOMETHING RIGHT NOW.
REX!
REX! ENOUGH ALREADY! PLEASE!
COME ON, MOM! THINGS WILL BE OKAY.
WE'LL FIND CLOUDIA, TOGETHER!
YOU'RE A SUPER MOM EVEN WITHOUT SUPER MOM STRENGTH.

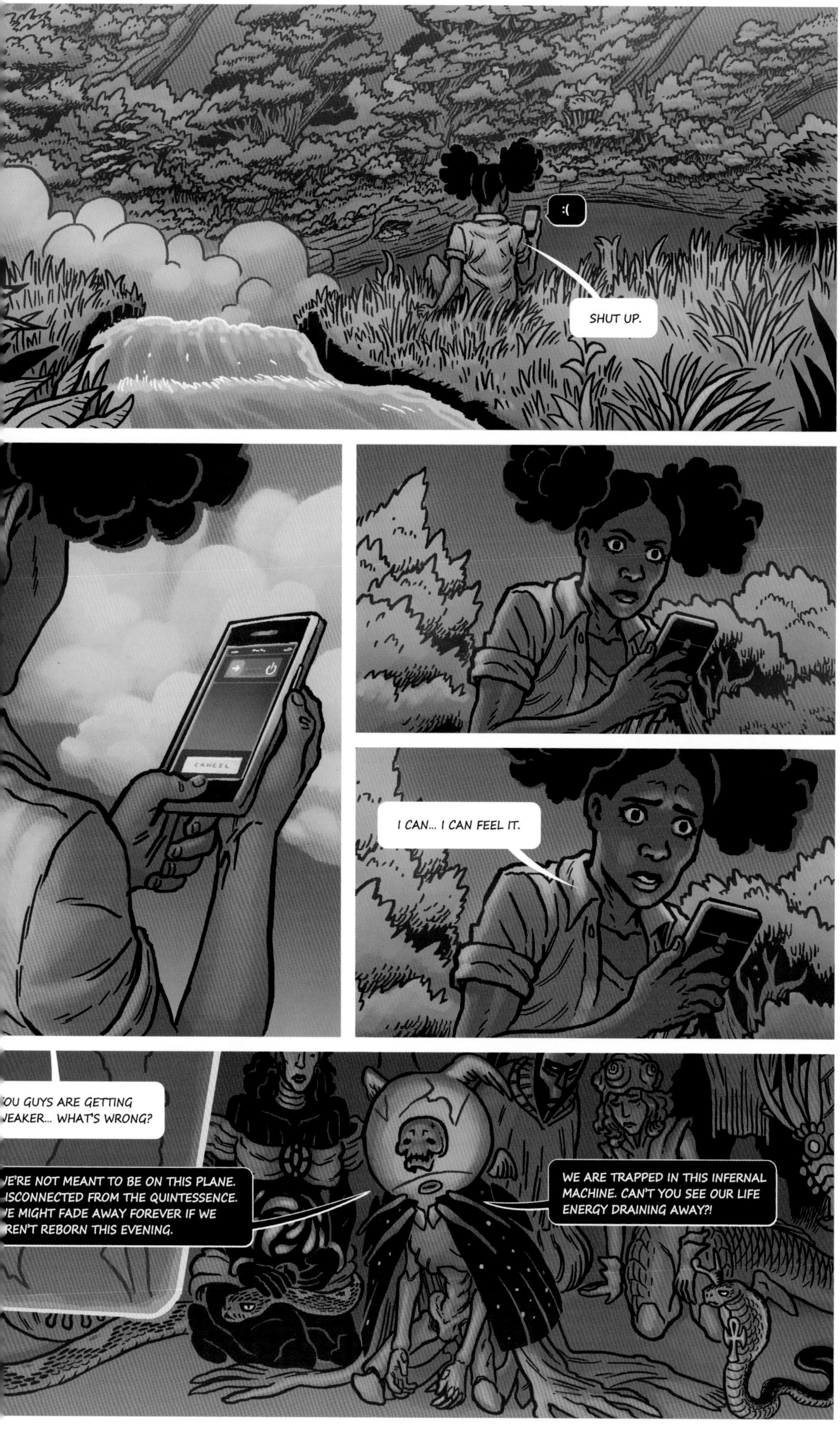
:(
SHUT UP.
I CAN... I CAN FEEL IT.
OU GUYS ARE GETTING
/EAKER... WHAT'S WRONG?
/E'RE NOT MEANT TO BE ON THIS PLANE.
ISCONNECTED FROM THE QUINTESSENCE.
/E MIGHT FADE AWAY FOREVER IF WE
REN'T REBORN THIS EVENING.
WE ARE TRAPPED IN THIS INFERNAL MACHINE. CAN'T YOU SEE OUR LIFE ENERGY DRAINING AWAY?!

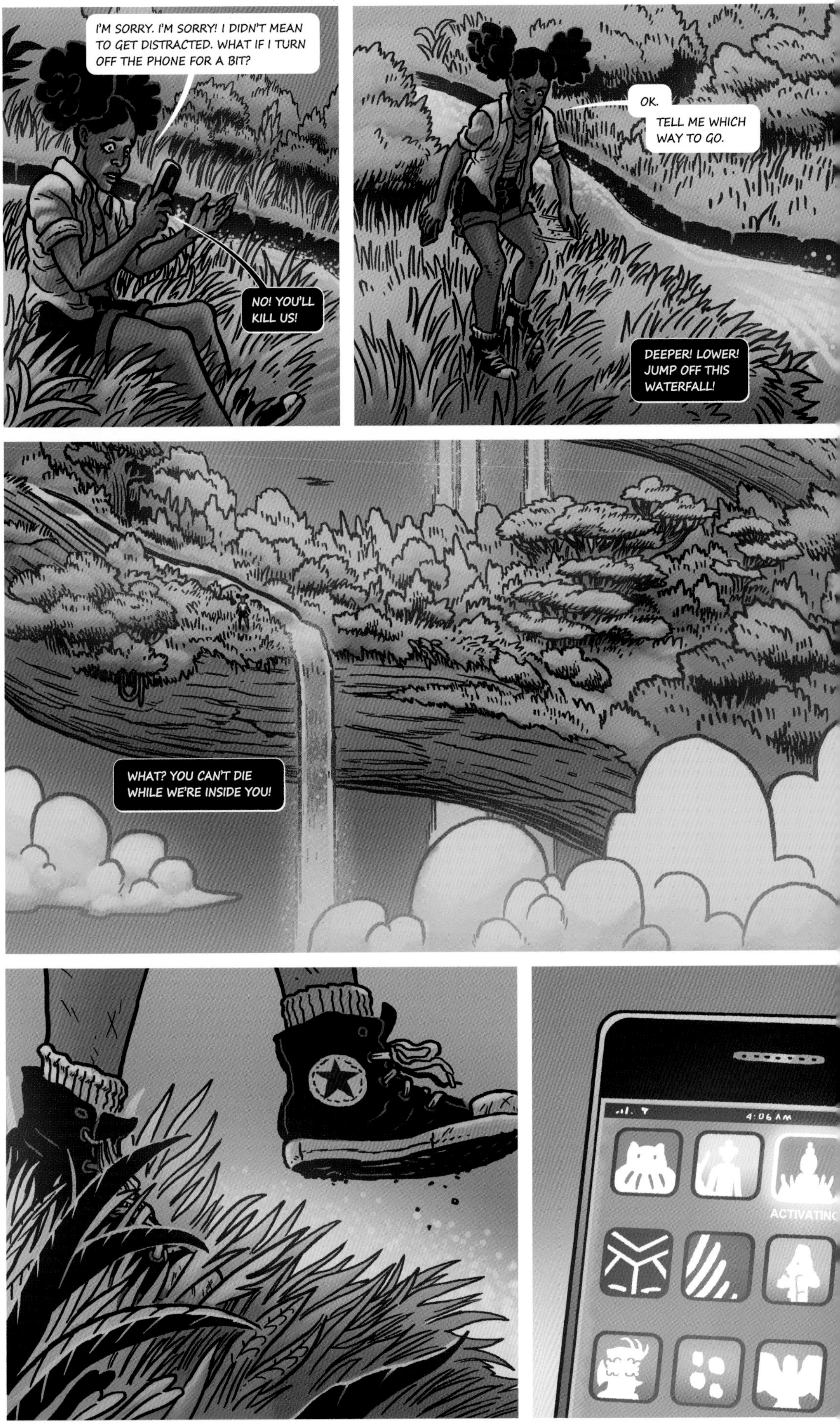
I'M SORRY. I'M SORRY! I DIDN'T MEAN TO GET DISTRACTED. WHAT IF I TURN OFF THE PHONE FOR A BIT?
NO! YOU'LL KILL US!
OK.
TELL ME WHICH WAY TO GO.
DEEPER! LOWER! JUMP OFF THIS WATERFALL!
WHAT? YOU CAN'T DIE WHILE WE'RE INSIDE YOU!
4:06 AM
ACTIVATING

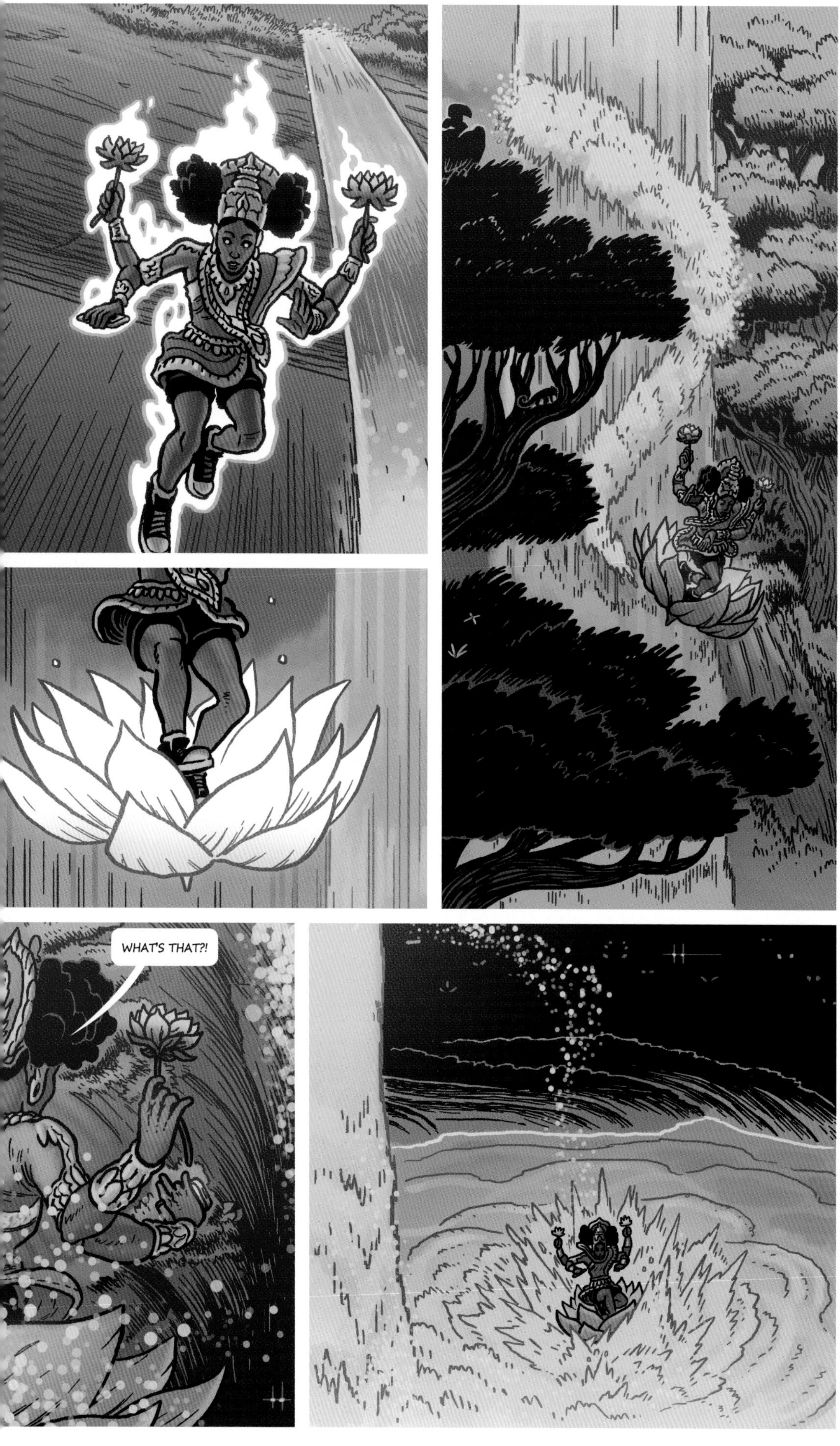
WHAT'S THAT?!

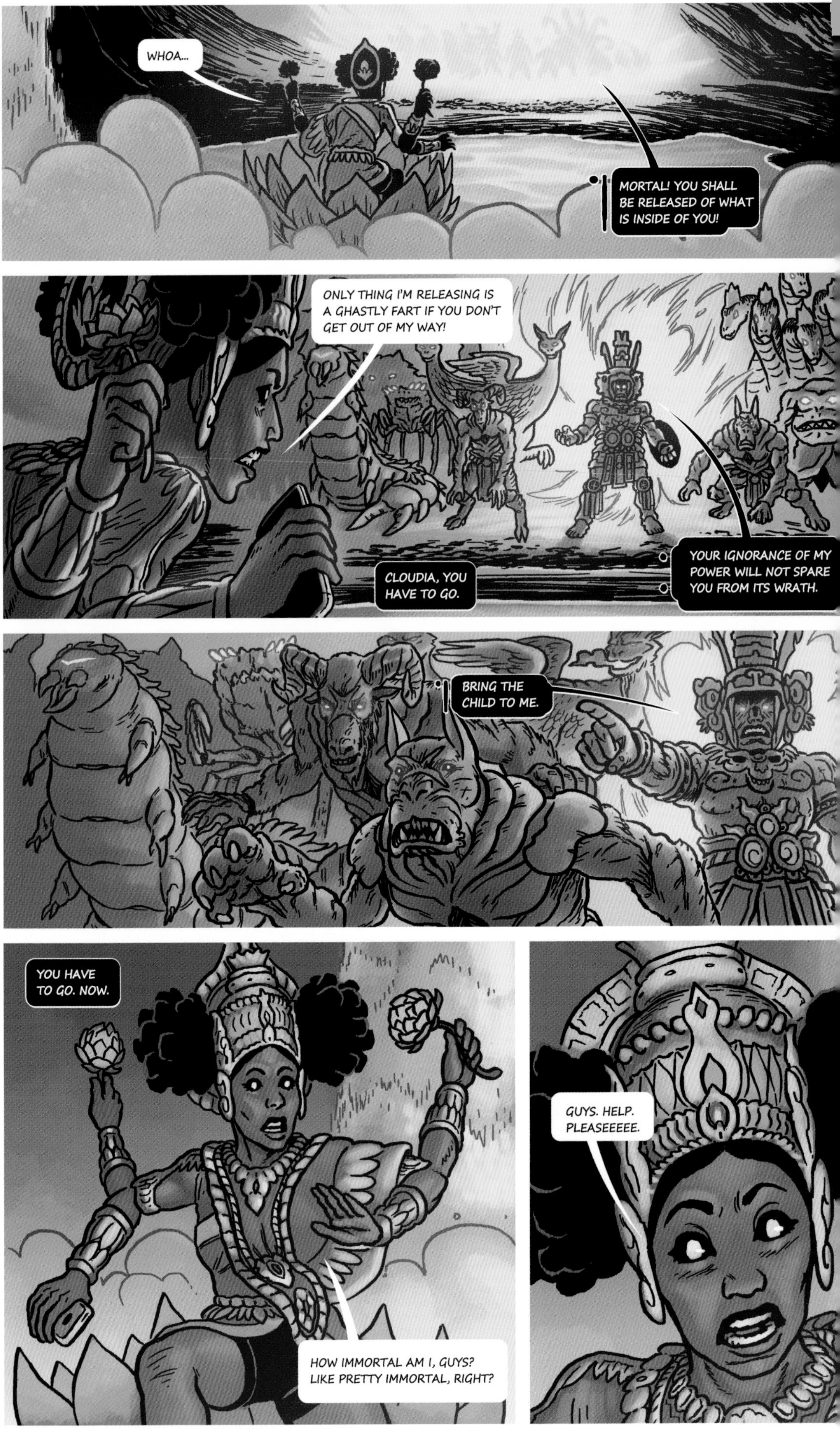
WHOA...
MORTAL! YOU SHALL BE RELEASED OF WHAT IS INSIDE OF YOU!
ONLY THING I'M RELEASING IS A GHASTLY FART IF YOU DON'T GET OUT OF MY WAY!
CLOUDIA, YOU HAVE TO GO.
YOUR IGNORANCE OF MY POWER WILL NOT SPARE YOU FROM ITS WRATH.
BRING THE CHILD TO ME.
YOU HAVE TO GO. NOW.
HOW IMMORTAL AM I, GUYS? LIKE PRETTY IMMORTAL, RIGHT?
GUYS. HELP. PLEASEEEEEE.

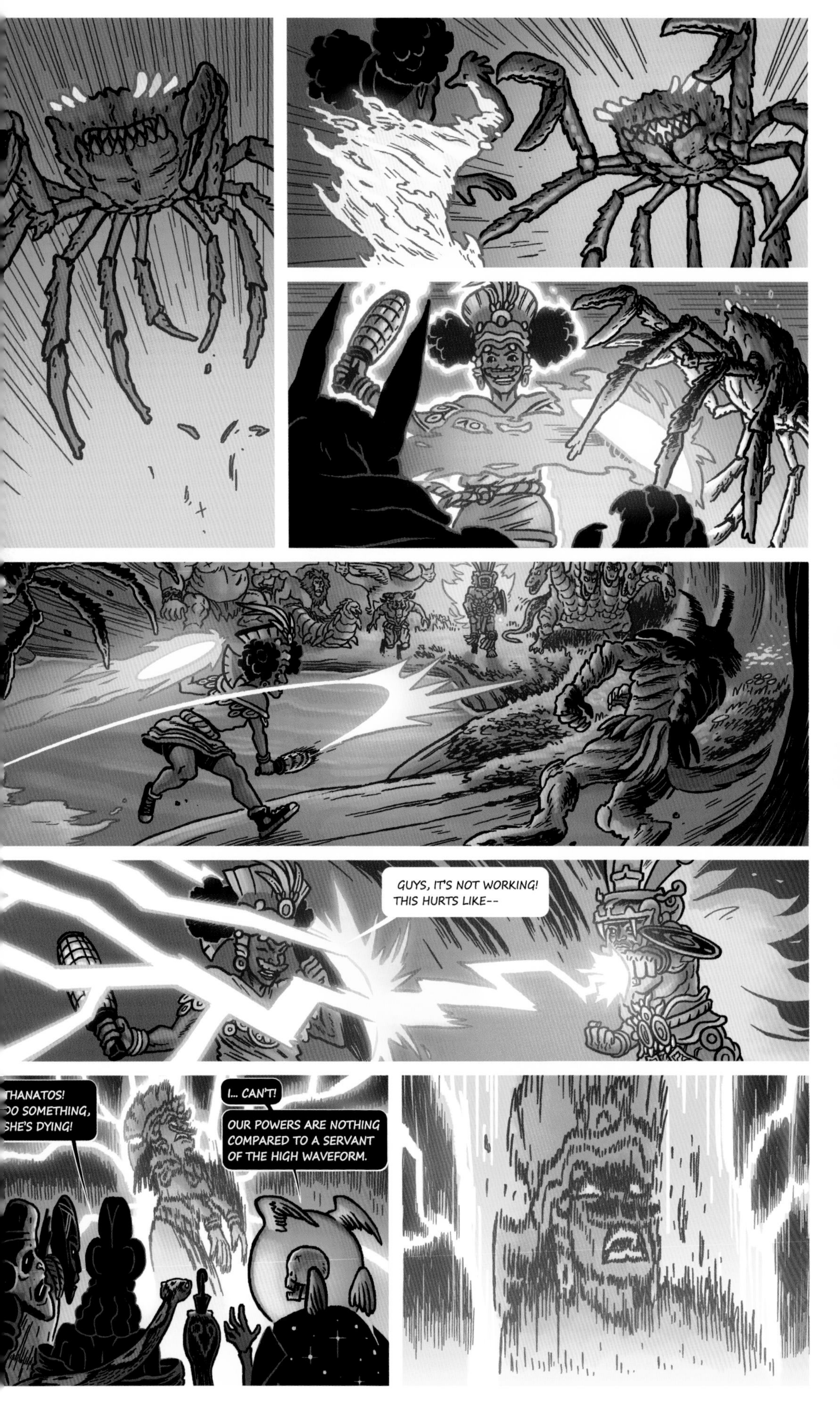
GUYS, IT'S NOT WORKING! THIS HURTS LIKE--
THANATOS! DO SOMETHING, SHE'S DYING!
I... CAN'T!
OUR POWERS ARE NOTHING COMPARED TO A SERVANT OF THE HIGH WAVEFORM.

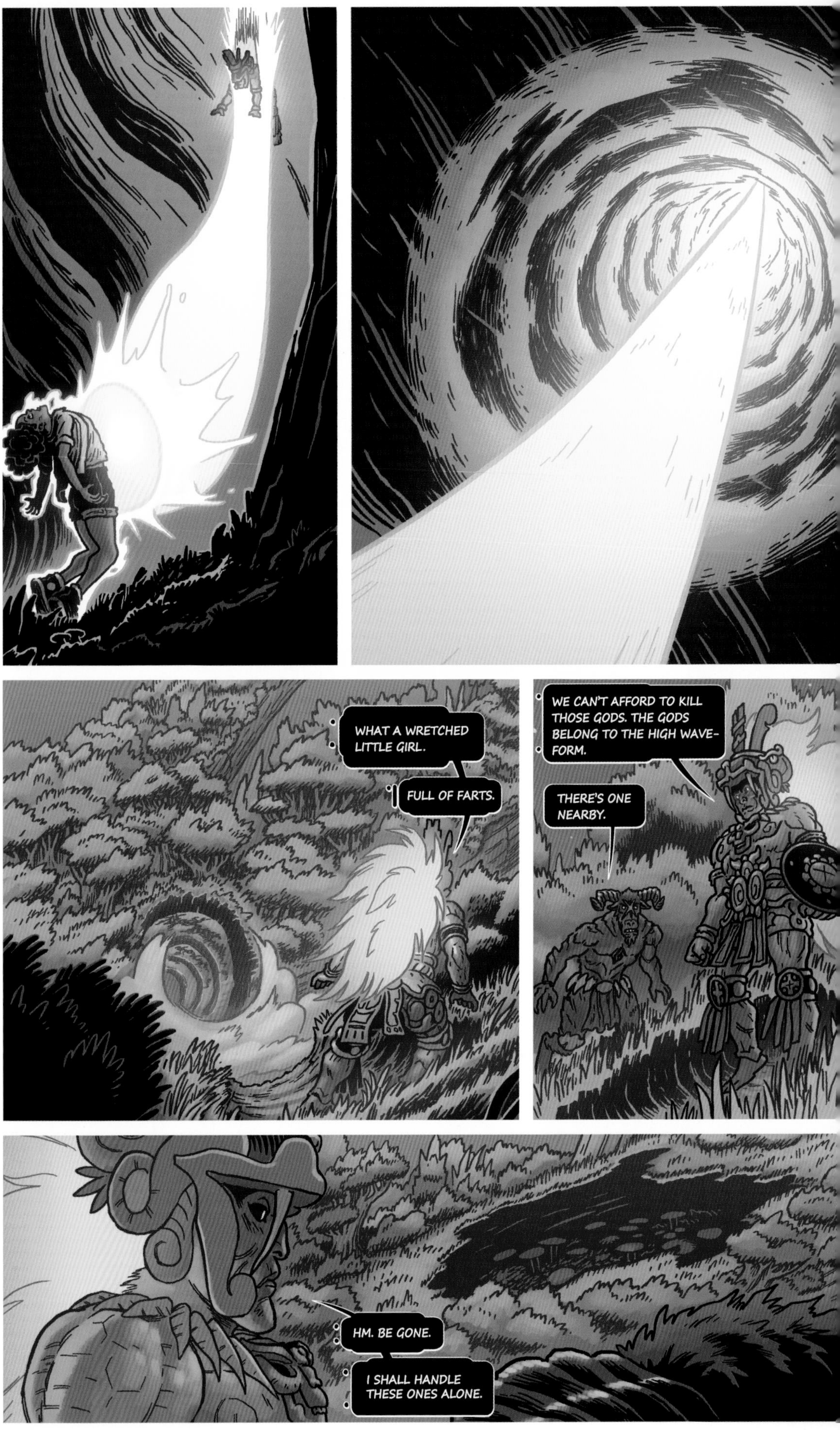
WHAT A WRETCHED LITTLE GIRL.
FULL OF FARTS.
WE CAN'T AFFORD TO KILL THOSE GODS. THE GODS BELONG TO THE HIGH WAVE-FORM.
THERE'S ONE NEARBY.
HM. BE GONE.
I SHALL HANDLE THESE ONES ALONE.

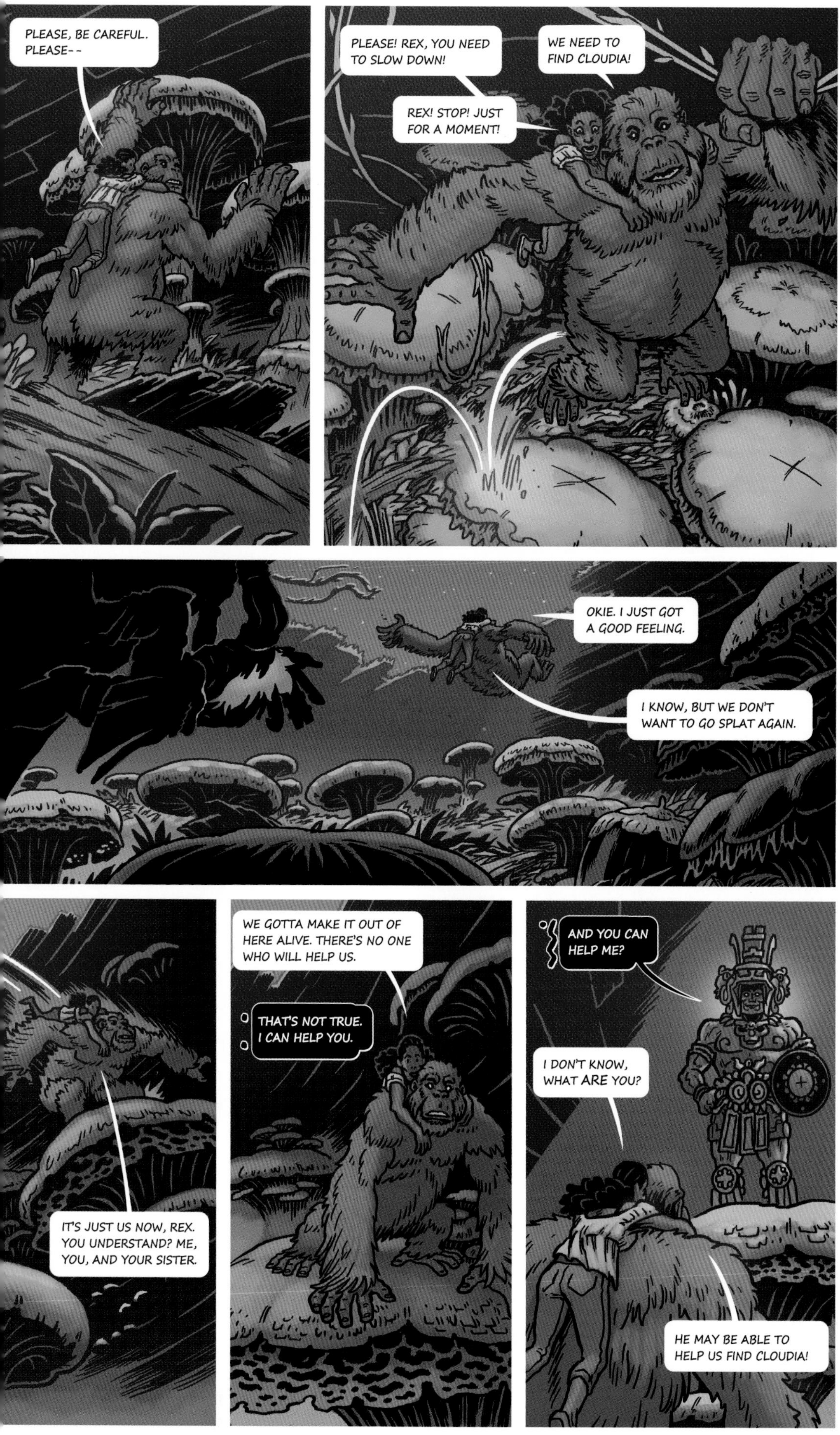
PLEASE, BE CAREFUL. PLEASE--
PLEASE! REX, YOU NEED TO SLOW DOWN!
WE NEED TO FIND CLOUDIA!
REX! STOP! JUST FOR A MOMENT!
OKIE. I JUST GOT A GOOD FEELING.
I KNOW, BUT WE DON'T WANT TO GO SPLAT AGAIN.
IT'S JUST US NOW, REX. YOU UNDERSTAND? ME, YOU, AND YOUR SISTER.
WE GOTTA MAKE IT OUT OF HERE ALIVE. THERE'S NO ONE WHO WILL HELP US.
THAT'S NOT TRUE. I CAN HELP YOU.
AND YOU CAN HELP ME?
I DON'T KNOW, WHAT ARE YOU?
HE MAY BE ABLE TO HELP US FIND CLOUDIA!

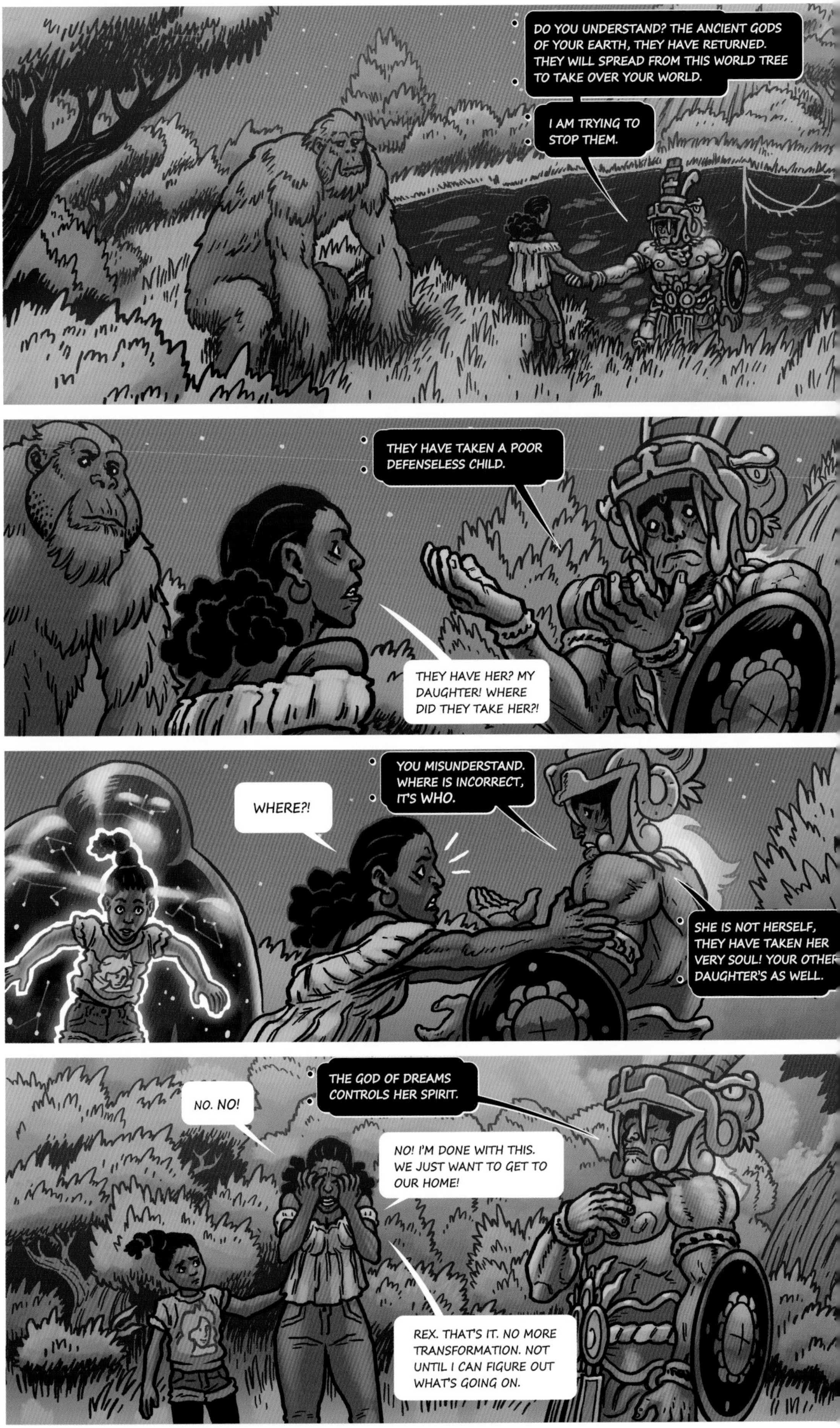
DO YOU UNDERSTAND? THE ANCIENT GODS OF YOUR EARTH, THEY HAVE RETURNED. THEY WILL SPREAD FROM THIS WORLD TREE TO TAKE OVER YOUR WORLD.
I AM TRYING TO STOP THEM.
THEY HAVE TAKEN A POOR DEFENSELESS CHILD.
THEY HAVE HER? MY DAUGHTER! WHERE DID THEY TAKE HER?!
WHERE?!
YOU MISUNDERSTAND. WHERE IS INCORRECT, IT'S WHO.
SHE IS NOT HERSELF, THEY HAVE TAKEN HER VERY SOUL! YOUR OTHER DAUGHTER'S AS WELL.
NO. NO!
THE GOD OF DREAMS CONTROLS HER SPIRIT.
NO! I'M DONE WITH THIS. WE JUST WANT TO GET TO OUR HOME!
REX. THAT'S IT. NO MORE TRANSFORMATION. NOT UNTIL I CAN FIGURE OUT WHAT'S GOING ON.

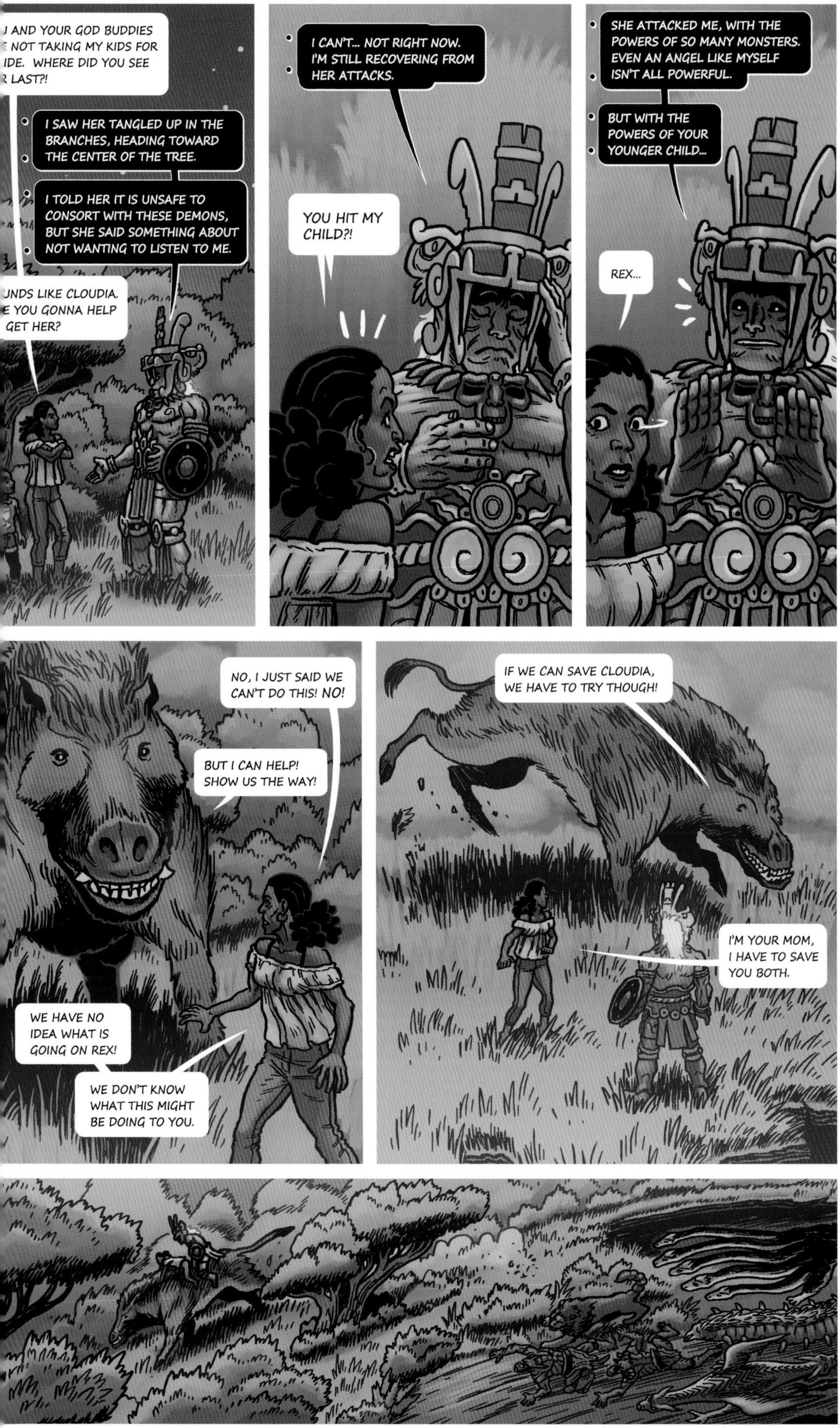

J AND YOUR GOD BUDDIES
: NOT TAKING MY KIDS FOR
IDE. WHERE DID YOU SEE
R LAST?!
I SAW HER TANGLED UP IN THE BRANCHES, HEADING TOWARD THE CENTER OF THE TREE.
I TOLD HER IT IS UNSAFE TO CONSORT WITH THESE DEMONS, BUT SHE SAID SOMETHING ABOUT NOT WANTING TO LISTEN TO ME.
UNDS LIKE CLOUDIA.
E YOU GONNA HELP
GET HER?
I CAN'T... NOT RIGHT NOW. I'M STILL RECOVERING FROM HER ATTACKS.
YOU HIT MY CHILD?!
SHE ATTACKED ME, WITH THE POWERS OF SO MANY MONSTERS. EVEN AN ANGEL LIKE MYSELF ISN'T ALL POWERFUL.
BUT WITH THE POWERS OF YOUR YOUNGER CHILD...
REX...
NO, I JUST SAID WE CAN'T DO THIS! NO!
BUT I CAN HELP! SHOW US THE WAY!
WE HAVE NO IDEA WHAT IS GOING ON REX!
WE DON'T KNOW WHAT THIS MIGHT BE DOING TO YOU.
IF WE CAN SAVE CLOUDIA, WE HAVE TO TRY THOUGH!
I'M YOUR MOM, I HAVE TO SAVE YOU BOTH.

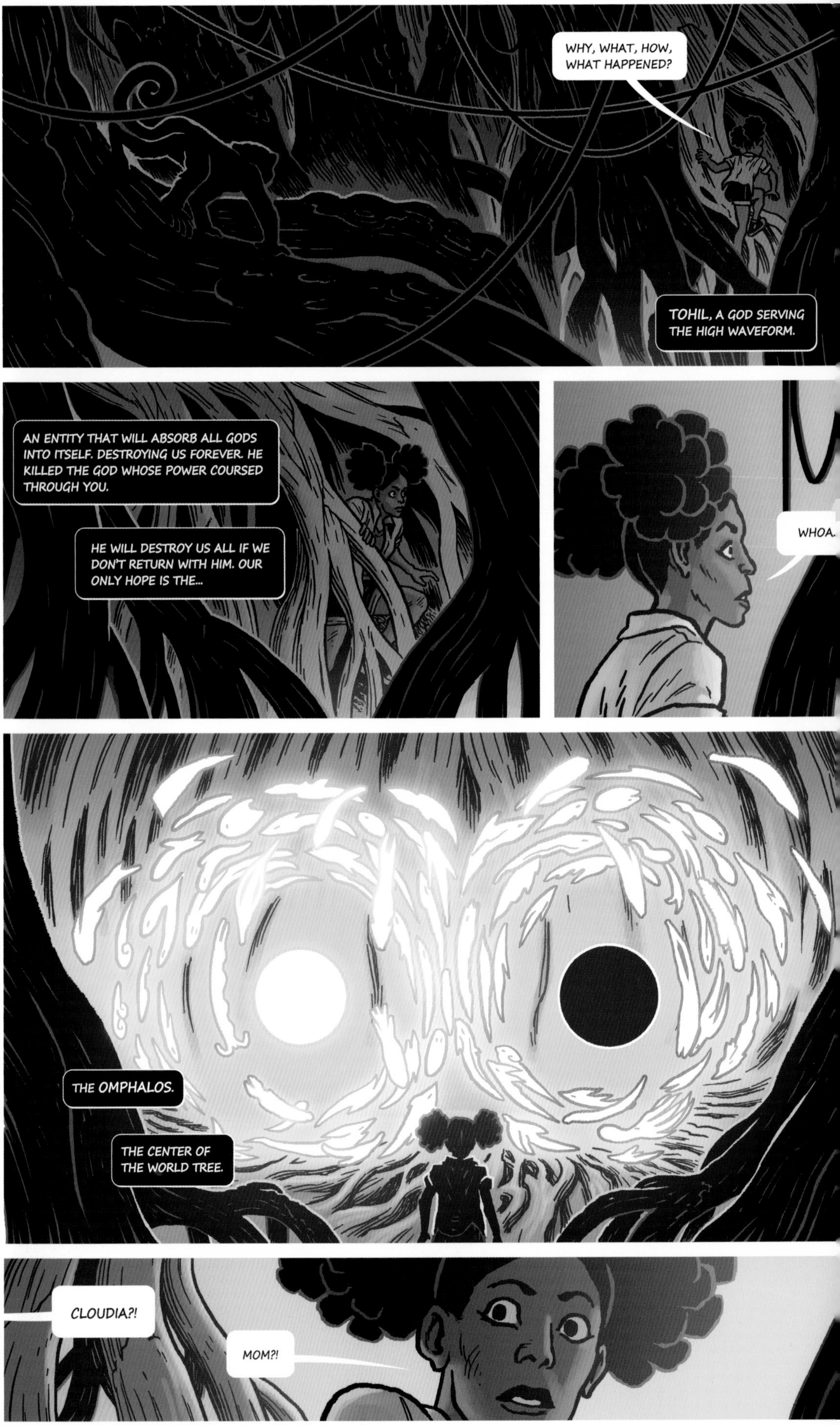

WHY, WHAT, HOW, WHAT HAPPENED?
TOHIL, A GOD SERVING THE HIGH WAVEFORM.
AN ENTITY THAT WILL ABSORB ALL GODS INTO ITSELF. DESTROYING US FOREVER. HE KILLED THE GOD WHOSE POWER COURSED THROUGH YOU.
HE WILL DESTROY US ALL IF WE DON'T RETURN WITH HIM. OUR ONLY HOPE IS THE...
WHOA.
THE OMPHALOS.
THE CENTER OF THE WORLD TREE.
CLOUDIA?!
MOM?!

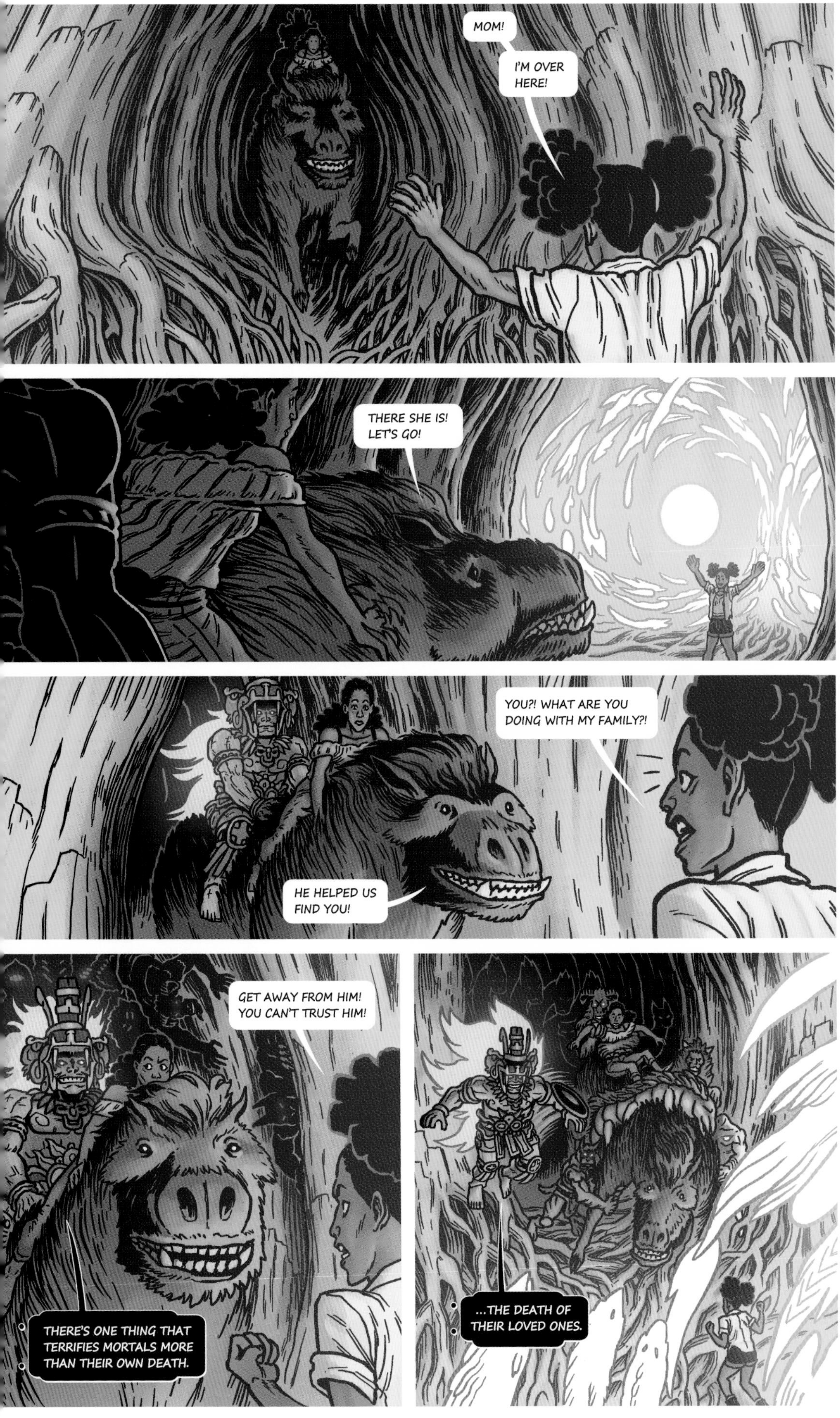
MOM!
I'M OVER HERE!
THERE SHE IS! LET'S GO!
YOU?! WHAT ARE YOU DOING WITH MY FAMILY?!
HE HELPED US FIND YOU!
GET AWAY FROM HIM! YOU CAN'T TRUST HIM!
THERE'S ONE THING THAT TERRIFIES MORTALS MORE THAN THEIR OWN DEATH.
...THE DEATH OF THEIR LOVED ONES.

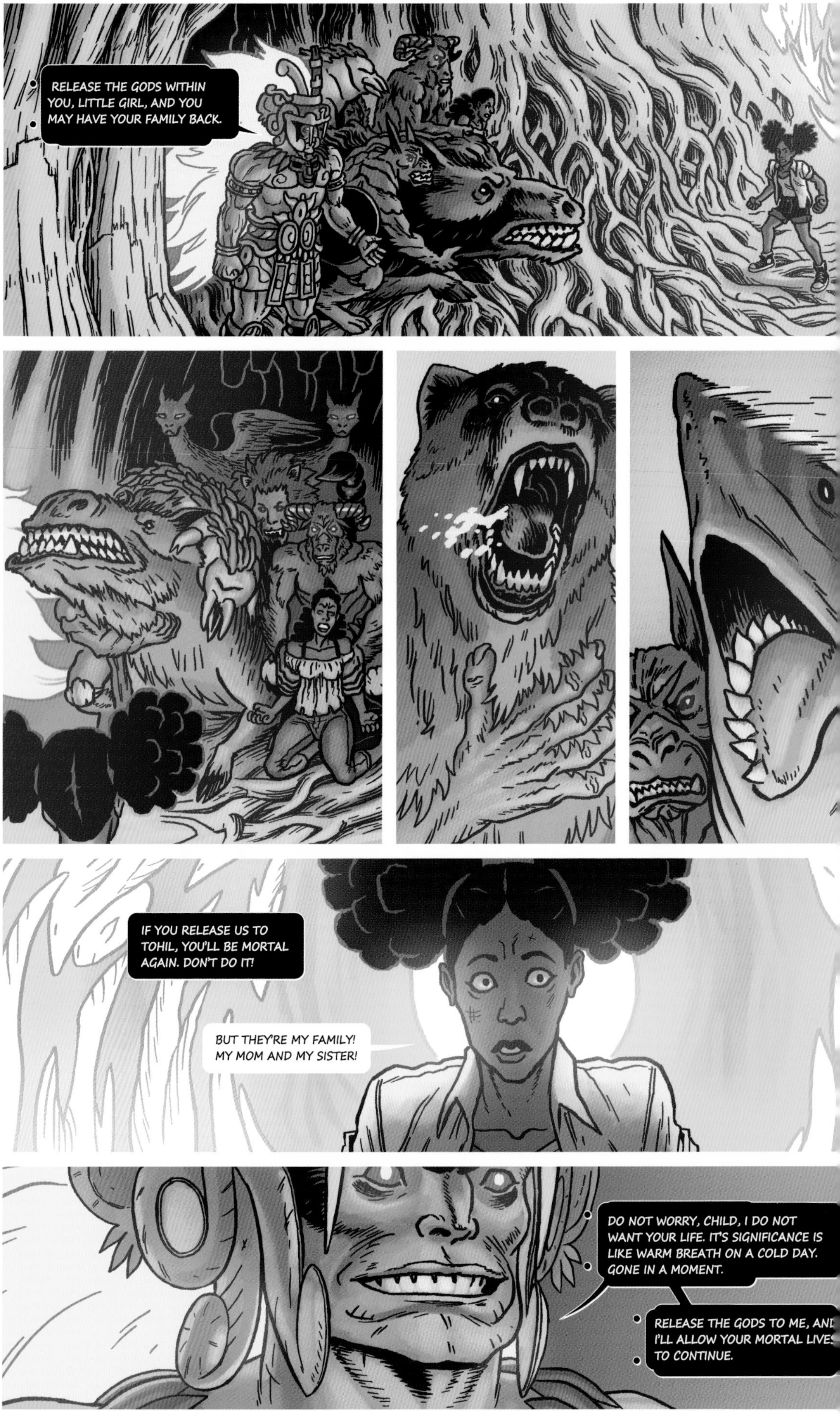
RELEASE THE GODS WITHIN YOU, LITTLE GIRL, AND YOU MAY HAVE YOUR FAMILY BACK.
IF YOU RELEASE US TO TOHIL, YOU'LL BE MORTAL AGAIN. DON'T DO IT!
BUT THEY'RE MY FAMILY! MY MOM AND MY SISTER!
DO NOT WORRY, CHILD, I DO NOT WANT YOUR LIFE. IT'S SIGNIFICANCE IS LIKE WARM BREATH ON A COLD DAY. GONE IN A MOMENT.
RELEASE THE GODS TO ME, AND I'LL ALLOW YOUR MORTAL LIVES TO CONTINUE.

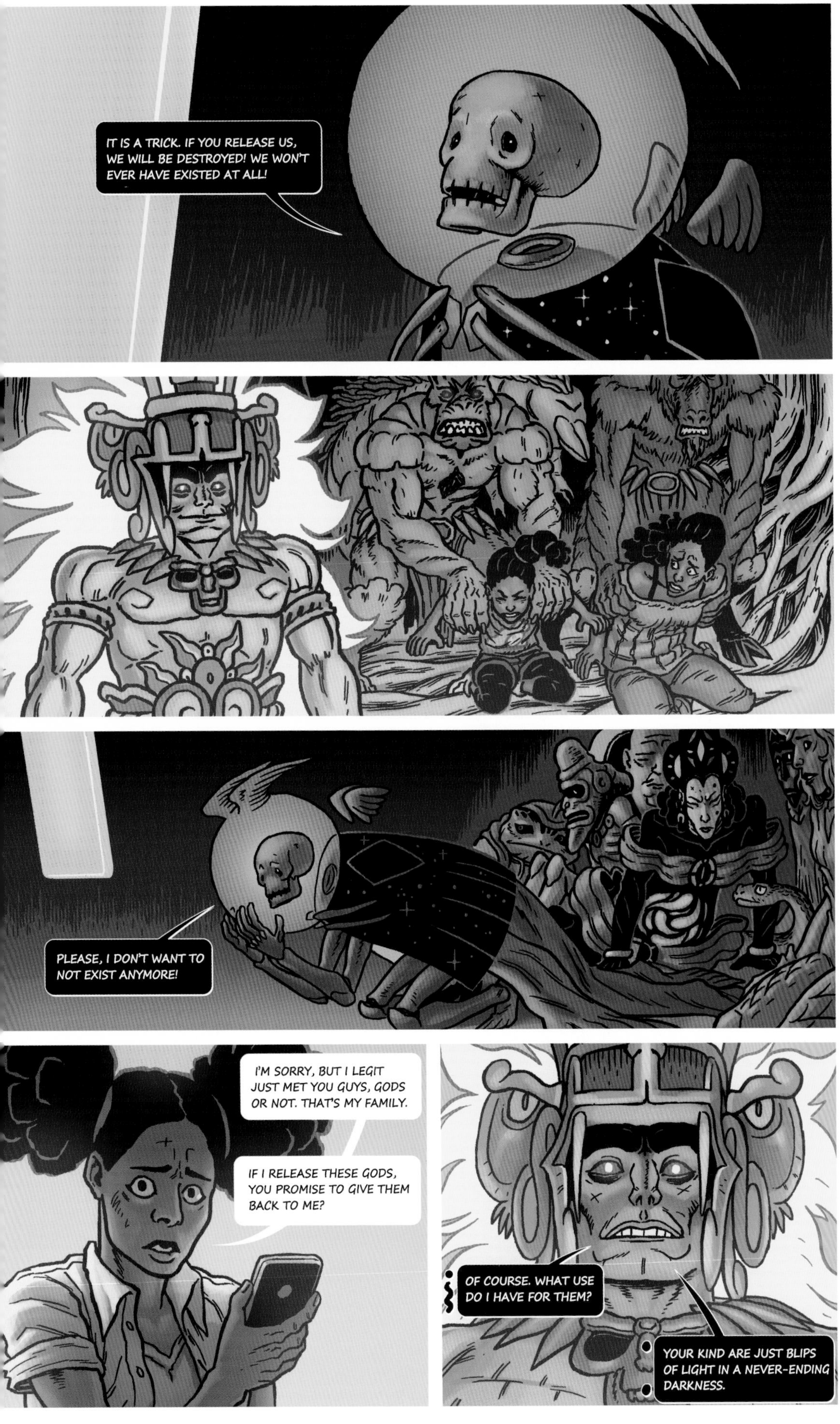
IT IS A TRICK. IF YOU RELEASE US, WE WILL BE DESTROYED! WE WON'T EVER HAVE EXISTED AT ALL!
PLEASE, I DON'T WANT TO NOT EXIST ANYMORE!
I'M SORRY, BUT I LEGIT JUST MET YOU GUYS, GODS OR NOT. THAT'S MY FAMILY.
IF I RELEASE THESE GODS, YOU PROMISE TO GIVE THEM BACK TO ME?
OF COURSE. WHAT USE DO I HAVE FOR THEM?
YOUR KIND ARE JUST BLIPS OF LIGHT IN A NEVER-ENDING DARKNESS.

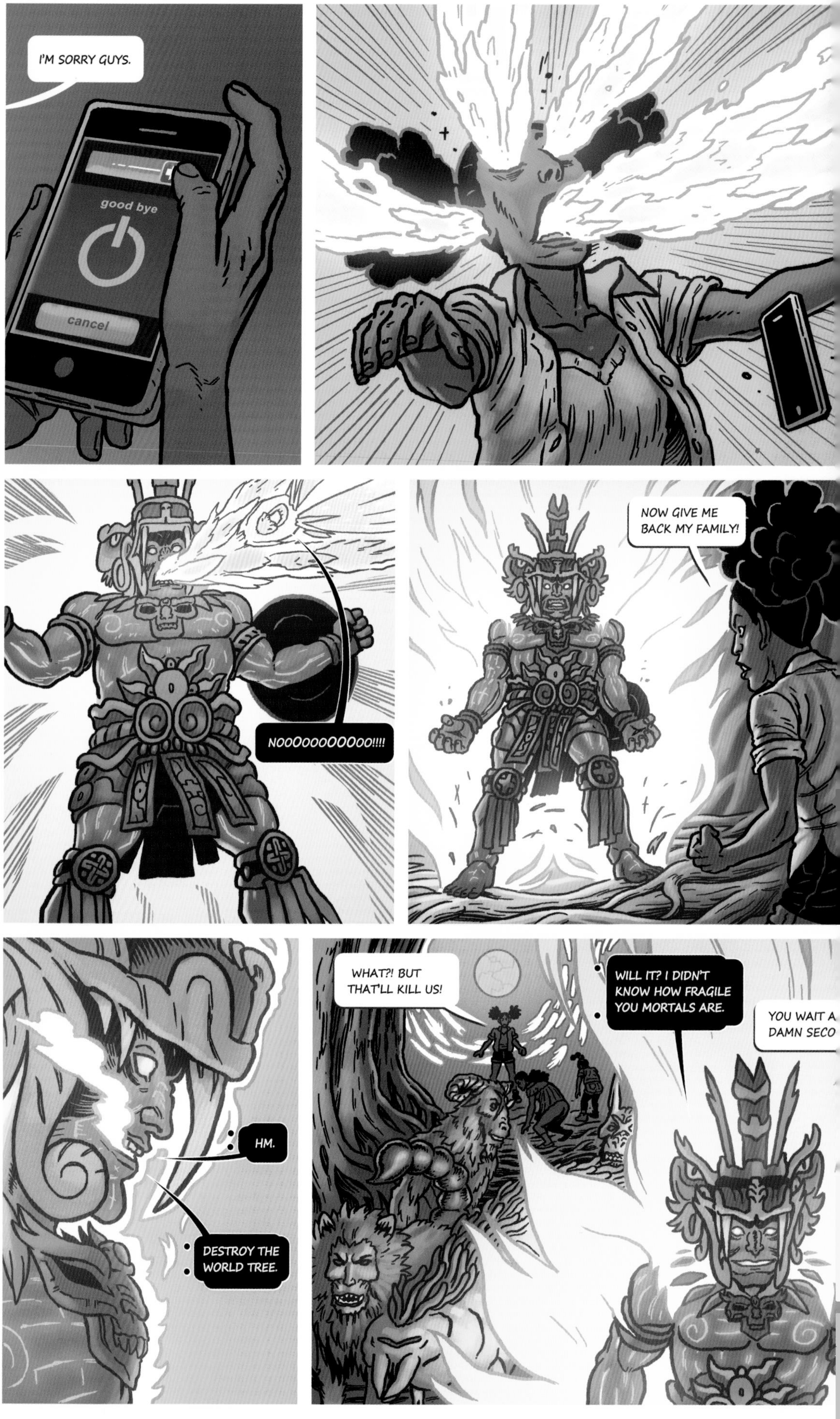
I'M SORRY GUYS.
good bye
cancel
NOOOOOOOOOOO!!!!
NOW GIVE ME BACK MY FAMILY!
HM.
DESTROY THE WORLD TREE.
WHAT?! BUT THAT'LL KILL US!
WILL IT? I DIDN'T KNOW HOW FRAGILE YOU MORTALS ARE.
YOU WAIT A DAMN SECO

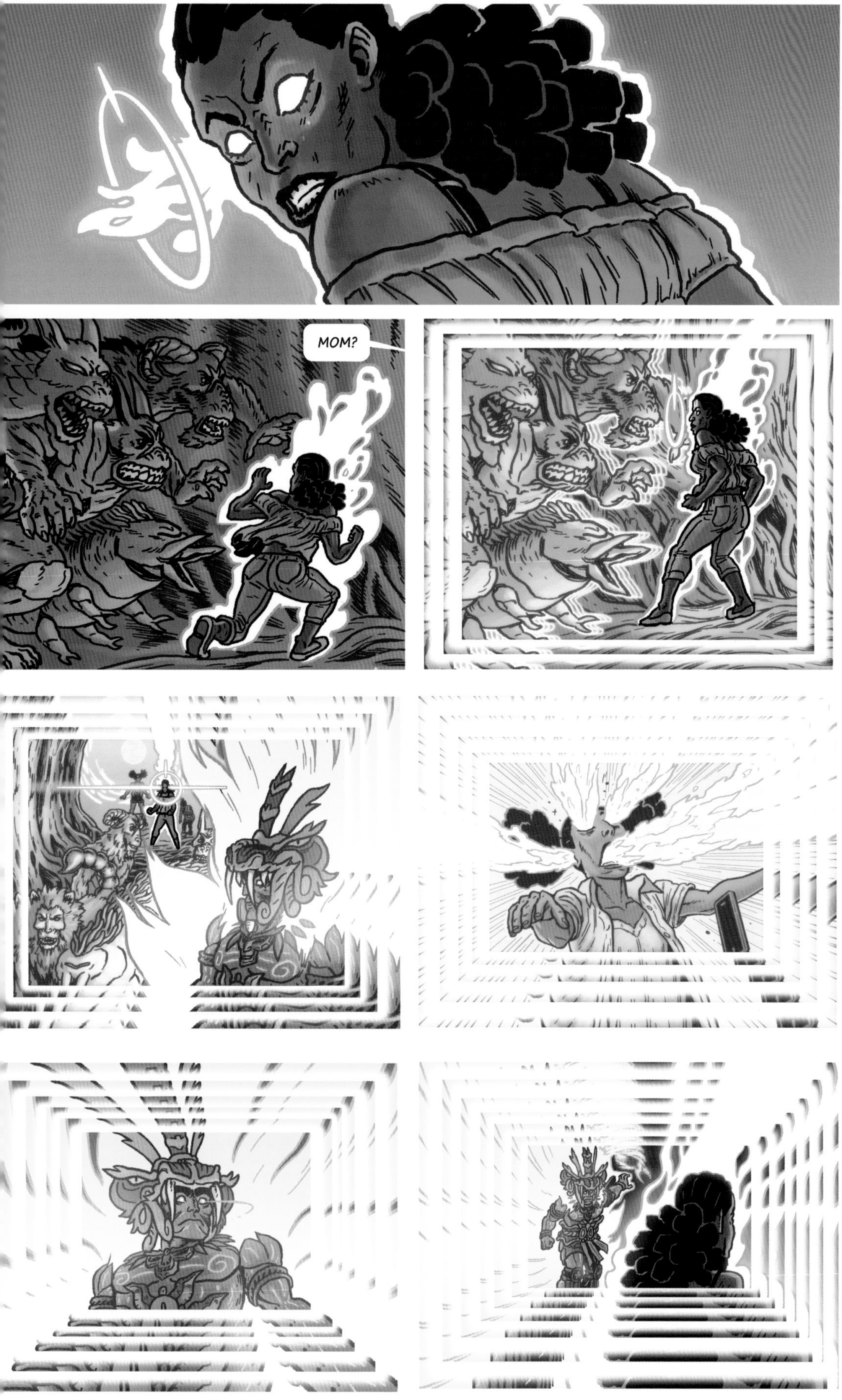
MOM?

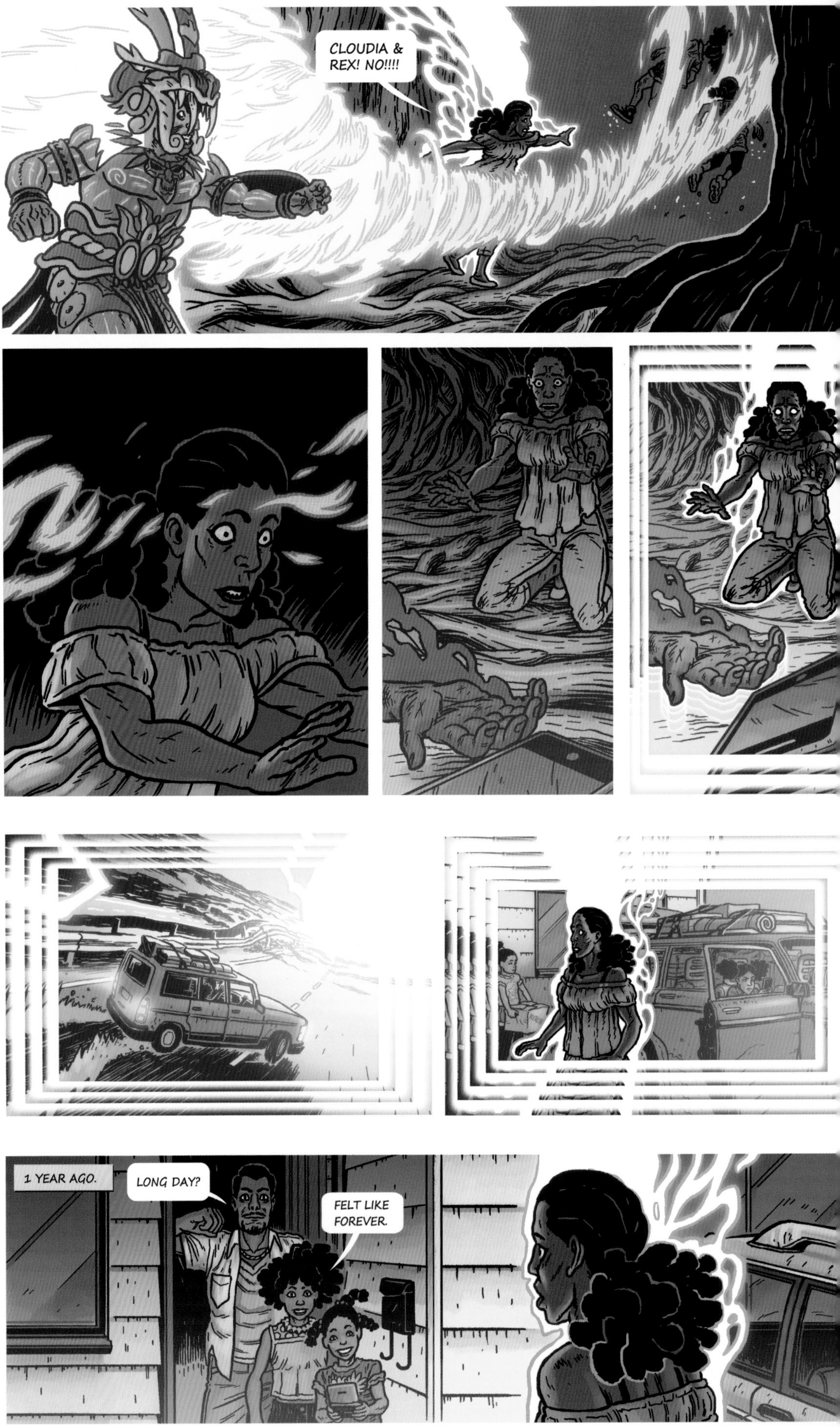
CLOUDIA & REX! NO!!!!
1 YEAR AGO.
LONG DAY?
FELT LIKE FOREVER.

CHAPTER THREE

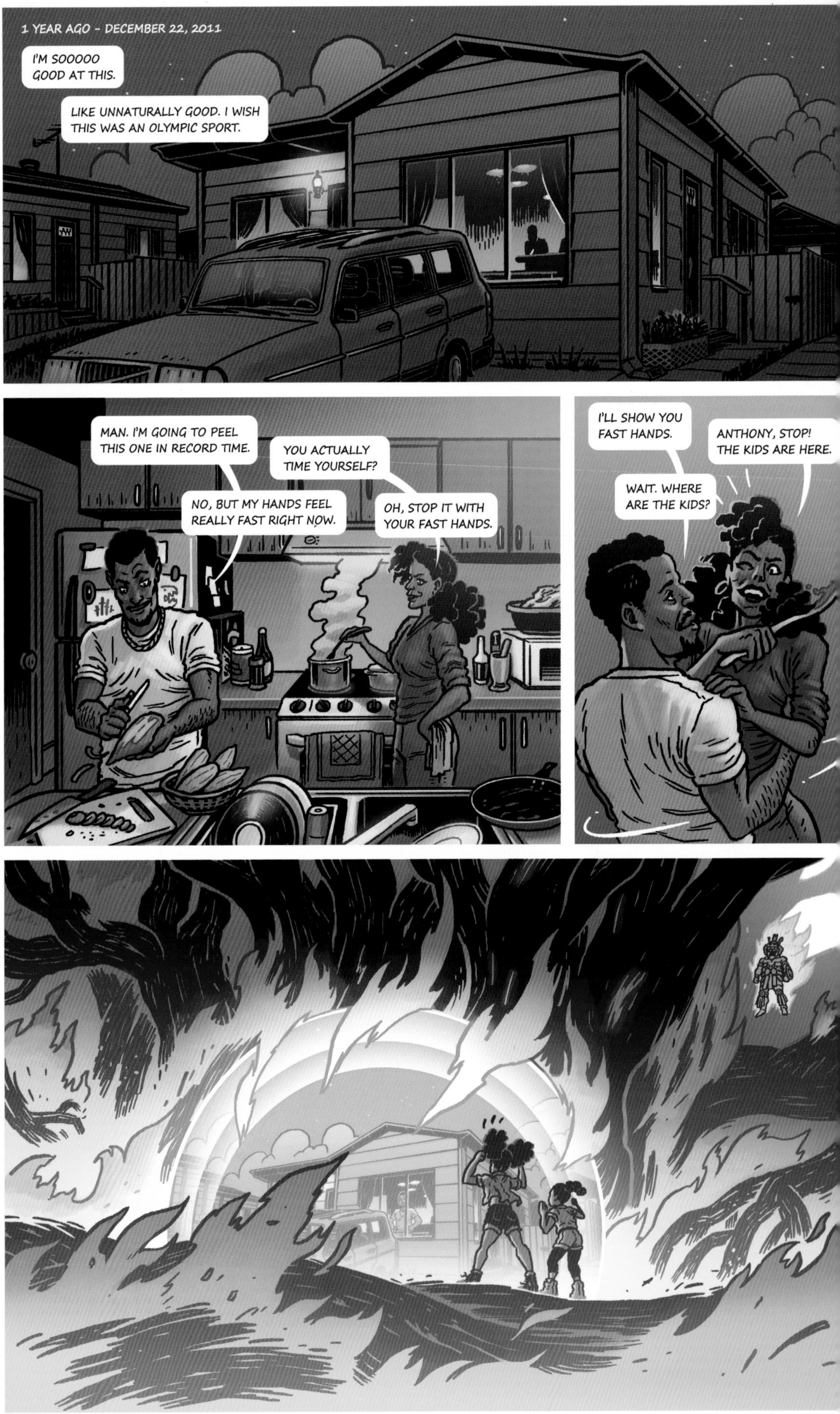
1 YEAR AGO - DECEMBER 22, 2011
I'M SOOOOO GOOD AT THIS.
LIKE UNNATURALLY GOOD. I WISH THIS WAS AN OLYMPIC SPORT.
MAN. I'M GOING TO PEEL THIS ONE IN RECORD TIME.
YOU ACTUALLY TIME YOURSELF?
NO, BUT MY HANDS FEEL REALLY FAST RIGHT NOW.
OH, STOP IT WITH YOUR FAST HANDS.
I'LL SHOW YOU FAST HANDS.
ANTHONY, STOP! THE KIDS ARE HERE.
WAIT. WHERE ARE THE KIDS?

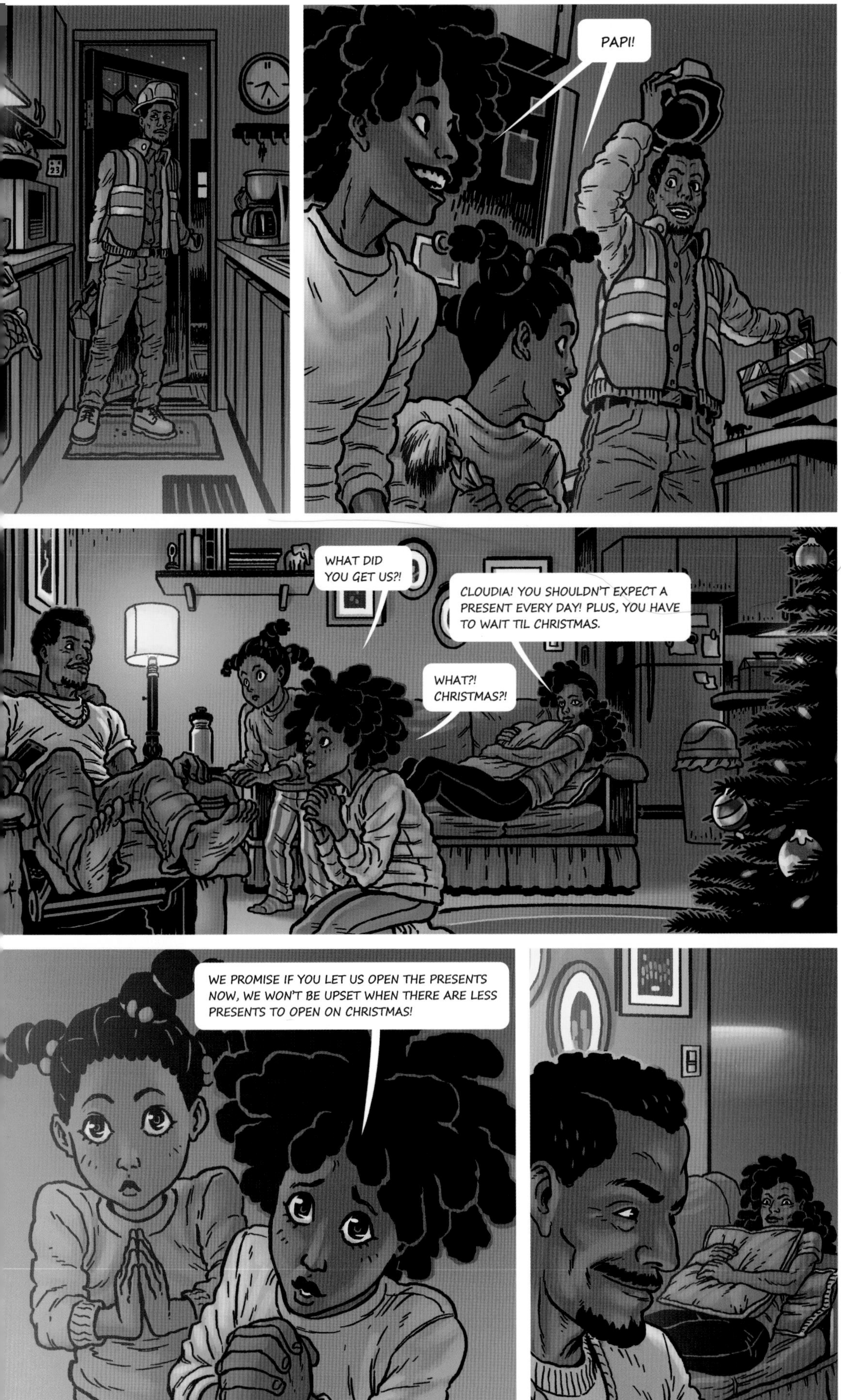
PAPI!
WHAT DID YOU GET US?!
CLOUDIA! YOU SHOULDN'T EXPECT A PRESENT EVERY DAY! PLUS, YOU HAVE TO WAIT TIL CHRISTMAS.
WHAT?! CHRISTMAS?!
WE PROMISE IF YOU LET US OPEN THE PRESENTS NOW, WE WON'T BE UPSET WHEN THERE ARE LESS PRESENTS TO OPEN ON CHRISTMAS!

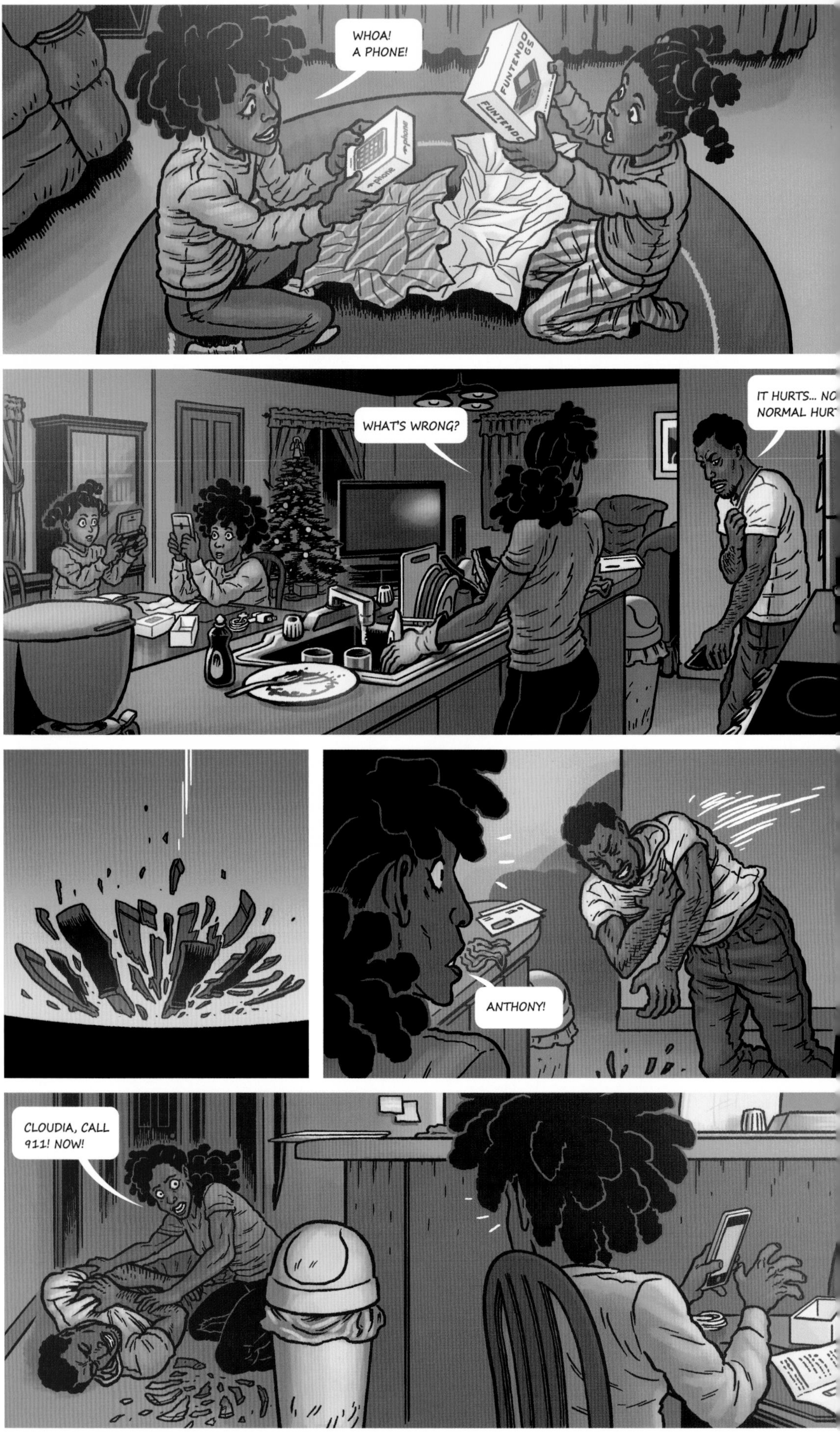
WHOA! A PHONE!
FUNTENDO GS
FUNTENDO
phone
WHAT'S WRONG?
IT HURTS... NO NORMAL HUR
ANTHONY!
CLOUDIA, CALL 911! NOW!

NCE
AMBU

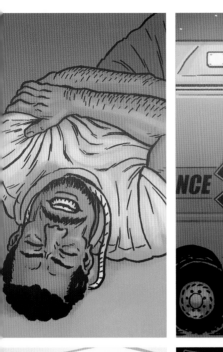

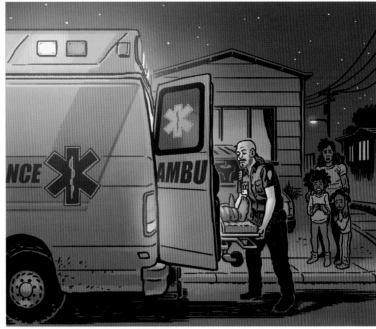

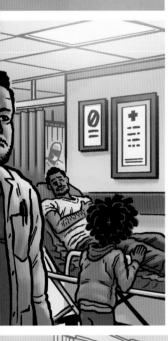

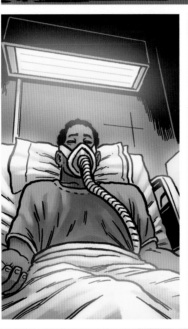

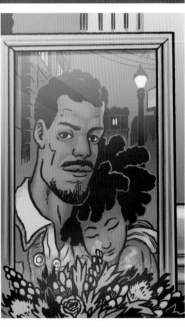

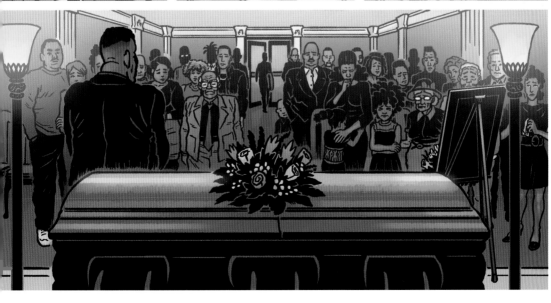

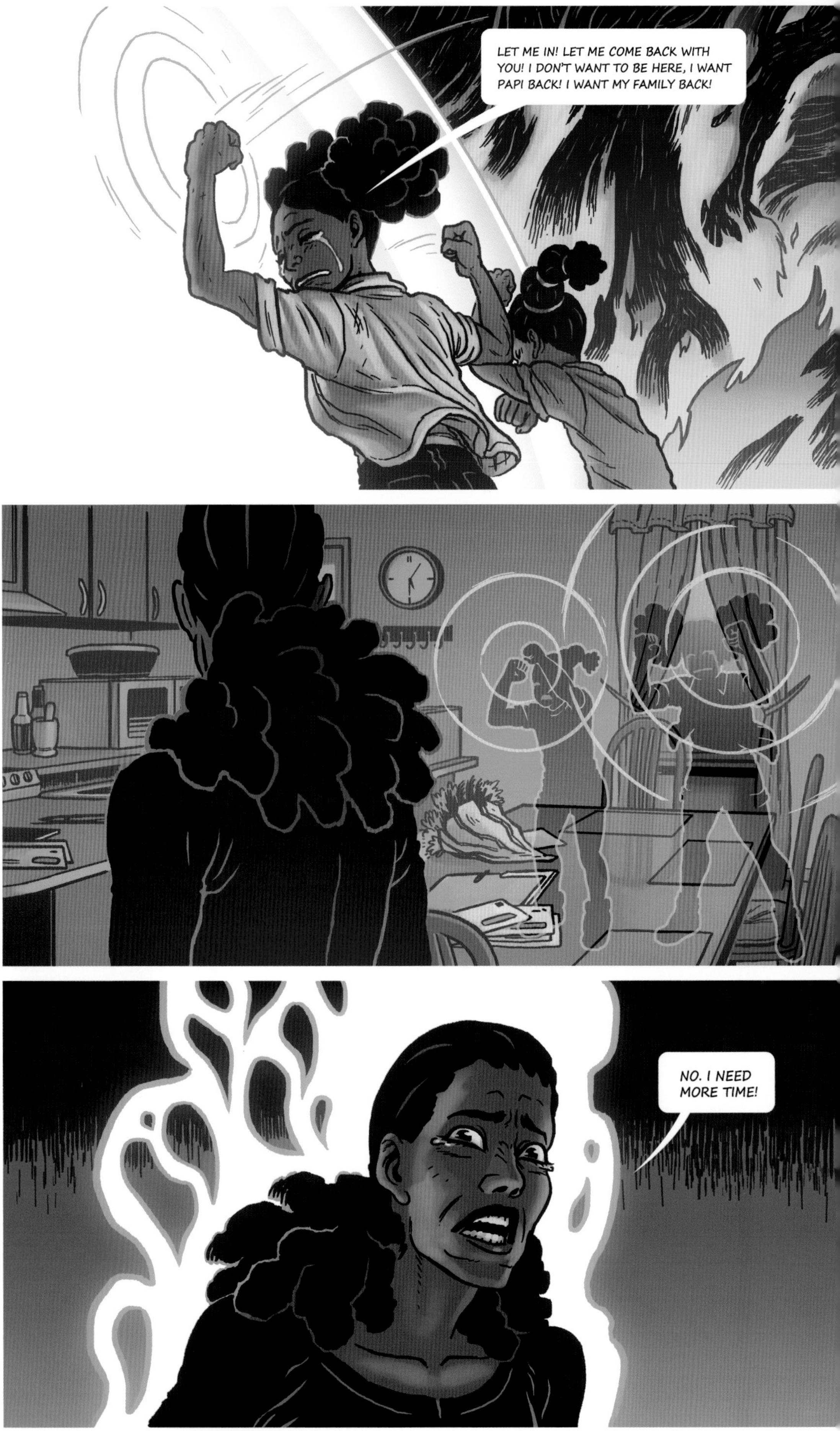
LET ME IN! LET ME COME BACK WITH YOU! I DON'T WANT TO BE HERE, I WANT PAPI BACK! I WANT MY FAMILY BACK!
NO. I NEED MORE TIME!

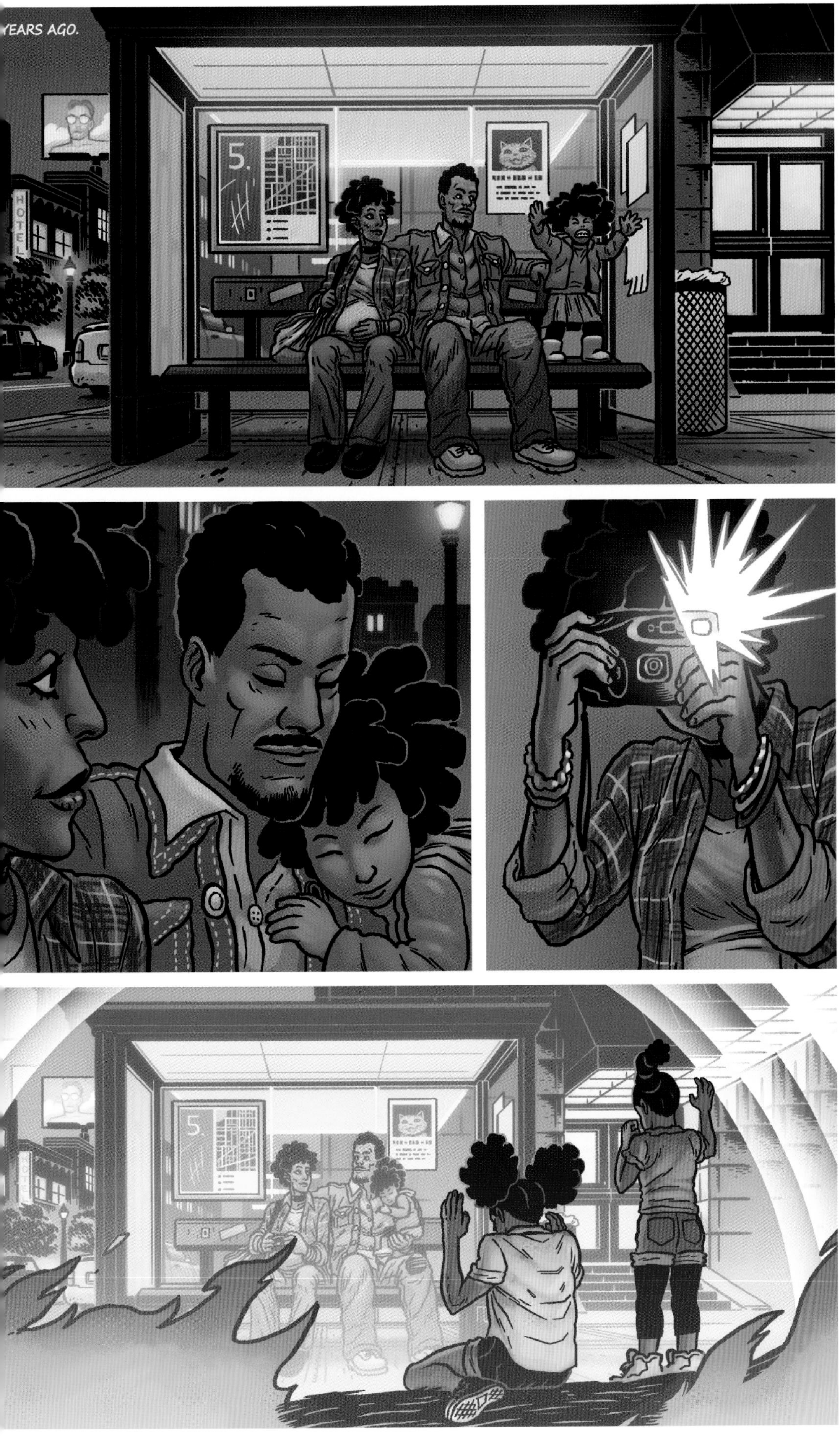

YEARS AGO.
HOTEL
5.

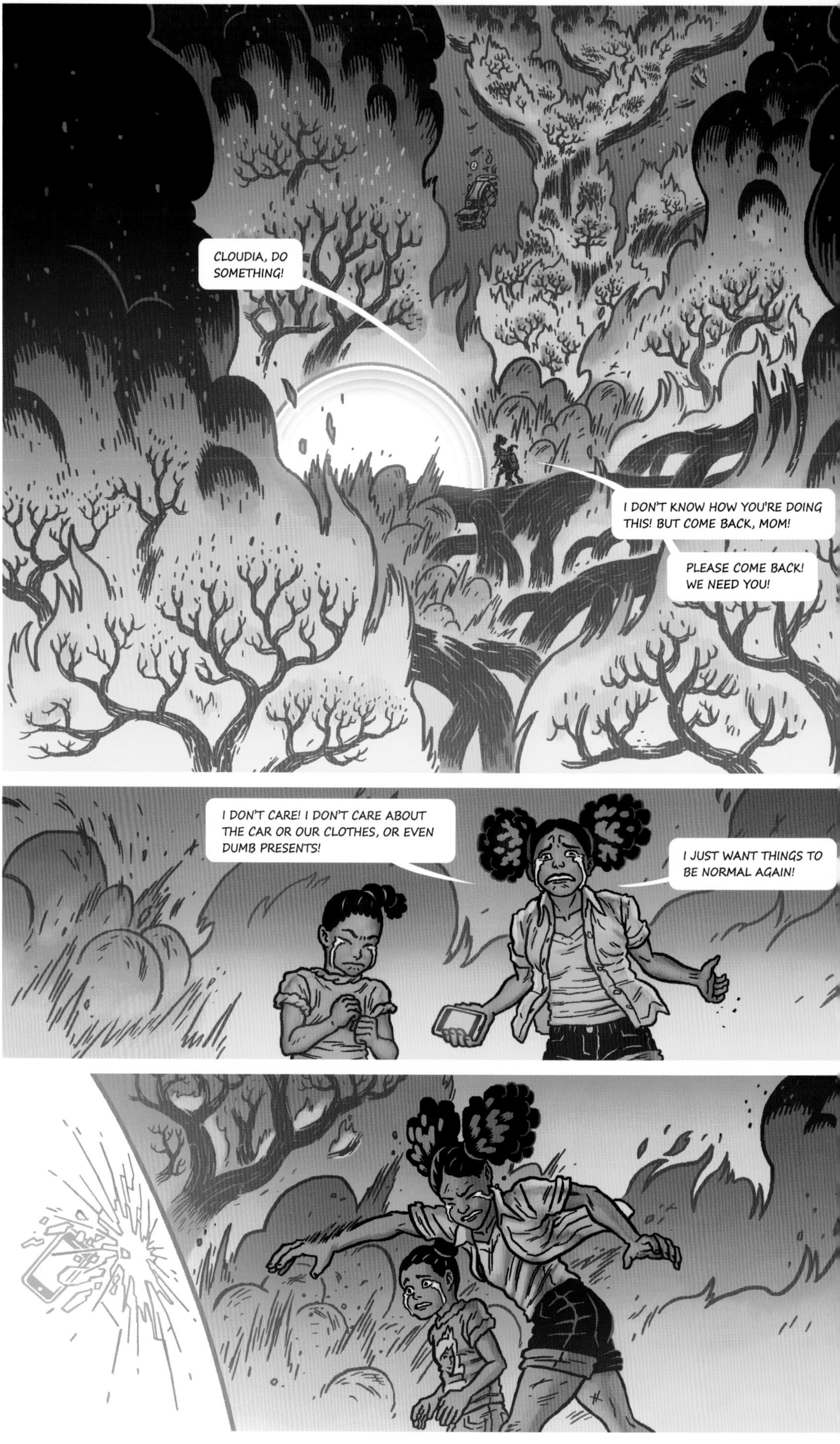

CLOUDIA, DO SOMETHING!
I DON'T KNOW HOW YOU'RE DOING THIS! BUT COME BACK, MOM!
PLEASE COME BACK! WE NEED YOU!
I DON'T CARE! I DON'T CARE ABOUT THE CAR OR OUR CLOTHES, OR EVEN DUMB PRESENTS!
I JUST WANT THINGS TO BE NORMAL AGAIN!

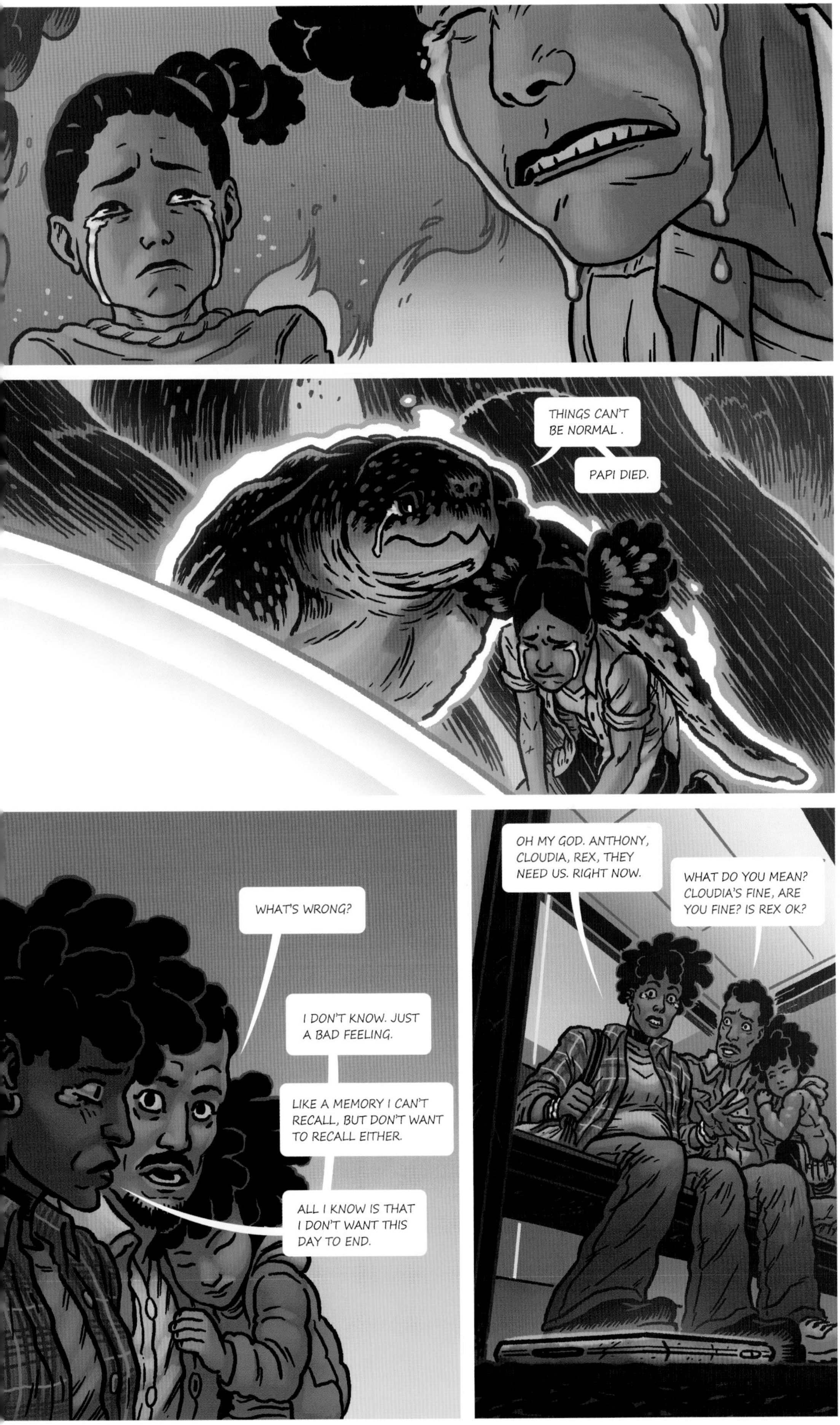
THINGS CAN'T BE NORMAL .
PAPI DIED.
WHAT'S WRONG?
I DON'T KNOW. JUST A BAD FEELING.
LIKE A MEMORY I CAN'T RECALL, BUT DON'T WANT TO RECALL EITHER.
ALL I KNOW IS THAT I DON'T WANT THIS DAY TO END.
OH MY GOD. ANTHONY, CLOUDIA, REX, THEY NEED US. RIGHT NOW.
WHAT DO YOU MEAN? CLOUDIA'S FINE, ARE YOU FINE? IS REX OK?

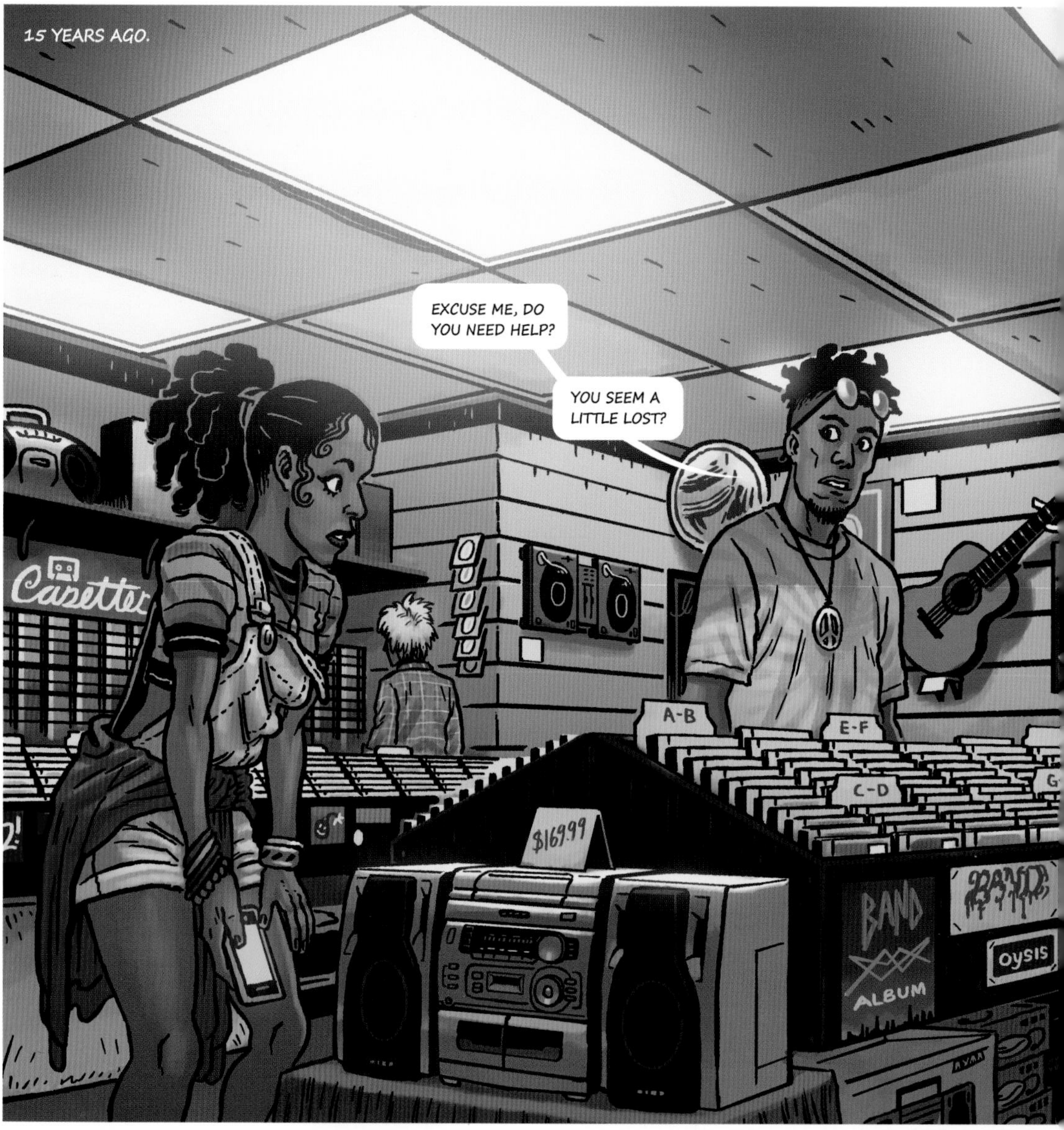
15 YEARS AGO.
EXCUSE ME, DO YOU NEED HELP?
YOU SEEM A LITTLE LOST?
Casette
A-B
E-F
C-D
$169.99
BAND ALBUM
oysis

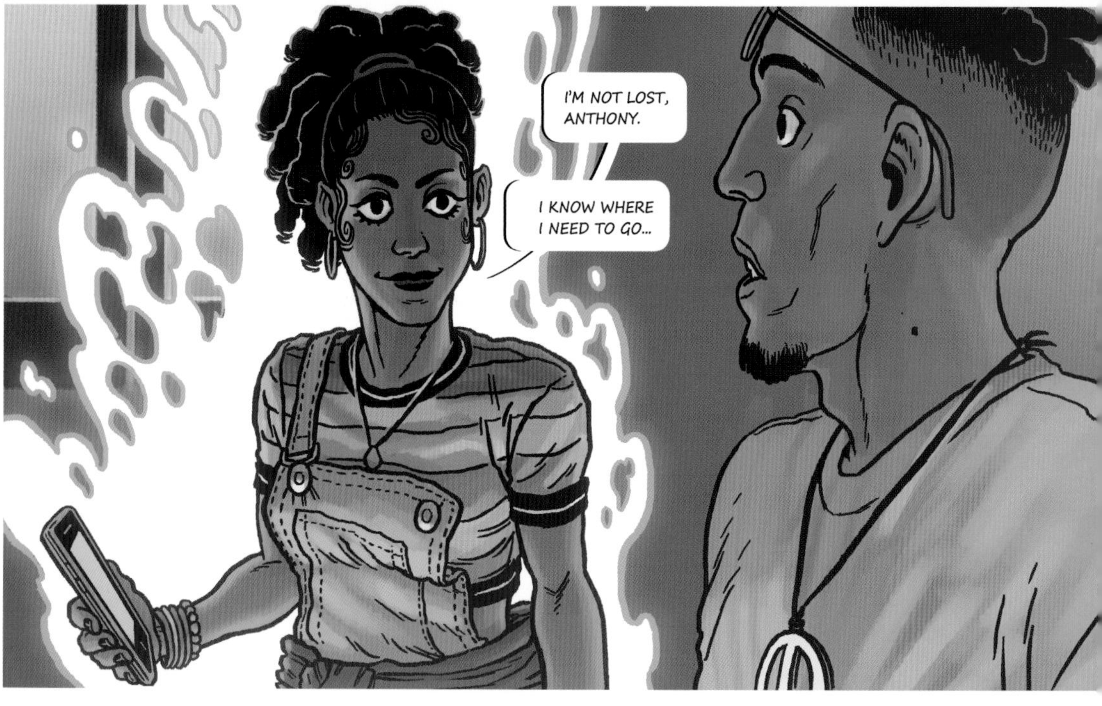
I'M NOT LOST, ANTHONY.
I KNOW WHERE I NEED TO GO...

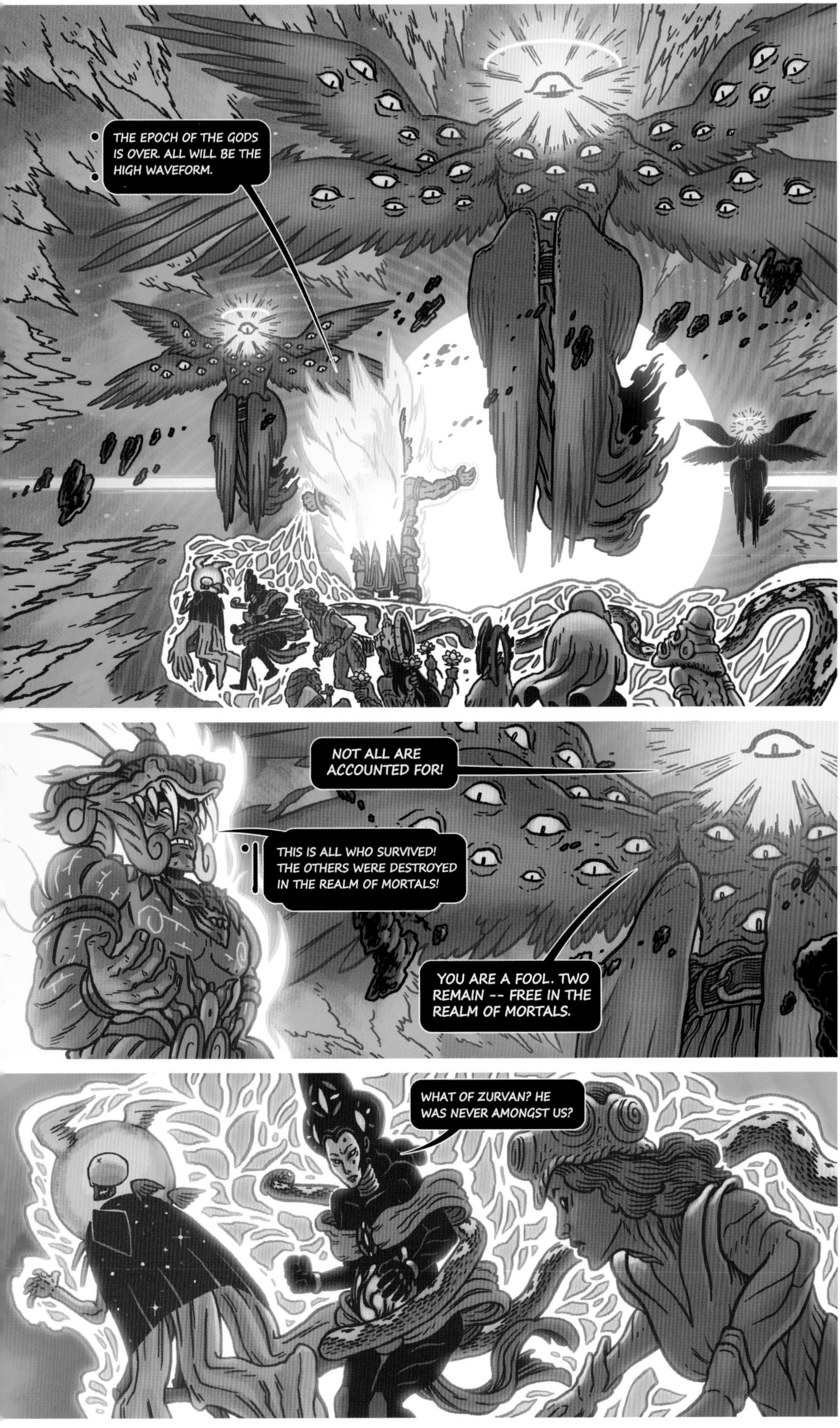
THE EPOCH OF THE GODS IS OVER. ALL WILL BE THE HIGH WAVEFORM.
NOT ALL ARE ACCOUNTED FOR!
THIS IS ALL WHO SURVIVED! THE OTHERS WERE DESTROYED IN THE REALM OF MORTALS!
YOU ARE A FOOL. TWO REMAIN -- FREE IN THE REALM OF MORTALS.
WHAT OF ZURVAN? HE WAS NEVER AMONGST US?

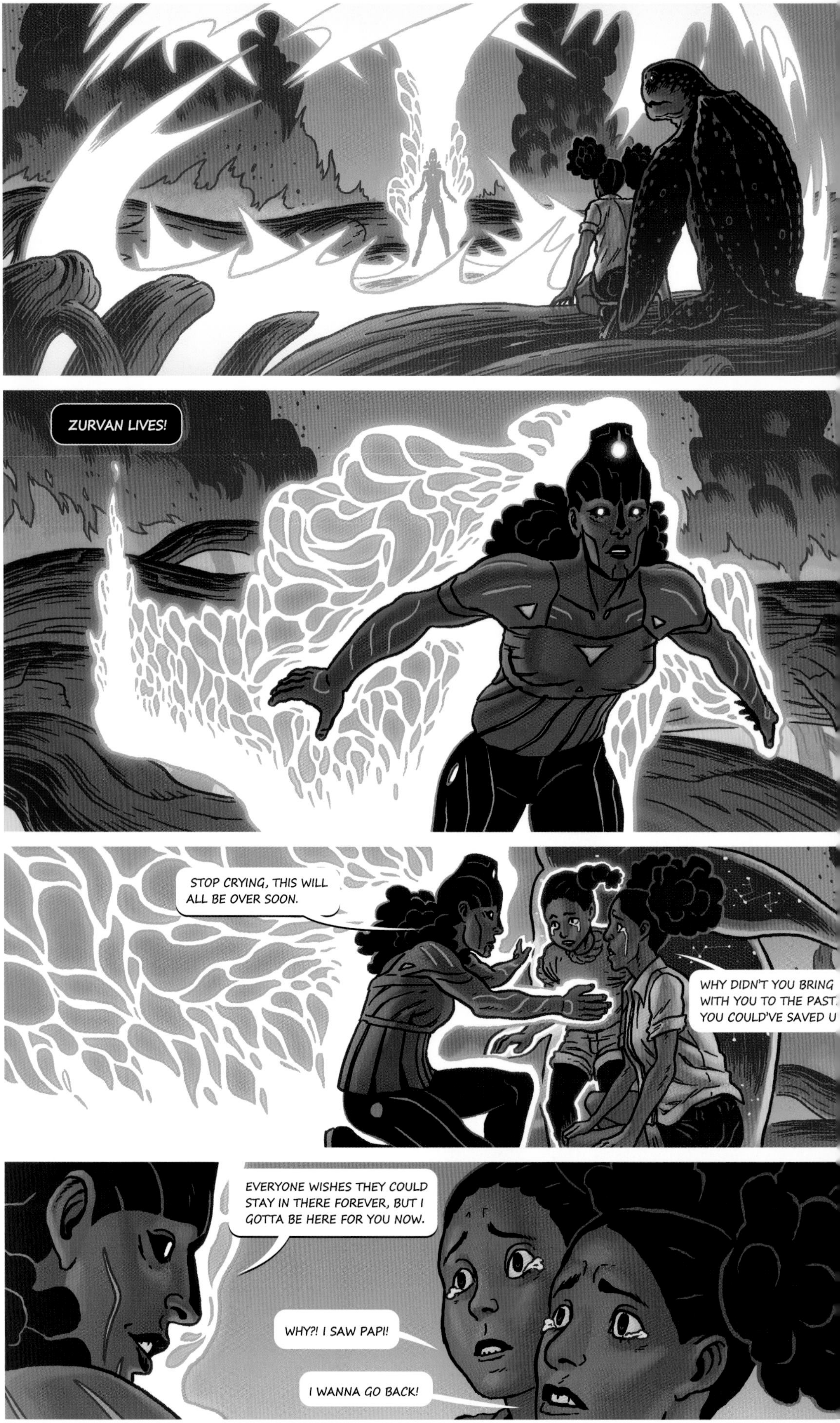
ZURVAN LIVES!
STOP CRYING, THIS WILL ALL BE OVER SOON.
WHY DIDN'T YOU BRING WITH YOU TO THE PAST. YOU COULD'VE SAVED U
EVERYONE WISHES THEY COULD STAY IN THERE FOREVER, BUT I GOTTA BE HERE FOR YOU NOW.
WHY?! I SAW PAPI!
I WANNA GO BACK!

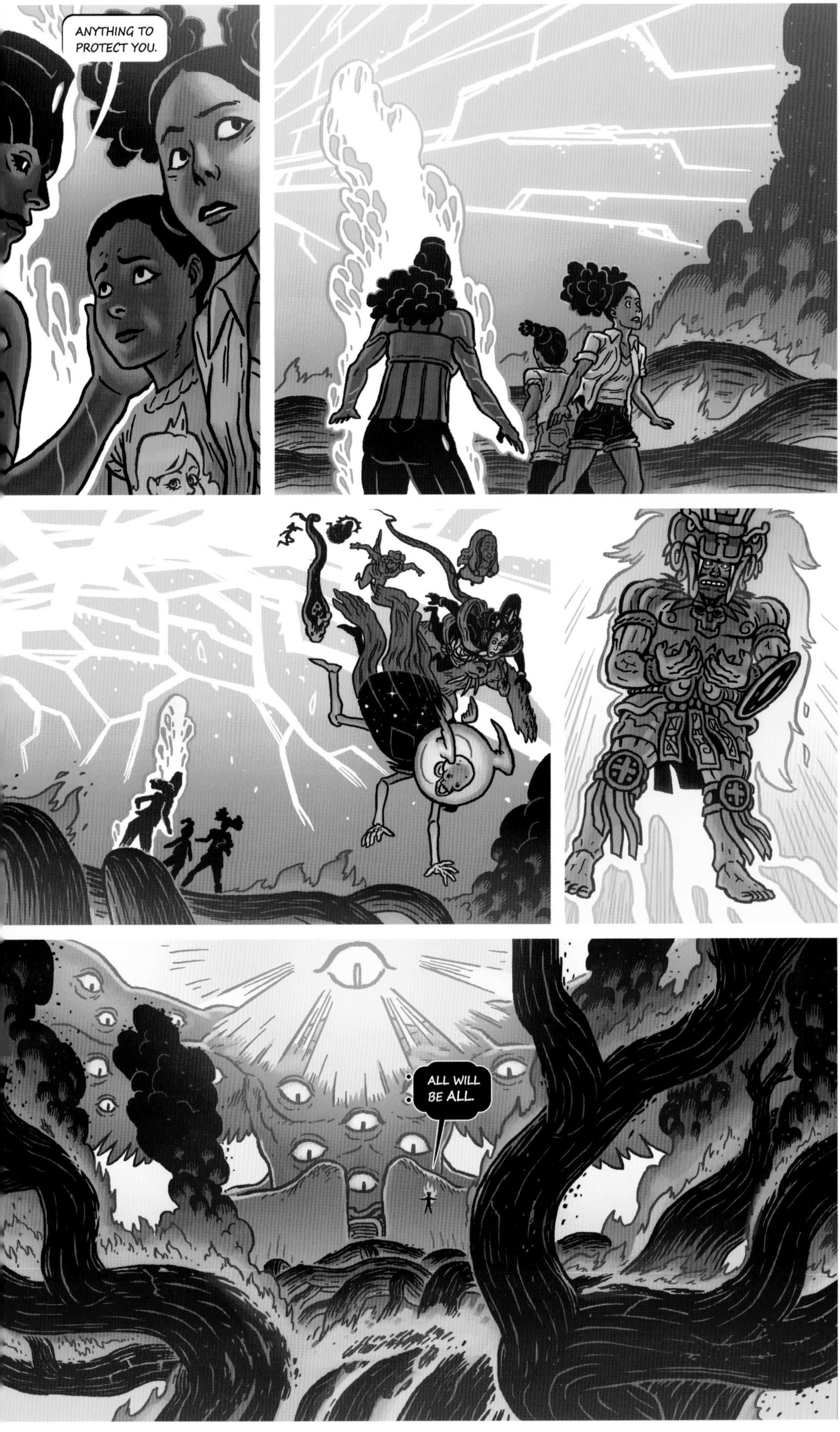
ANYTHING TO PROTECT YOU.
ALL WILL BE ALL.

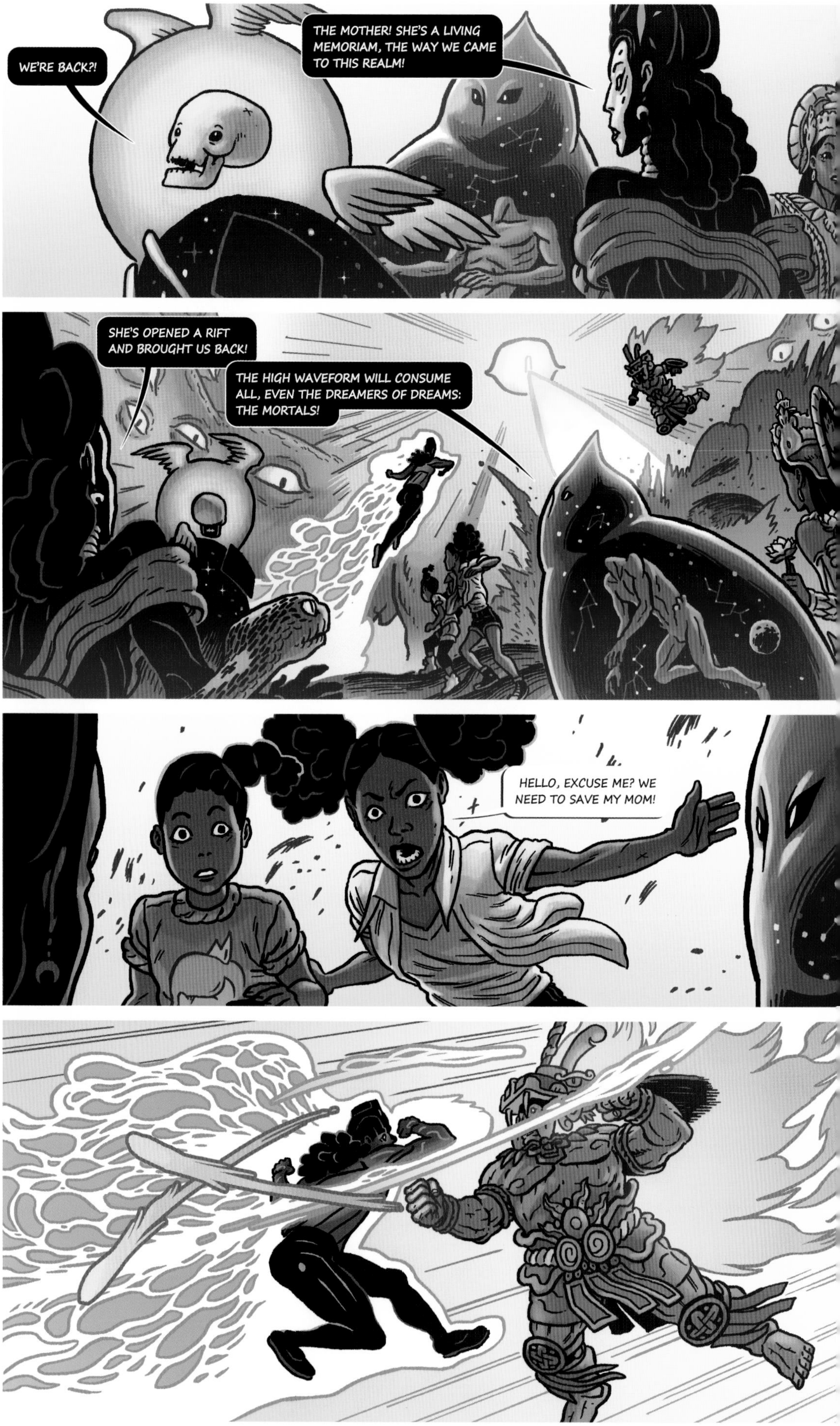
WE'RE BACK?!
THE MOTHER! SHE'S A LIVING MEMORIAM, THE WAY WE CAME TO THIS REALM!
SHE'S OPENED A RIFT AND BROUGHT US BACK!
THE HIGH WAVEFORM WILL CONSUME ALL, EVEN THE DREAMERS OF DREAMS: THE MORTALS!
HELLO, EXCUSE ME? WE NEED TO SAVE MY MOM!

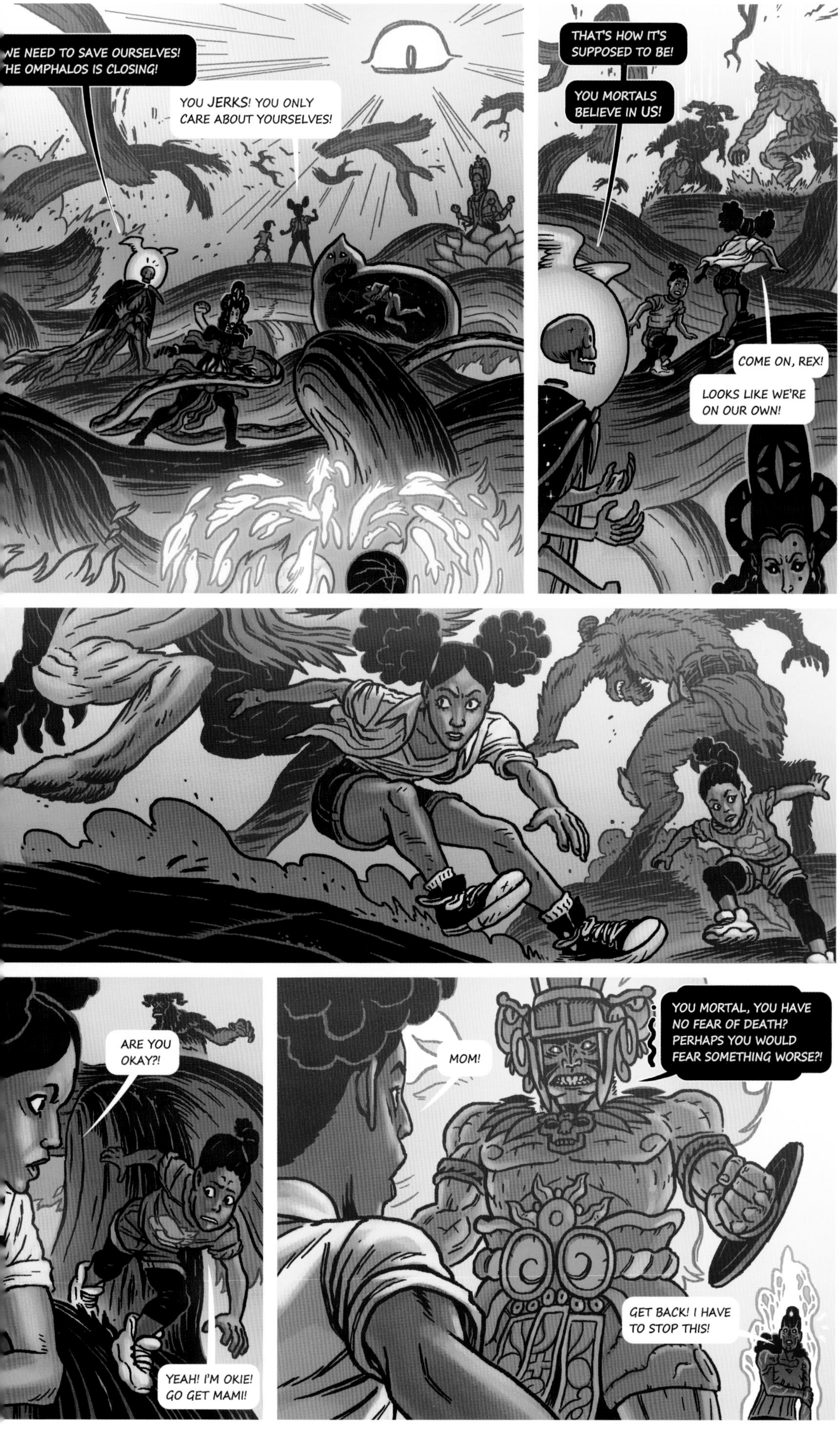
WE NEED TO SAVE OURSELVES! THE OMPHALOS IS CLOSING!
YOU JERKS! YOU ONLY CARE ABOUT YOURSELVES!
THAT'S HOW IT'S SUPPOSED TO BE!
YOU MORTALS BELIEVE IN US!
COME ON, REX!
LOOKS LIKE WE'RE ON OUR OWN!
ARE YOU OKAY?!
YEAH! I'M OKIE! GO GET MAMI!
MOM!
YOU MORTAL, YOU HAVE NO FEAR OF DEATH? PERHAPS YOU WOULD FEAR SOMETHING WORSE?!
GET BACK! I HAVE TO STOP THIS!

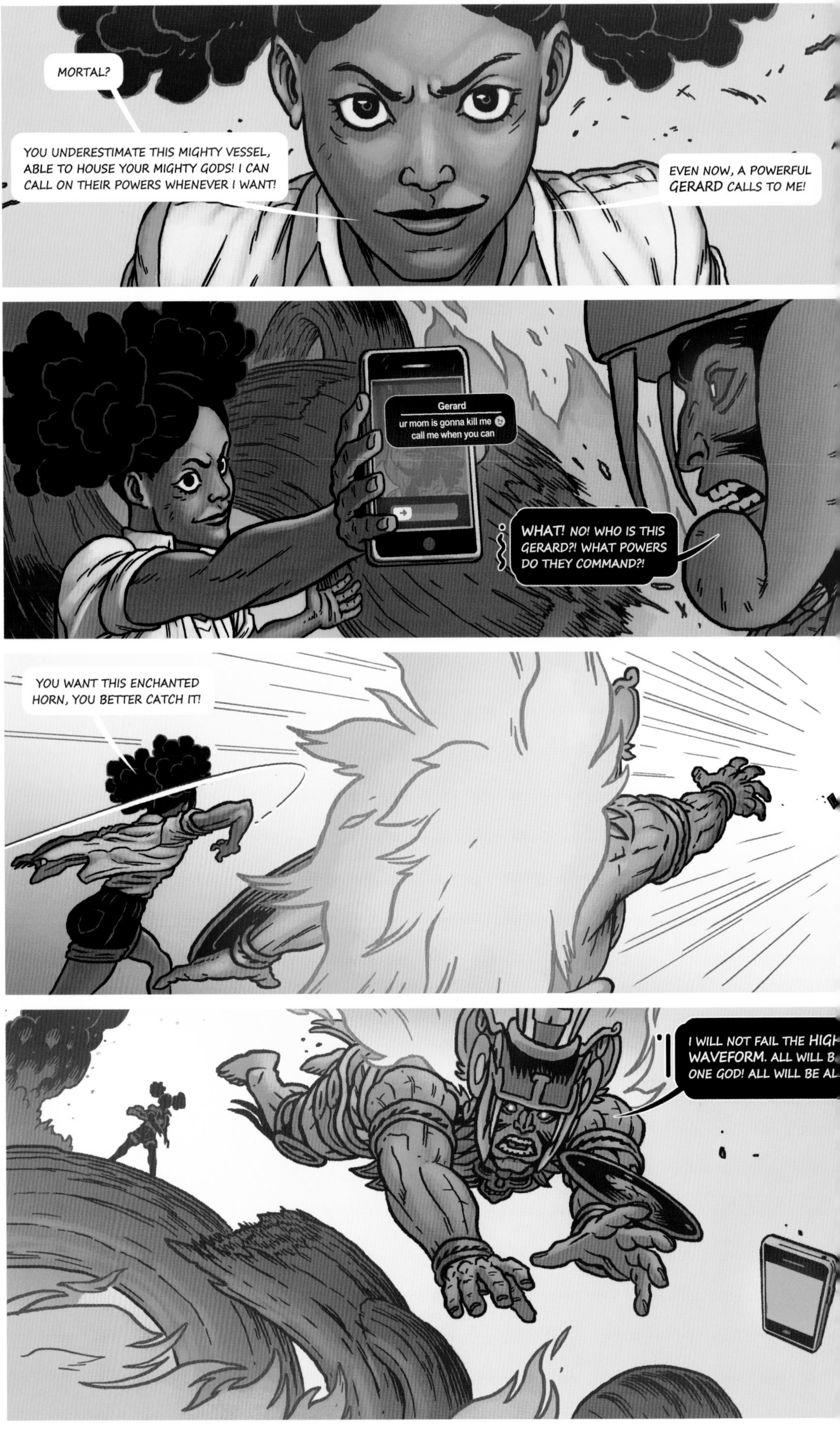
MORTAL?
YOU UNDERESTIMATE THIS MIGHTY VESSEL, ABLE TO HOUSE YOUR MIGHTY GODS! I CAN CALL ON THEIR POWERS WHENEVER I WANT!
EVEN NOW, A POWERFUL GERARD CALLS TO ME!
Gerard
ur mom is gonna kill me
call me when you can
WHAT! NO! WHO IS THIS GERARD?! WHAT POWERS DO THEY COMMAND?!
YOU WANT THIS ENCHANTED HORN, YOU BETTER CATCH IT!
I WILL NOT FAIL THE HIG
WAVEFORM. ALL WILL B
ONE GOD! ALL WILL BE AL

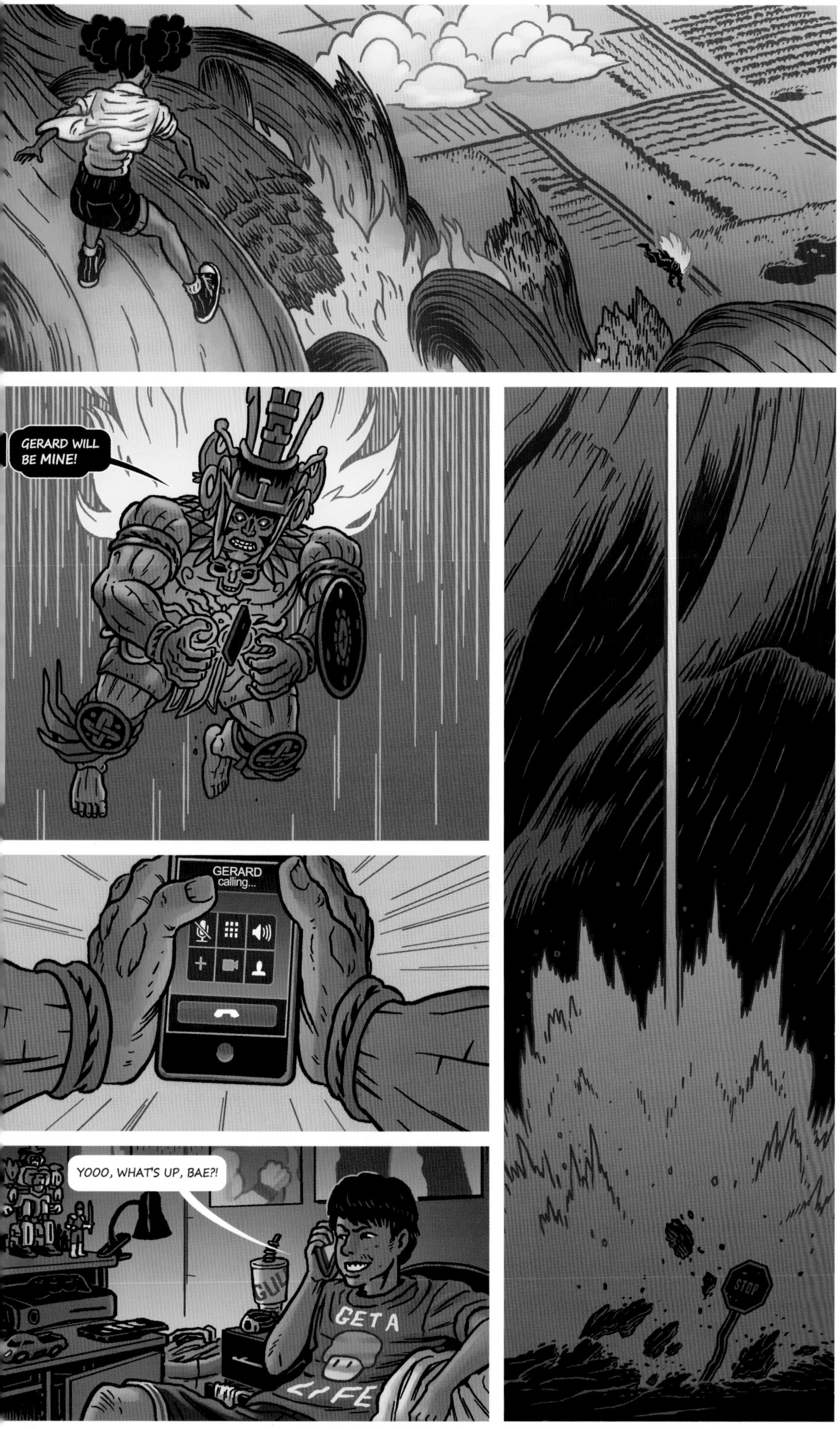
GERARD WILL BE MINE!
GERARD
calling...
YOOO, WHAT'S UP, BAE?!
GET A
LIFE
STOP

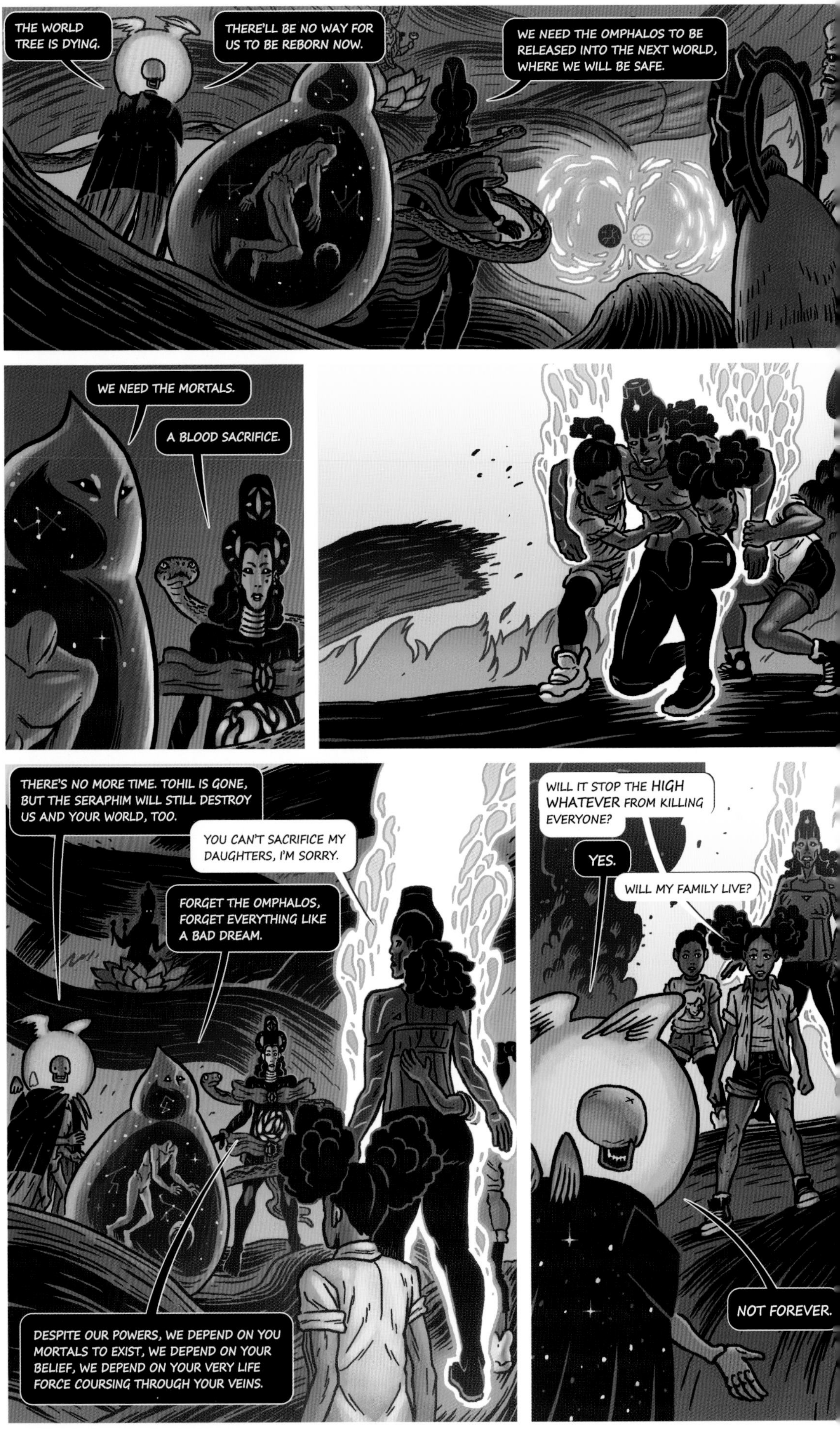
THE WORLD TREE IS DYING.
THERE'LL BE NO WAY FOR US TO BE REBORN NOW.
WE NEED THE OMPHALOS TO BE RELEASED INTO THE NEXT WORLD, WHERE WE WILL BE SAFE.
WE NEED THE MORTALS.
A BLOOD SACRIFICE.
THERE'S NO MORE TIME. TOHIL IS GONE, BUT THE SERAPHIM WILL STILL DESTROY US AND YOUR WORLD, TOO.
YOU CAN'T SACRIFICE MY DAUGHTERS, I'M SORRY.
FORGET THE OMPHALOS, FORGET EVERYTHING LIKE A BAD DREAM.
DESPITE OUR POWERS, WE DEPEND ON YOU MORTALS TO EXIST, WE DEPEND ON YOUR BELIEF, WE DEPEND ON YOUR VERY LIFE FORCE COURSING THROUGH YOUR VEINS.
WILL IT STOP THE HIGH WHATEVER FROM KILLING EVERYONE?
YES.
WILL MY FAMILY LIVE?
NOT FOREVER.

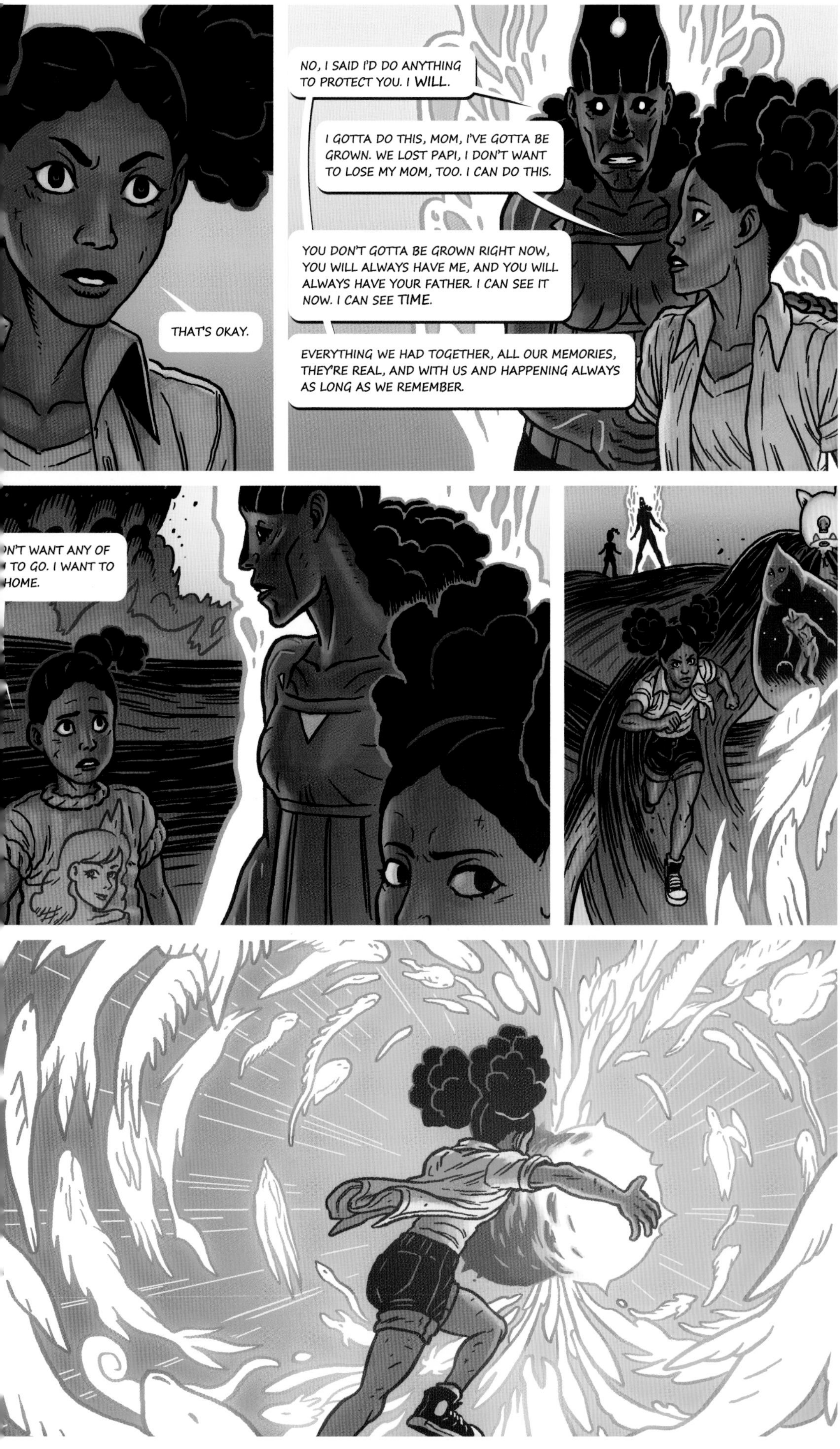
THAT'S OKAY.
NO, I SAID I'D DO ANYTHING TO PROTECT YOU. I WILL.
I GOTTA DO THIS, MOM, I'VE GOTTA BE GROWN. WE LOST PAPI, I DON'T WANT TO LOSE MY MOM, TOO. I CAN DO THIS.
YOU DON'T GOTTA BE GROWN RIGHT NOW, YOU WILL ALWAYS HAVE ME, AND YOU WILL ALWAYS HAVE YOUR FATHER. I CAN SEE IT NOW. I CAN SEE TIME.
EVERYTHING WE HAD TOGETHER, ALL OUR MEMORIES, THEY'RE REAL, AND WITH US AND HAPPENING ALWAYS AS LONG AS WE REMEMBER.
N'T WANT ANY OF TO GO. I WANT TO HOME.

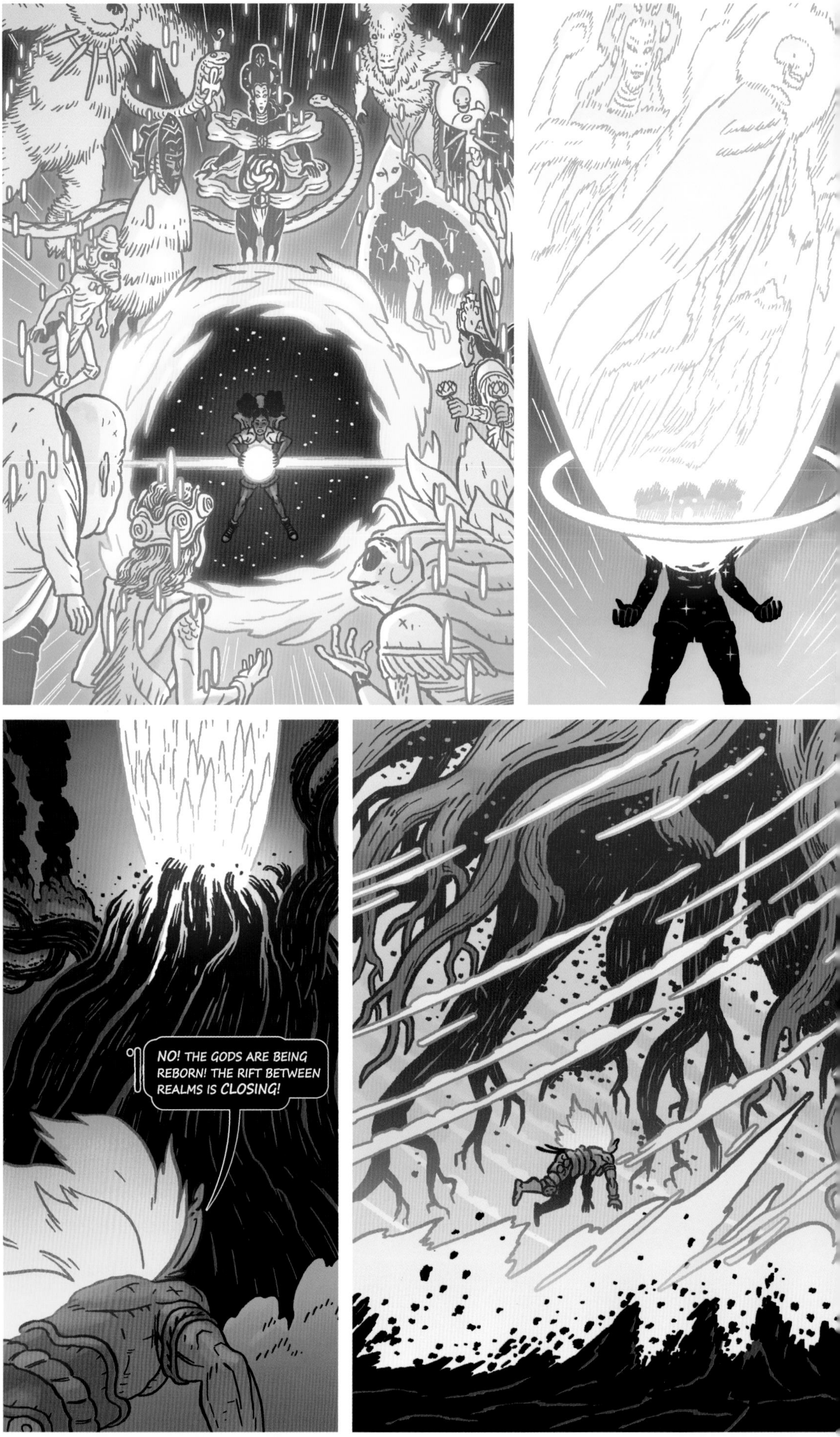
NO! THE GODS ARE BEING REBORN! THE RIFT BETWEEN REALMS IS CLOSING!

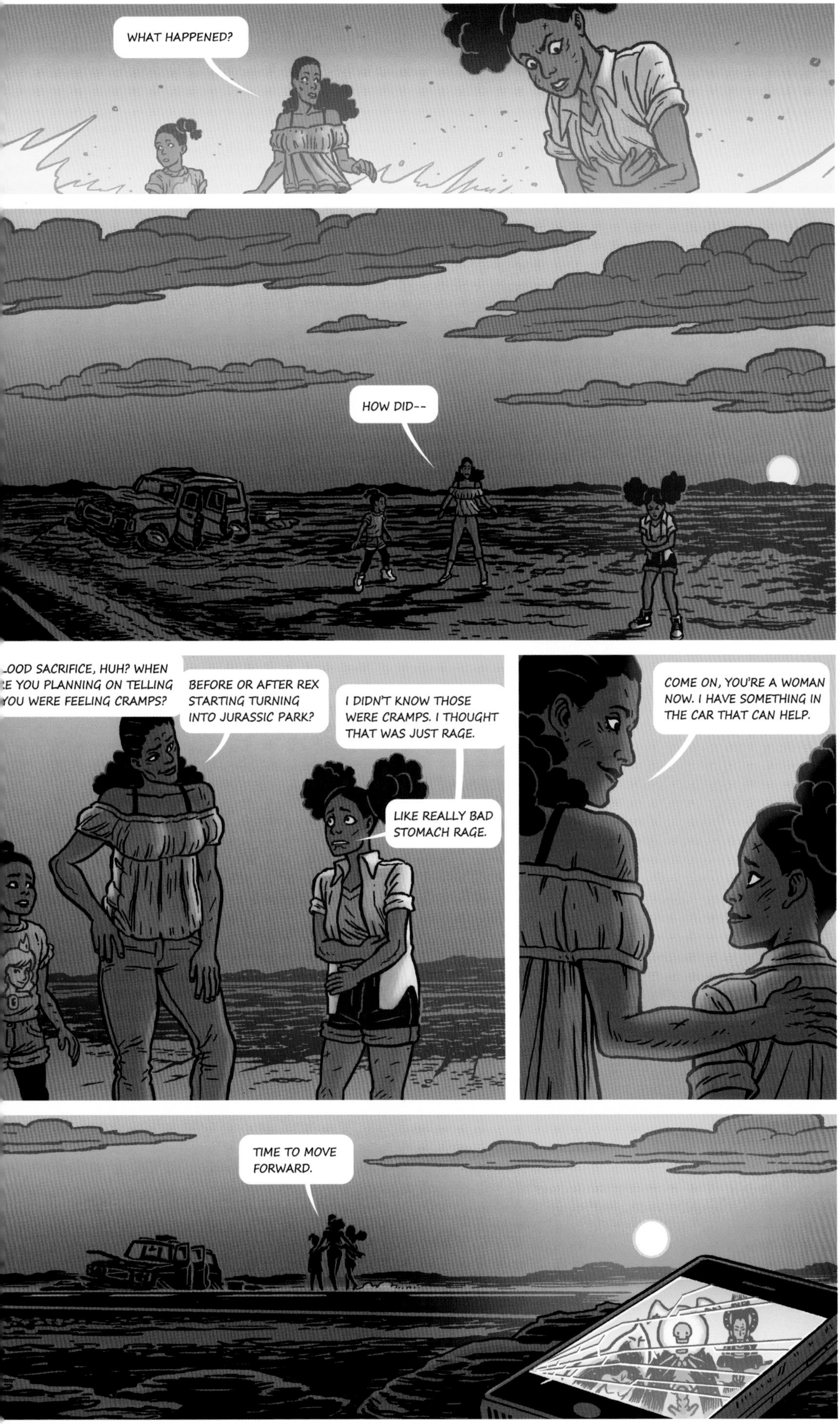
WHAT HAPPENED?
HOW DID--
LOOD SACRIFICE, HUH? WHEN E YOU PLANNING ON TELLING YOU WERE FEELING CRAMPS?
BEFORE OR AFTER REX STARTING TURNING INTO JURASSIC PARK?
I DIDN'T KNOW THOSE WERE CRAMPS. I THOUGHT THAT WAS JUST RAGE.
LIKE REALLY BAD STOMACH RAGE.
COME ON, YOU'RE A WOMAN NOW. I HAVE SOMETHING IN THE CAR THAT CAN HELP.
TIME TO MOVE FORWARD.

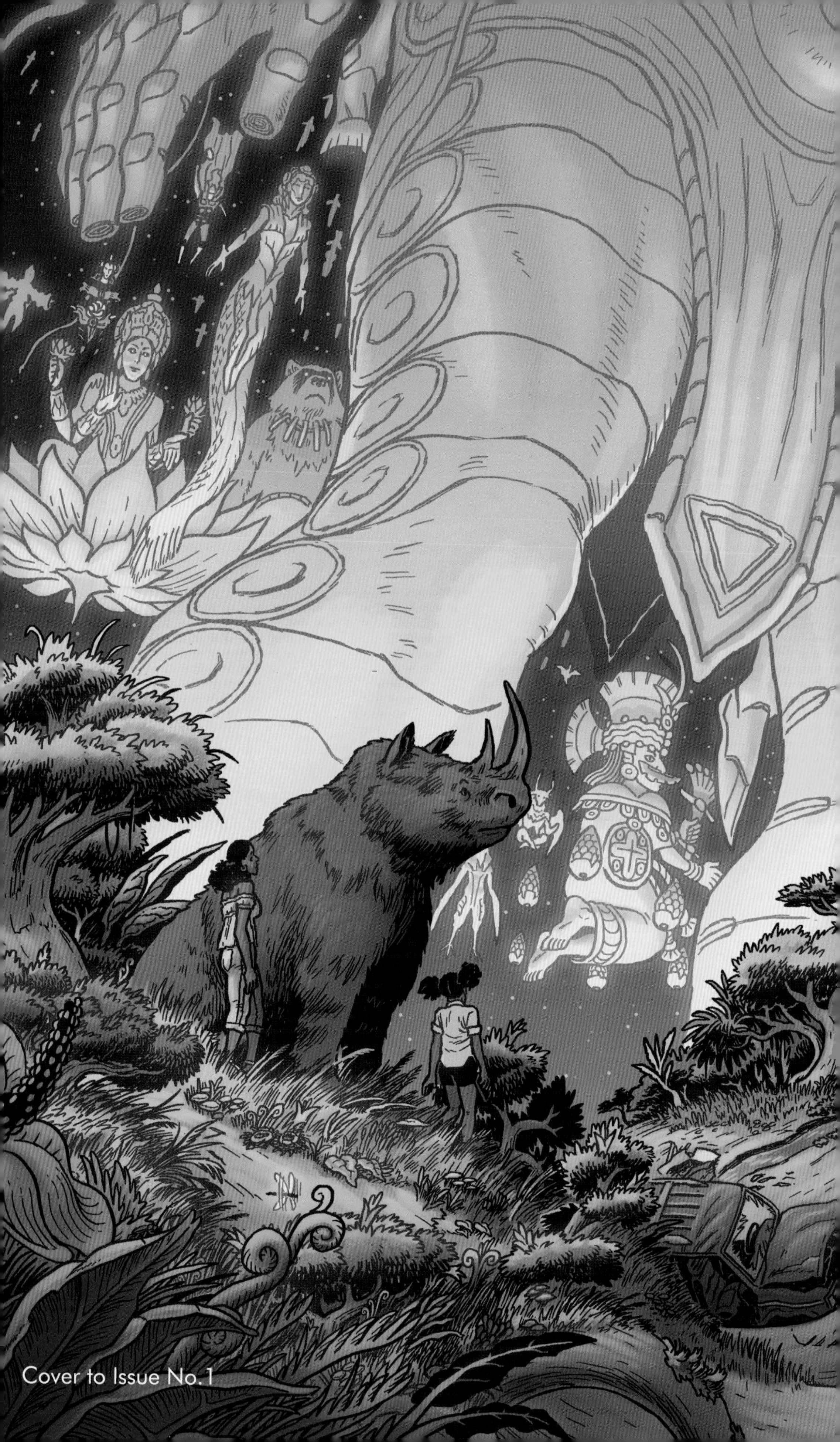

Cover to Issue No.1

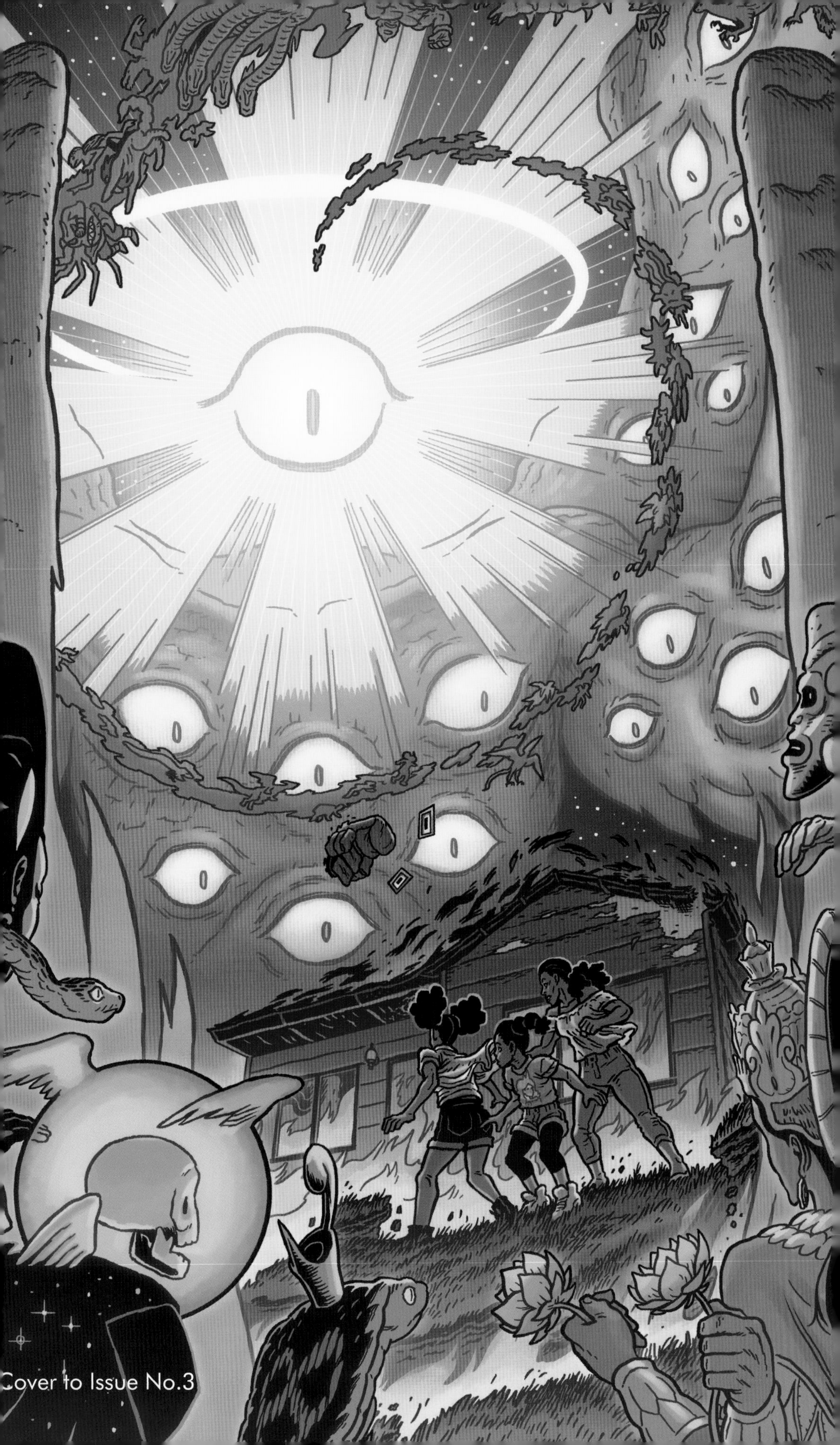

Cover to Issue No.3

PRODUCTION GALLER

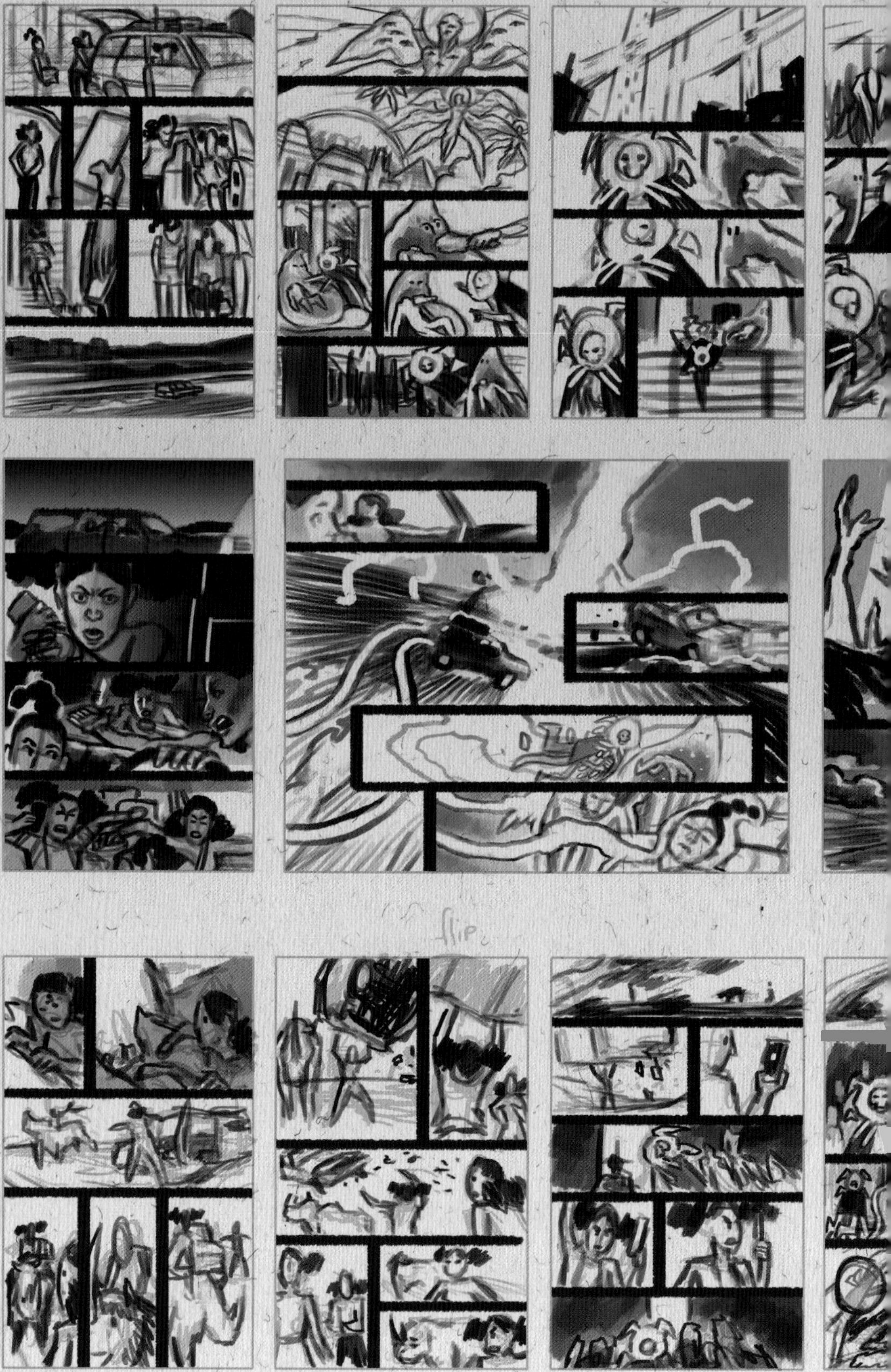
flip

Layout Thumbnails for Issue No.1

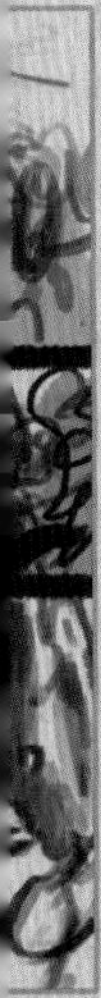

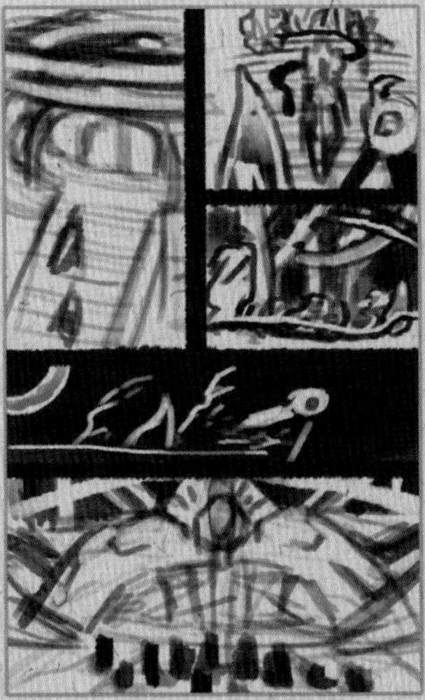

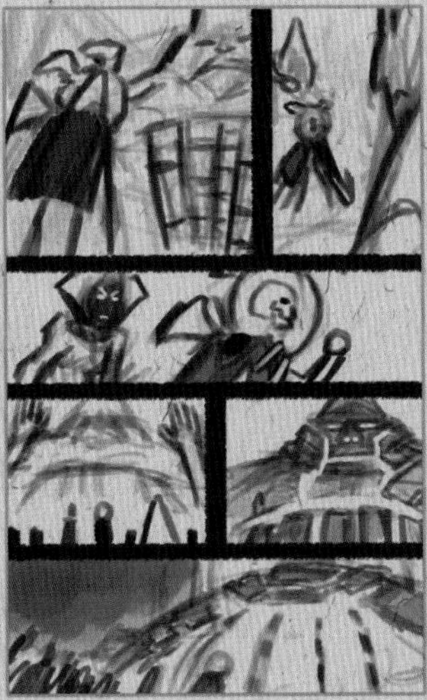

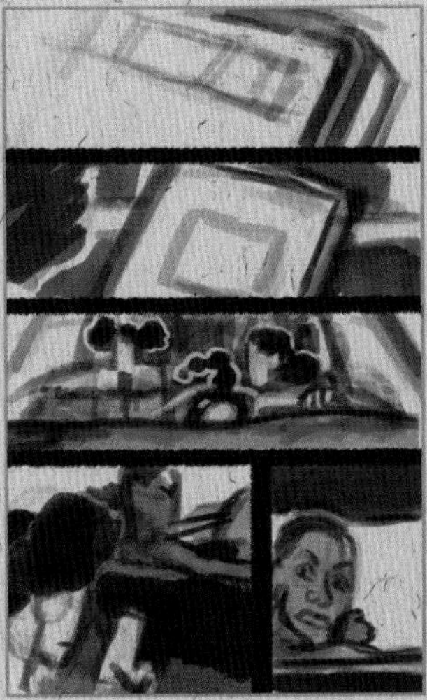

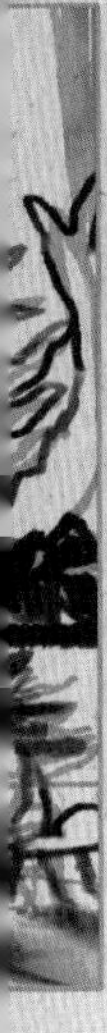

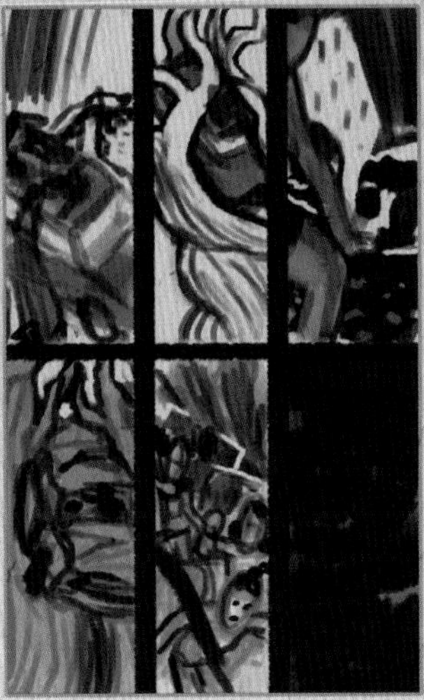

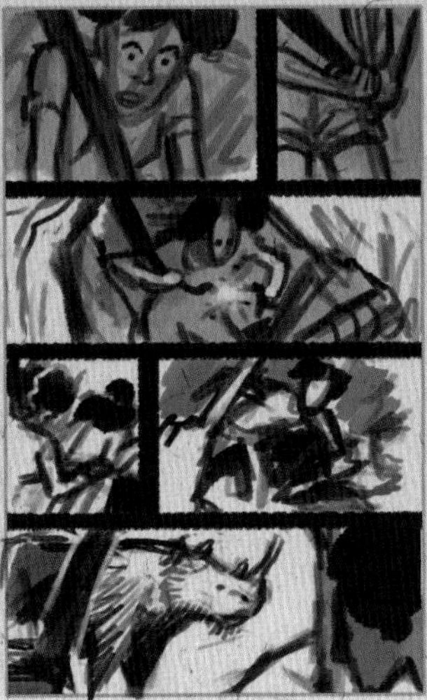

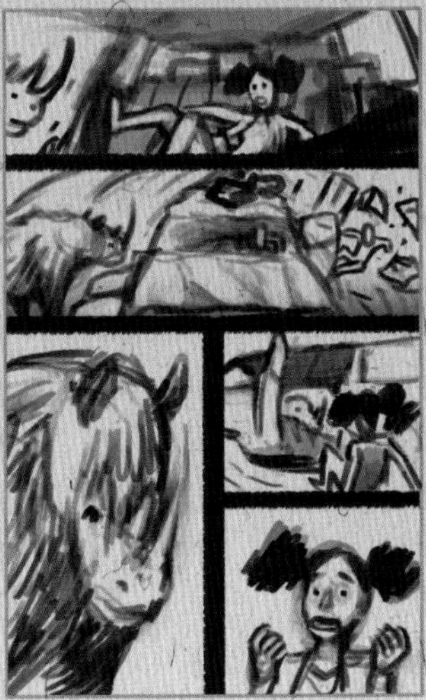

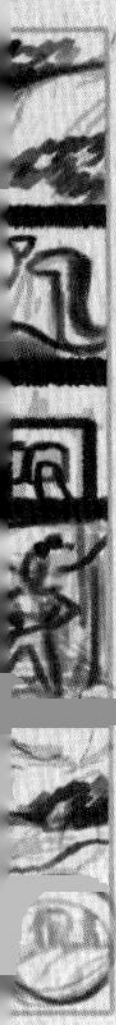

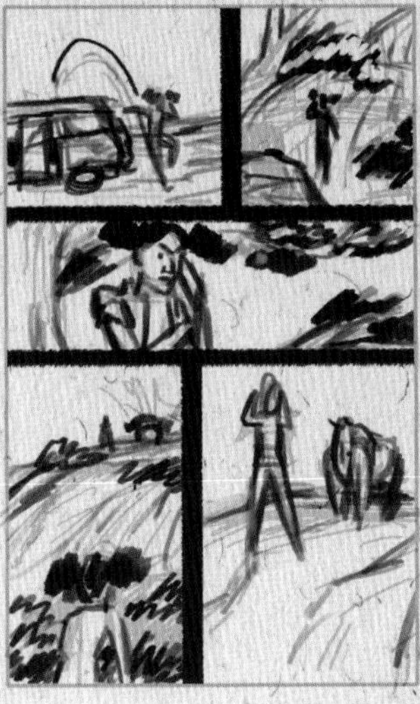

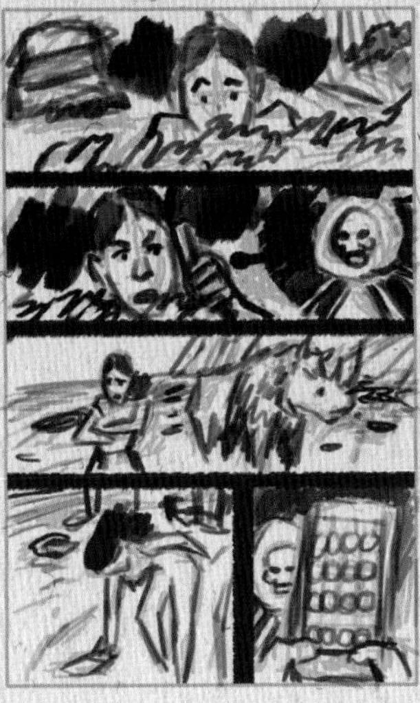

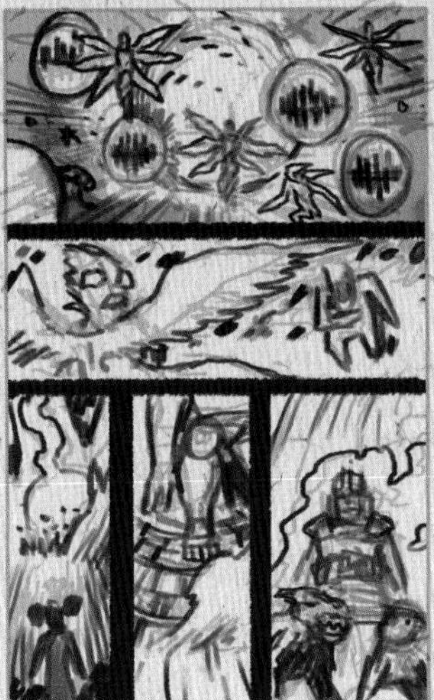

Cover Art Process for Issue No.1

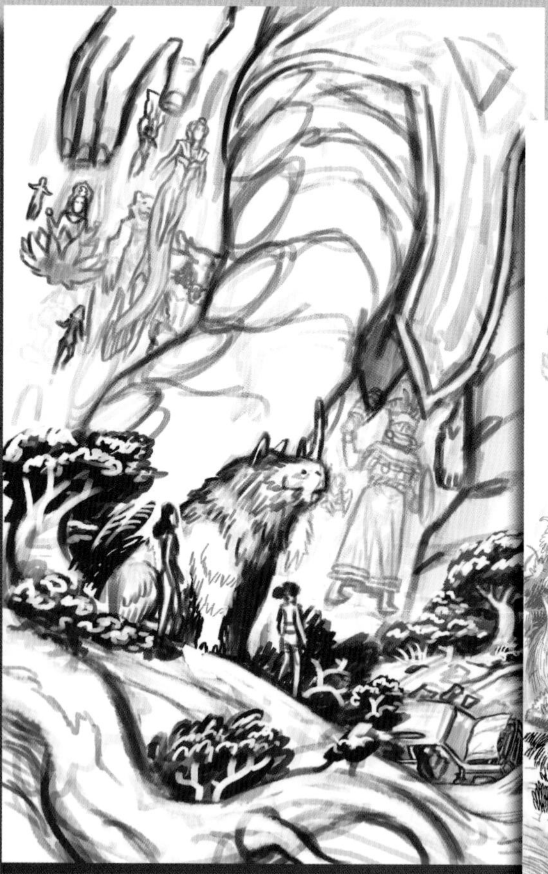

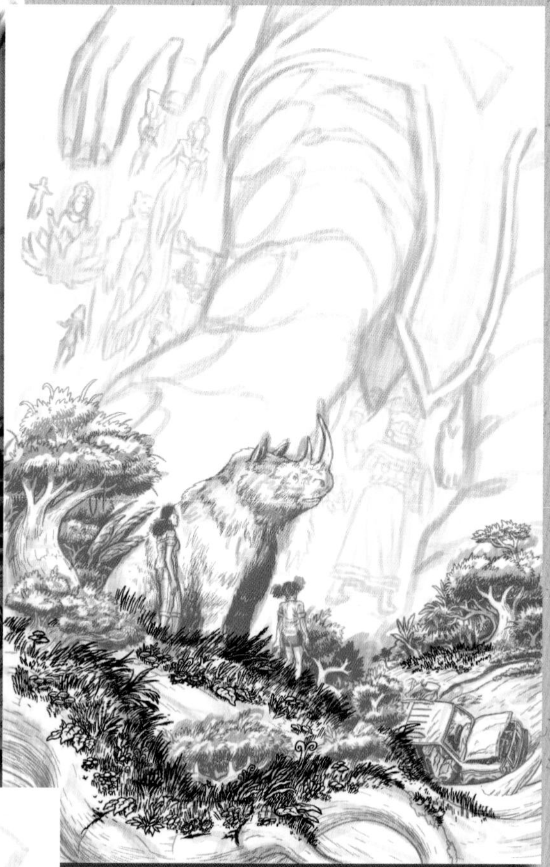

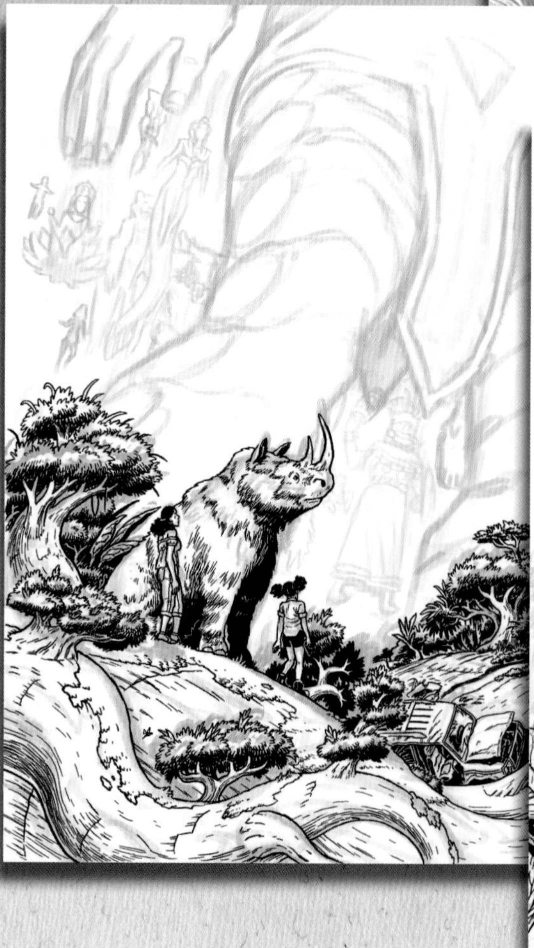

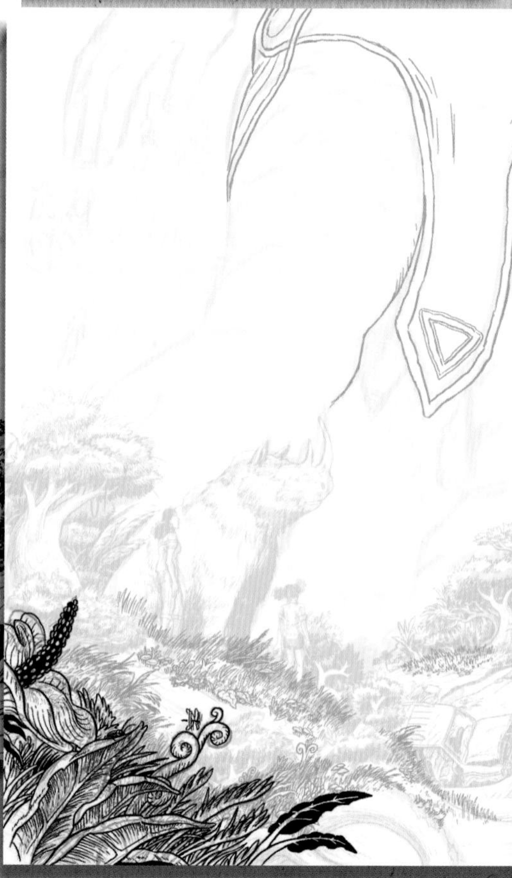

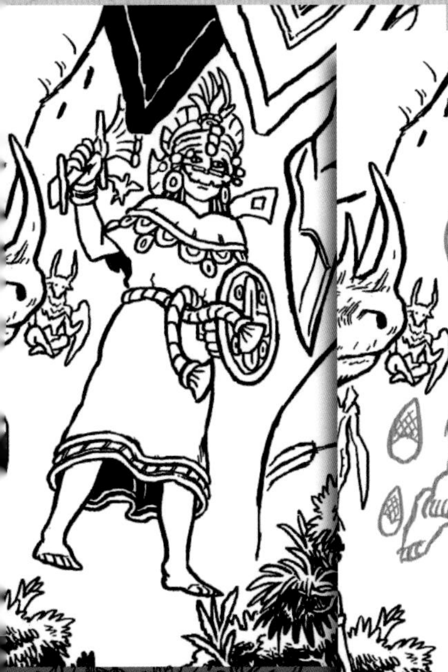
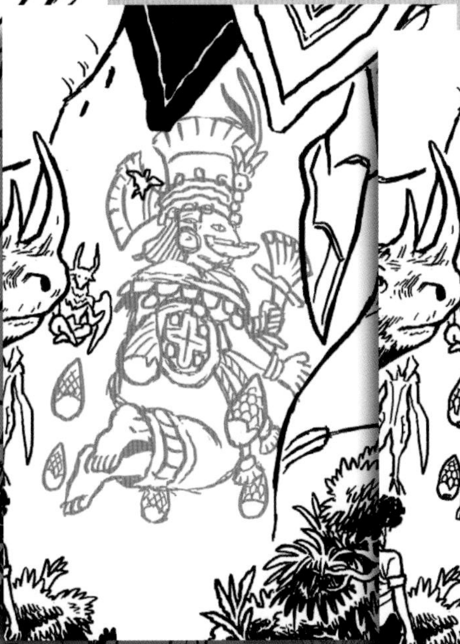
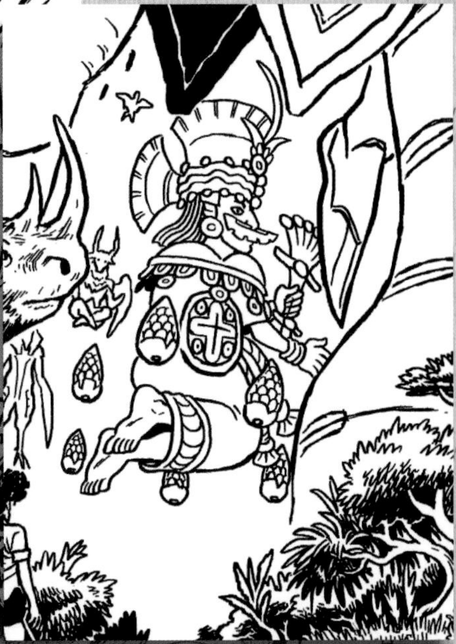
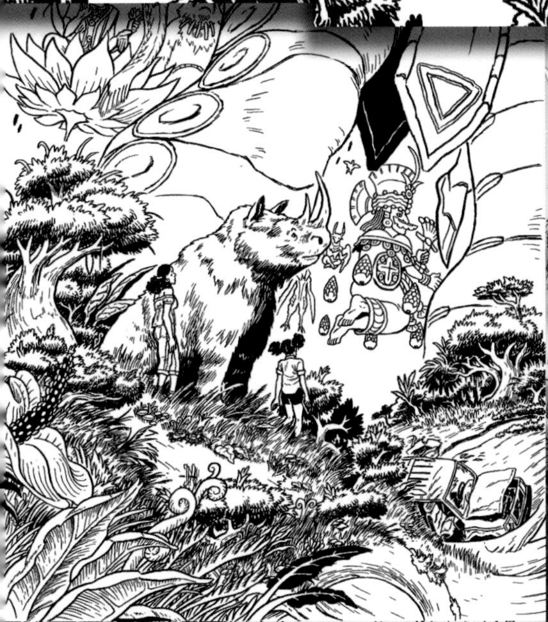
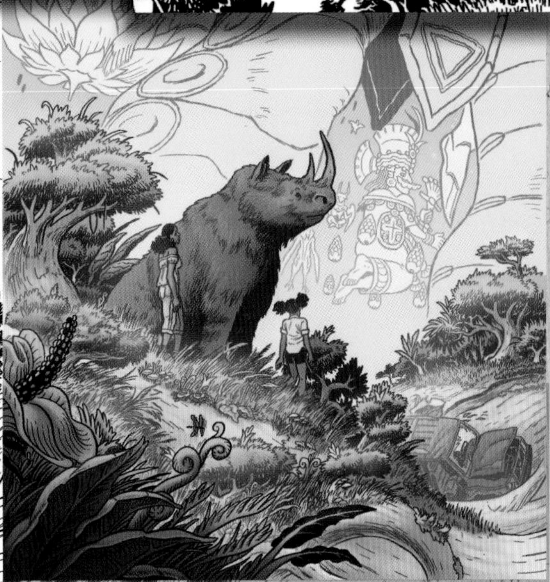
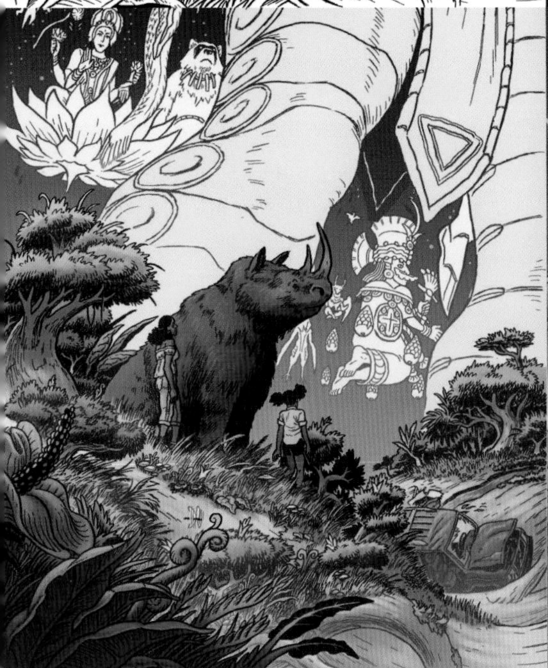
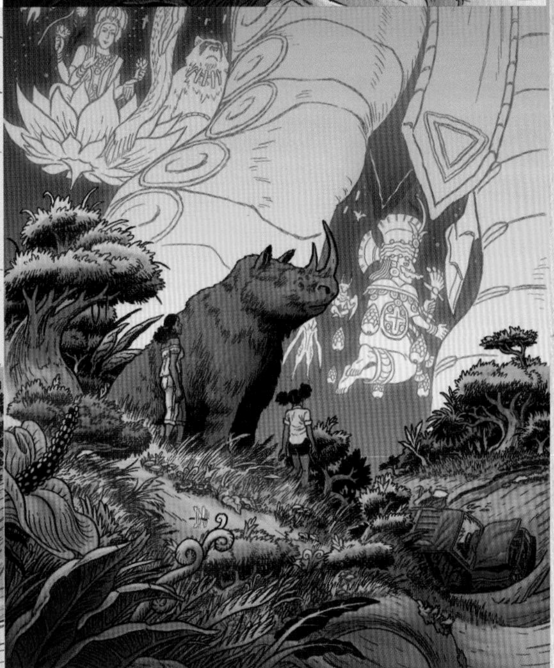

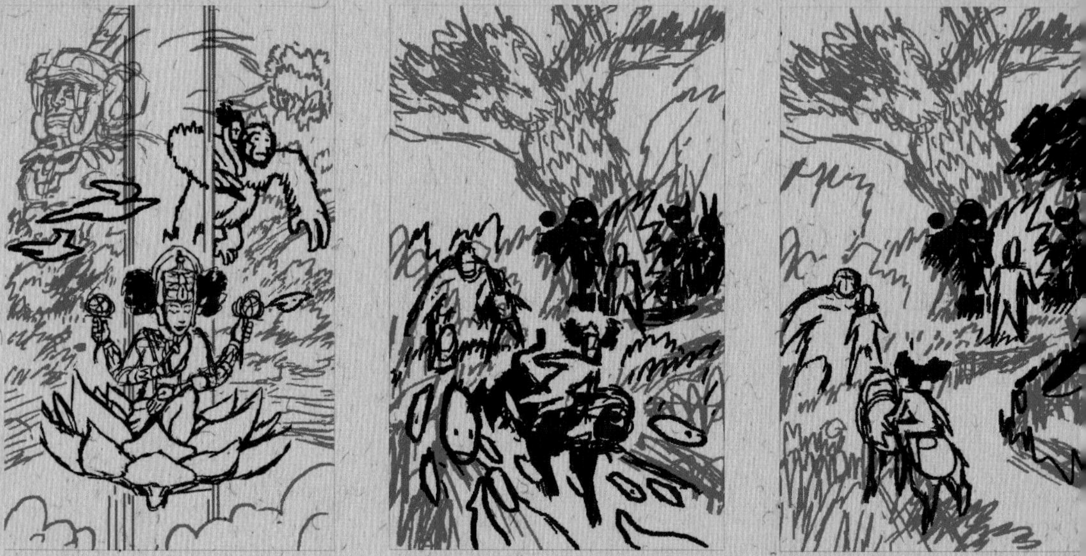

Unused concept sketches for Issue No. 2 cov

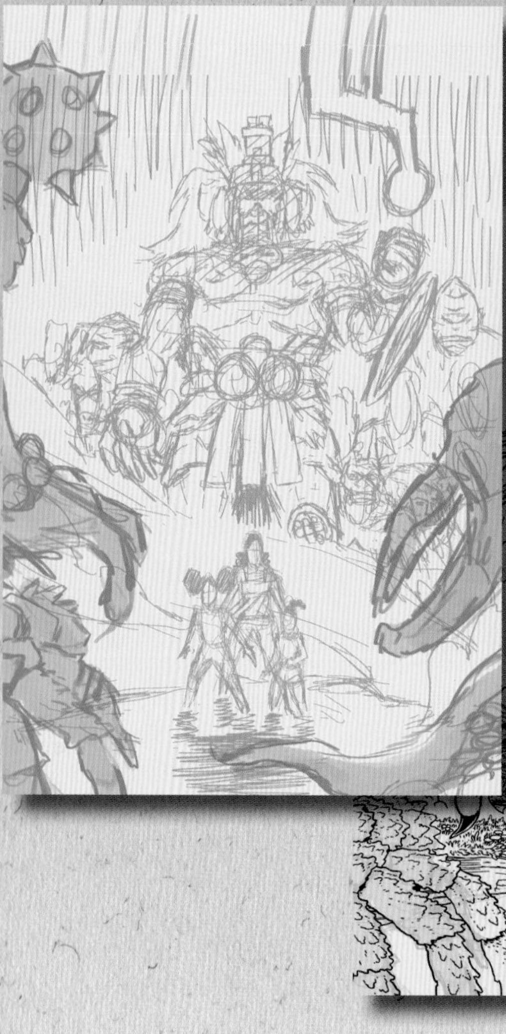

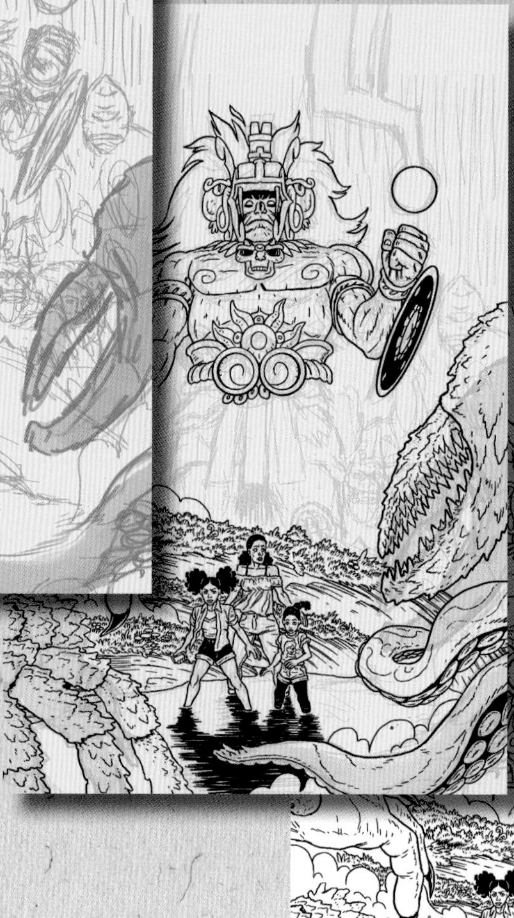

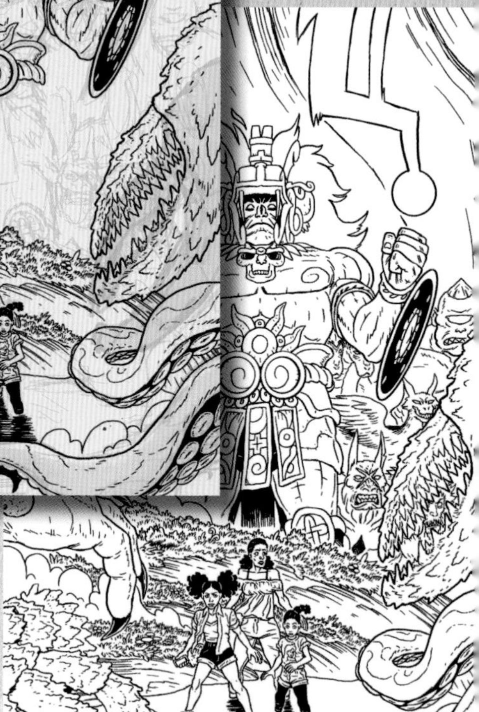

Cover Art Process for Issue No.2

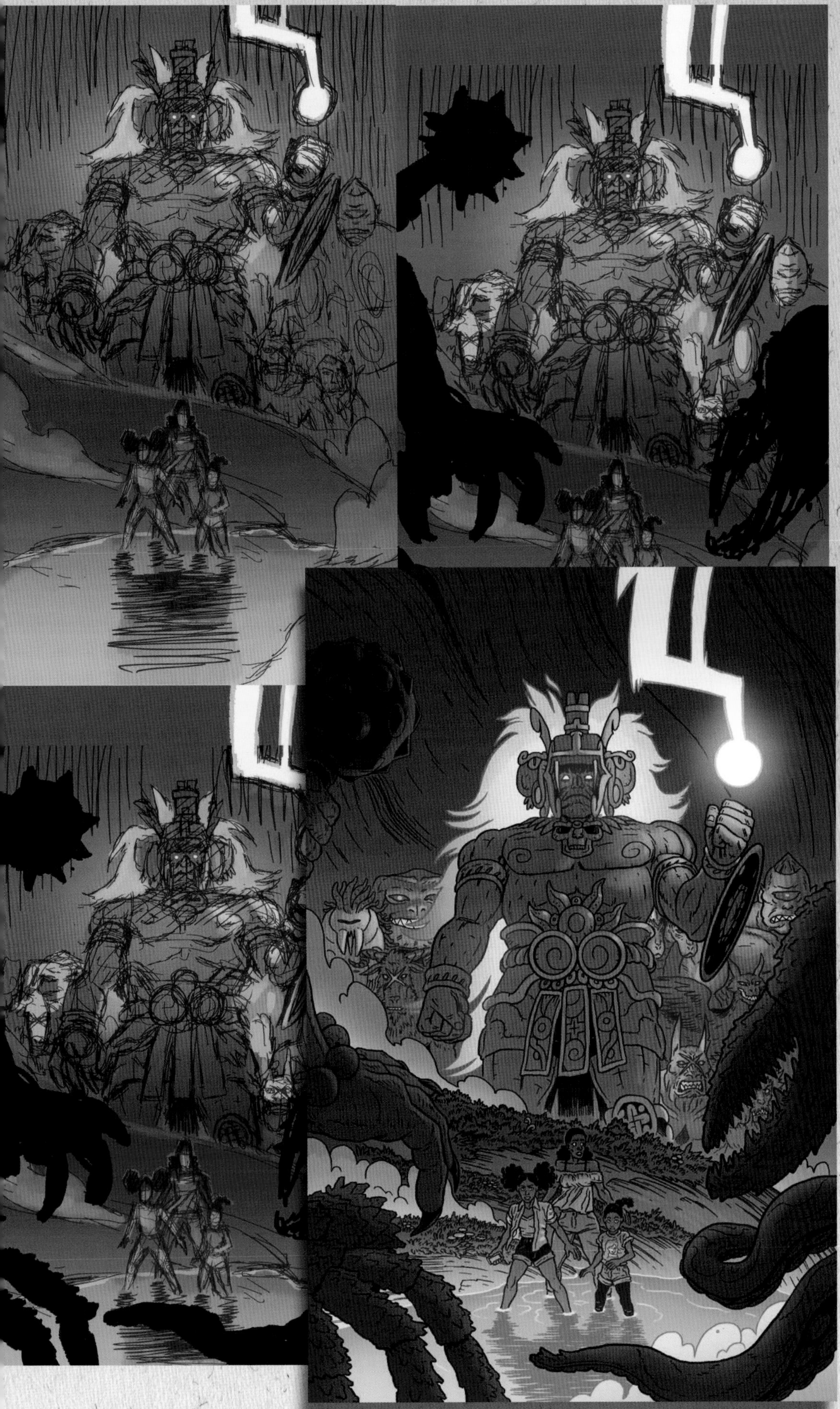

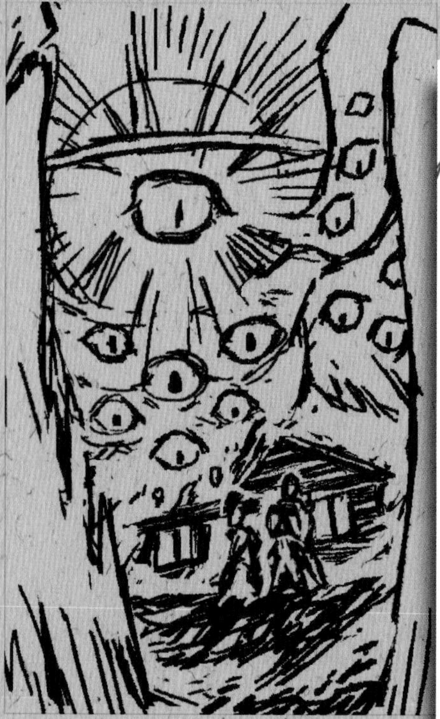
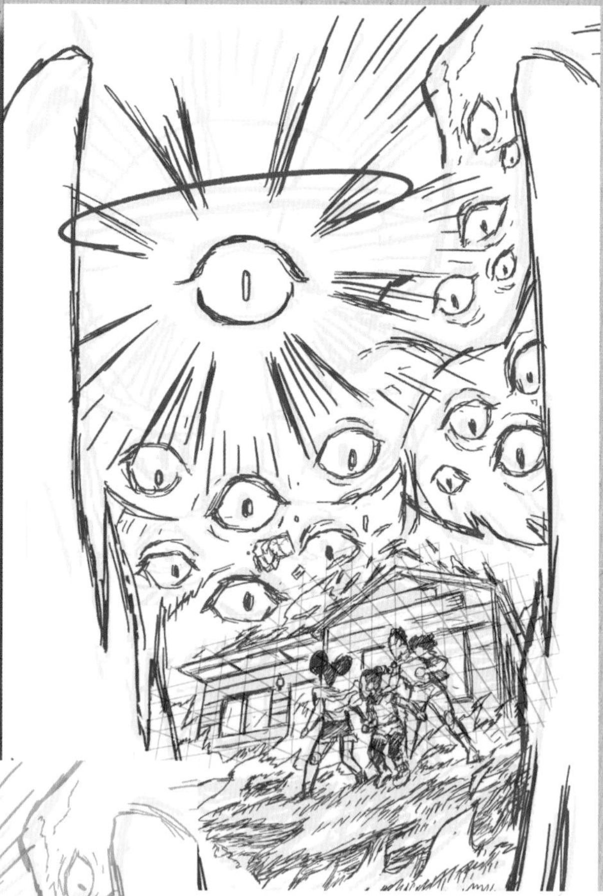
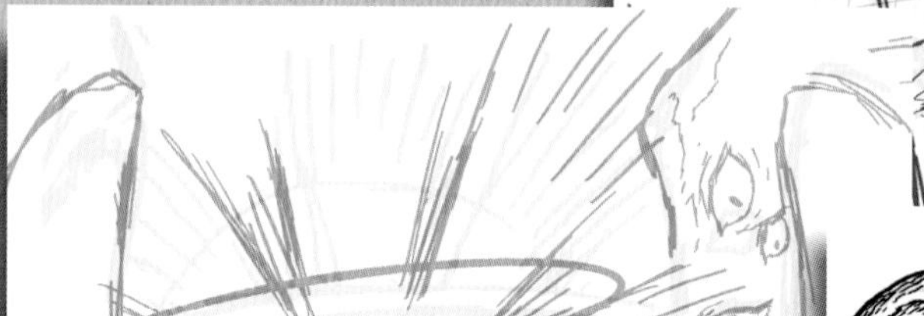
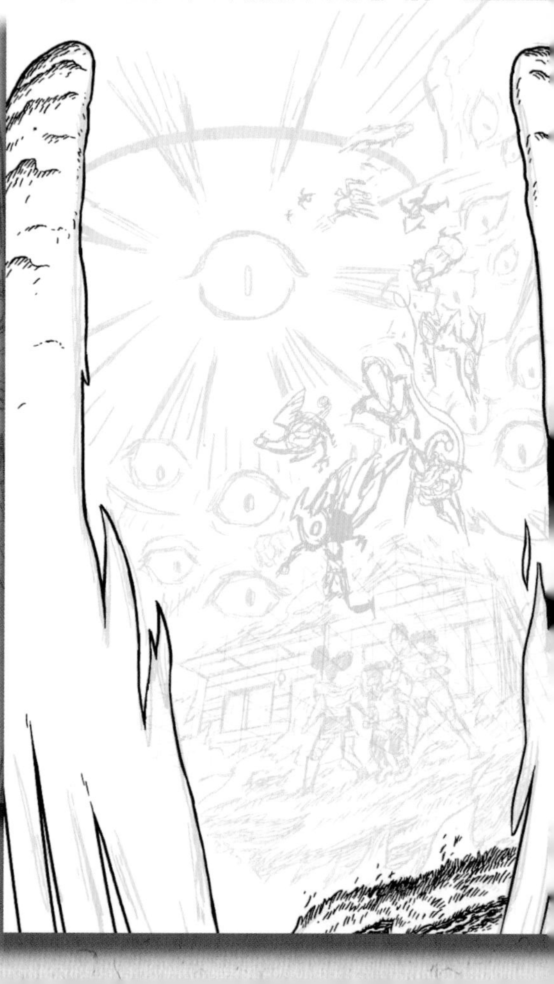

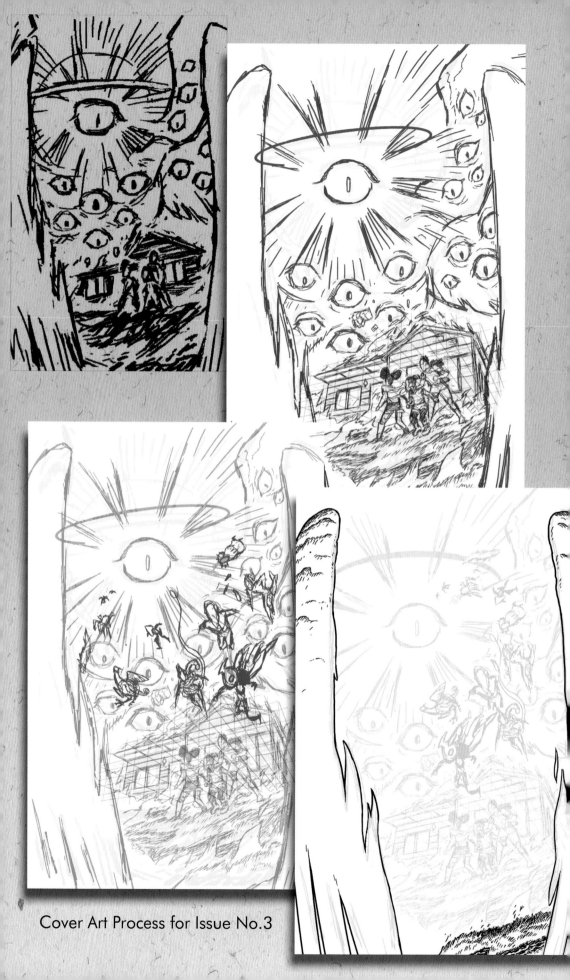

Cover Art Process for Issue No.3

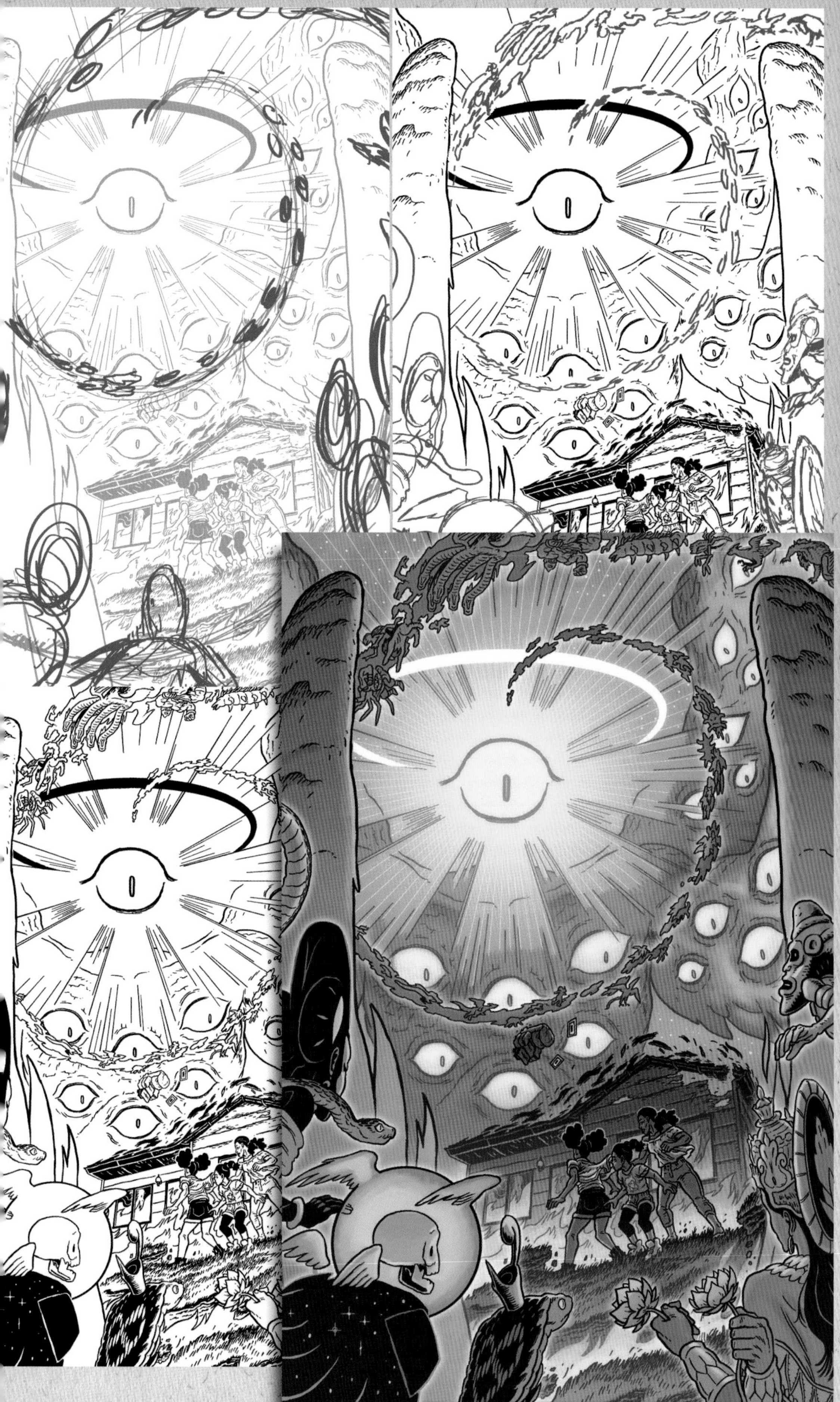

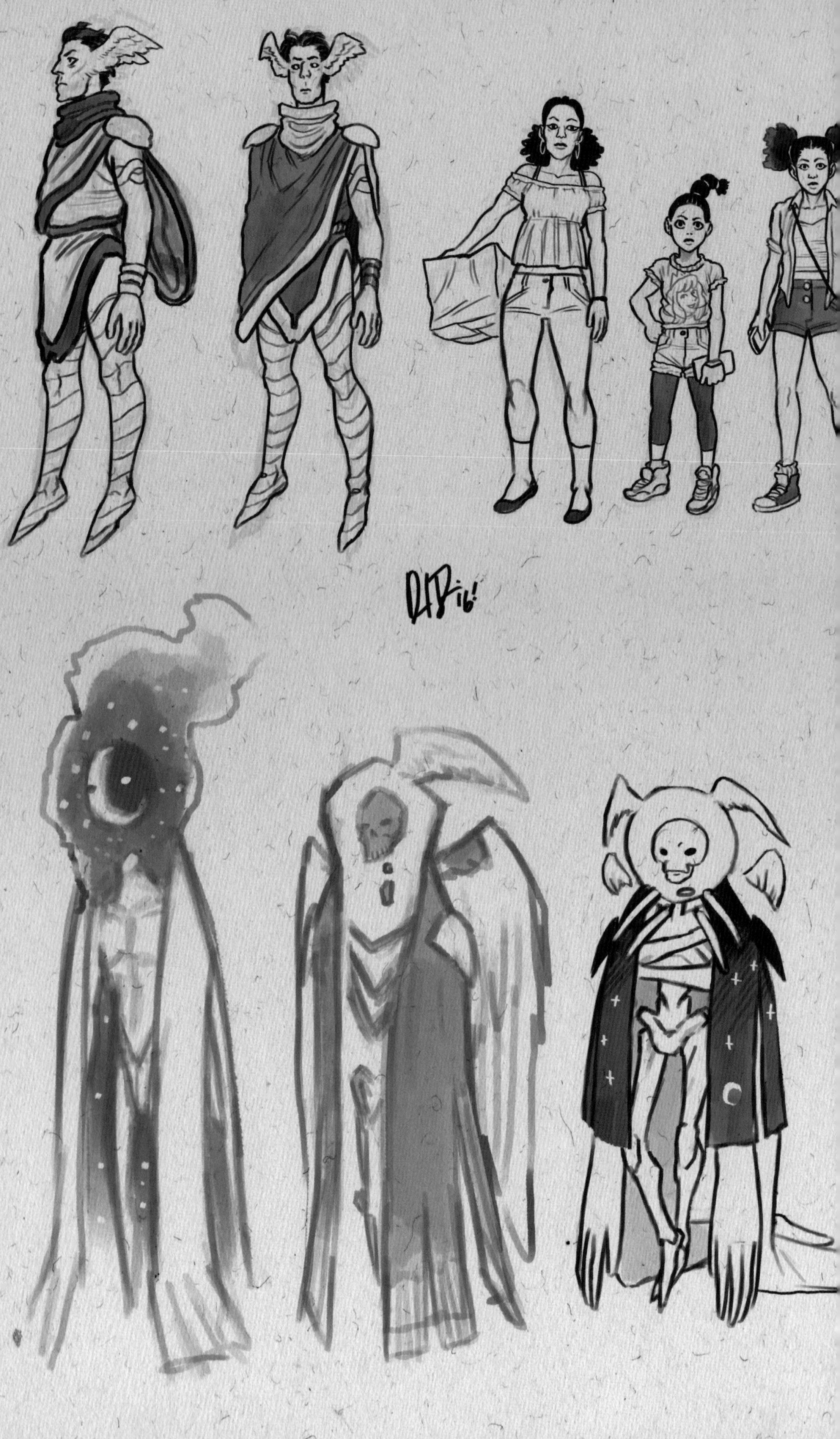

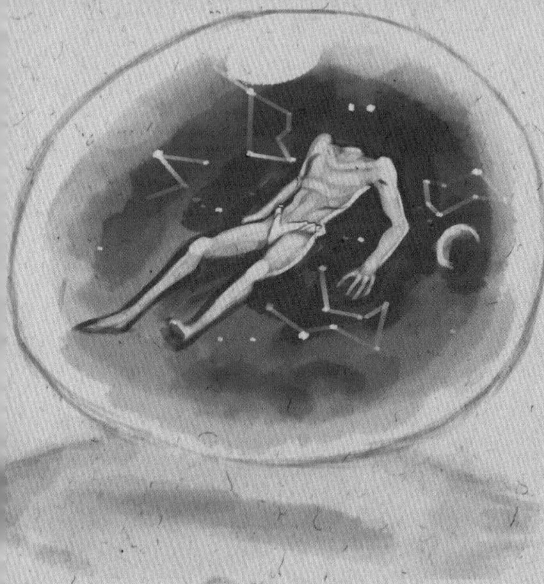

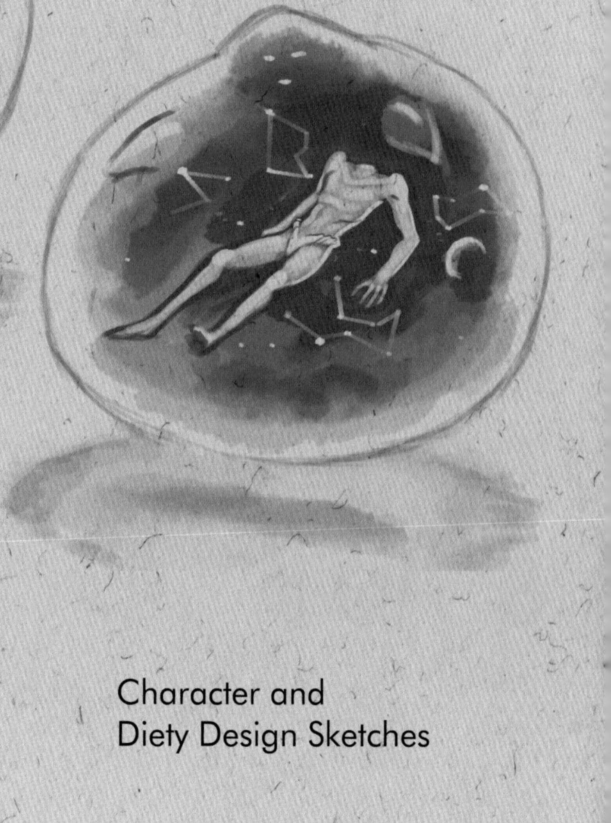

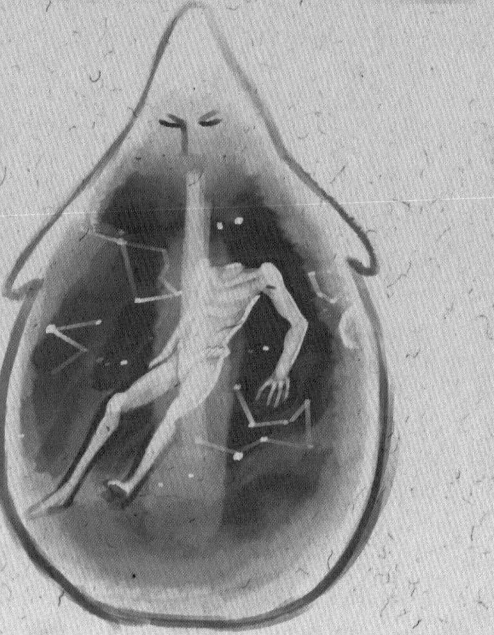

Character and
Diety Design Sketches

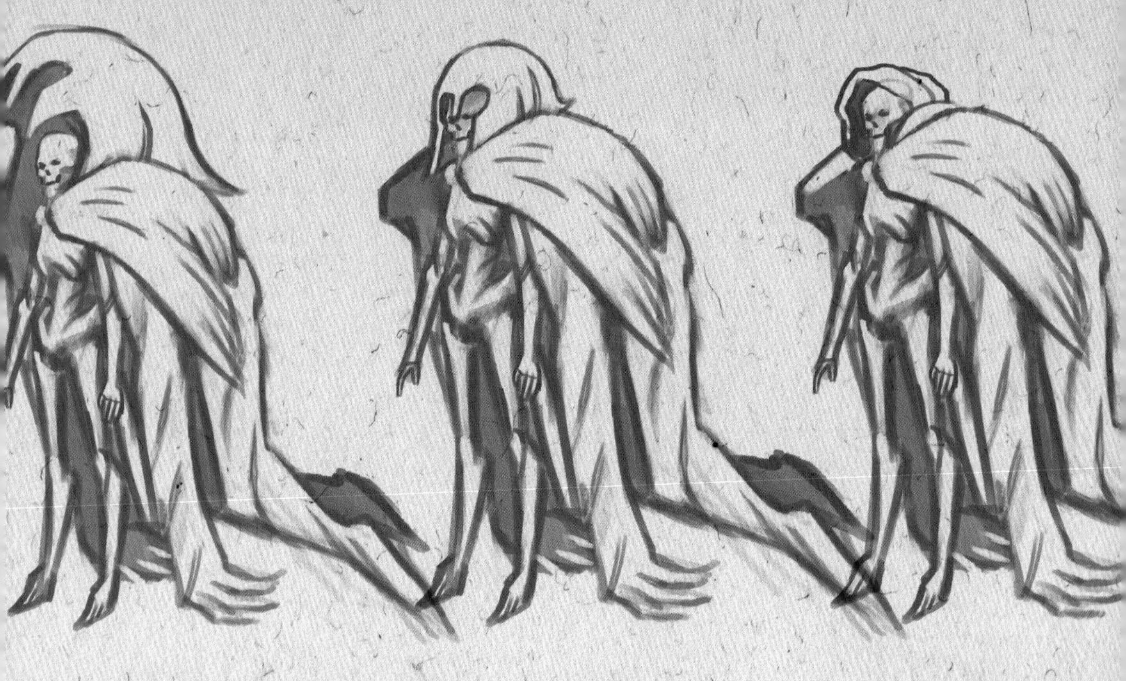

Ulises Farinas is a writer/artist from Elizabeth, New Jersey. He is the writer of *Judge Dredd* from IDW and the writer/artist of *Motro* from Oni Press. He has written for *Godzilla, Regular Show,* and is the creator of *Gamma* from Dark Horse, *Oort* from Stela, and *Cloudia & Rex* from Lion Forge under his new publishing label Buño. He is currently creating and editing books for Buño with a collection of talent from around the comic industry.

Erick Freitas is a gut-punching, nose-breaking, nostalgia-cracking writer, creator, and producer from Elizabeth, New Jersey. He is currently writing *Judge Dredd: Blessed Earth* with Ulises Farinas, and has written for *Amazing Forest, Judge Dredd: Mega City Zero, Motro, Godzilla, Regular Show,* and now *Cloudia & Rex.* When he isn't writing, he's scouting locations for TV & film productions such as *Iron Fist, The Defenders, Younger,* and *The Good Wife.* Follow him on Instagram @ErrFreitas and on Twitter @Err_Freitas.

Daniel Irizarri is coffee-addicted Puerto Rican comic book artist/hermit. His work can be found in *Americatown, This City This Fire, Judge Dredd: The Blessed Earth* and his own sci-fi and fantasy short stories. He lives with his cat Lexington in Mayagüez, Puerto Rico, and enjoys going out to eat with his friends or a good round of *Overwatch.* Check out his work on instagram @ danielirizarri.